Changeling Press, LLC

ChangelingPress.com

The Outcasts Duet

Marteeka Karland

The Outcasts Duet
Marteeka Karland

ISBN: 978-1-60521-836-6

Publisher:
Changeling Press LLC
315 N. Centre St.
Martinsburg, WV 25404
ChangelingPress.com

Printed in the U.S.A.

Editor: Katriena Knights
Cover Artist: Marteeka Karland

The individual stories in this anthology have been previously released in E-Book format.

Table of Contents

Mating the Triad (The Outcasts 1)
Marteeka Karland

A Thief On The Run...
Exiled to the Outlands, Mia struggles to find shelter, food, and safety. Her aggressive style of survival is what got her kicked out of the city in the first place, but in the Outlands, it means the difference between life and a very cruel death.

A Triad In Need Of A Mate...
Mia's sheer viciousness in defending herself catches the notice of one of the most powerful triads in the Outlands. Not only do they covet her body, but they're eager to tame the little hellcat. At least, that's what Mia believes.

How Can Such A Strong Woman Submit?
Not one to simply be taken care of, Mia refuses to be treated as anything other than an equal -- even in times of battle. How can she prove to three powerful warriors she's not only the one for them, but an asset in every aspect of their lives?

Chapter One

"Mia Cook. For the crime of theft from a noble house, your punishment is banishment to the Outlands." The pious judge looked down at me from his throne. With a sneer, I spat in his general direction, expecting to get backhanded by one of several guards surrounding the dais. When nothing happened, I did it again for good measure. The judges always looked at us lowborns with contempt and superiority. I wanted to do some *real* lawbreaking. Like ripping off the guy's nuts. With my teeth.

I didn't resist when two guards dragged me to the center of the great room where court was held daily. Once an accused had been judged guilty, he or she stood in the ceremonial circle for all to see. Maybe it was me, but it seemed like they were just looking for reasons to banish any lowborns in the city. My crime? I'd stolen a bowl of bread. Granted, it wasn't just any bowl of bread -- it was spoonbread. A Kentucky Outback delight. At least it had been back in the day. Earth hadn't always been so medieval. There had been a time when whole festivals were dedicated to Kentucky spoonbread. Now, a dish like that was a delicacy, available only to the wealthy. Nobles. It was also my very favorite thing in the whole goddamned city.

Spoonbread is a "wet" bread dish made of cornmeal. You bake it, serve it with real butter, and eat it with a spoon. Like a pudding or custard, only not hardly as moist. In my opinion, the punishment was worth getting to eat the entire bowl -- which I had, fighting for the last spoonful after I'd been caught.

Especially since it had been a couple of days since I'd had anything to eat. I knew when I stole it what my punishment would be if I were caught. But, honestly, you should try this shit. It's worth the ordeal.

Which means the damned guards got to parade me through the whole of the middle- and low-born sections. Naked. After my little "spat" with the judge, I doubted I could conjure enough sympathy to get one of them to cover me with a cape until we got to the gate.

"You will be sent forth into the wildness beyond the walls of our hallowed city. Such is the way of all heathens. May the Heavenly Father in all his wisdom give you what you deserve in the Outland where He punishes all heathens."

As the bastard spoke, the guards stripped the clothing from my body. When my outfit proved too difficult to remove easily, they simply cut the material, throwing everything into a great fire pit next to the circle. There was no way I could simply snag something on the way out to cover myself.

Just to be contrary, I stood proud, refusing to cover myself with my arms. Lifting my chin, I looked into the eyes of the man who'd passed judgment on me. He was old. Like *really* old. Thin hanks of long gray hair hung all over his head. His look was kind of comical since he was balding in places. If he'd been intelligent, he'd have cut it neatly, or simply shaved the shit off. What hair he had did little to cover the age-spotted skin. I knew my fucking with him was working when a most unbecoming blush splotched his already splotchy skin. Am I a bitch for loving the fact that he was old, ugly, and probably couldn't get it up long enough to enjoy a woman? Probably a good thing. He was the kind of man to take advantage of his position.

As if he'd heard my thoughts, the judge leaned forward in his chair behind his desk. "The little bitch still has no respect for her betters. Why not show the little thief what she's in for? Show her what happens to thieves who don't learn their place." An evil smile should have graced his less-than-perfect features, but, of course, the little bastard kept his pious expression firmly intact. How he managed that when he'd just ordered his guards to rape me was beyond my understanding.

"I will kill you," I bit out.

He sat back, a small smile on his face. "I imagine you will. At least, in your dreams, between bouts of torture."

One of the guards sneered, looking as if he'd been hoping for this development. A second guard muscled his way around the first one, growling a little. He was the clear Alpha there. No one challenged him as he took his place next to me, gripping my upper arm tightly. Obviously, he intended to be the one to carry out my extra punishment.

Fucker.

He was thickly muscled and stood over a head taller than me. His battle-scarred face seemed to match his body, if his heavily muscled arms were any indications. Scars crisscrossed his skin as if he had taken many blows. By not covering them as most men did, he signaled he was proud of his badges of honor. None in the guard challenged him. At present anyway.

As the guy pulled me closer to him, he whispered, "I'll make this pleasurable for you if you'll not fight. If you do, one of the others will challenge me. If they manage to take you, they won't even try to be gentle, let alone give you pleasure."

"So it's either fight and get hurt or submit and not get hurt. Either way, I'm fucked. Literally."

He fisted my hair, tilting my head back so I had to look up at him, then whispered for my ears alone even as he bared his teeth menacingly. His actions and expressions seemed more for the surrounding crowd -- and the judge -- than anything else. Despite the rough handling, he didn't really hurt me. "You're strong. You fought well when they took you. If I hadn't been there, you might even have escaped."

I remembered the bastard now. He had indeed been the one to capture me, wrapping his big, brawny arms around my slim body and squeezing until they were like a boa constrictor around me. Still, I'd fought until I'd passed out from lack of oxygen.

"You might fight them off again, but they're not alone this time. If you can brave this with me, I'll see to it you have some place to go in the Outlands. It may well be a hard life, but it will be life. If you're good at sex, it can be very profitable."

"Great," I said sarcastically. "I'm going from a thief to a whore."

"Better than from a thief to dead," he bit out, clearly losing patience with me. "Consider this a test. Pass, and you will be rewarded. Fail, and the Outlands can have you. No simpering female can survive out there."

"Fine," I said, "but if you're lying to me, know that I will find a way to come back and cut out your balls."

He grunted in acknowledgement before turning me away from him so that his chest was at my back. "I believe you, little warrior." He gripped my shoulders, yanking me back against him. His cock pressed against my lower back through his trousers. *Impressive* size...

"You know he's only doing this because he can't get it up himself. Right?" I wasn't quiet with my jab, sneering at the judge as I spoke. If the increasing redness to his face and head was any indication, he'd definitely heard me. Well, that and the indignant sounding spluttering he made.

"Just so," the guard said at my ear. "Why not show him what he's missing? We'll both get pleasure, he'll be filled with longing and embarrassment, and you'll get to live."

"How do I know you're not just looking for a quick fuck before you turn me out on my own?"

"You don't," he said, his grip on me tightening. "Even if I am, why not take a few minutes of pleasure before what could be your death?" His big hands held me fast as he grazed his mouth down the side of my throat, nipping for good measure, making me yelp in surprise.

"I can probably manage that," I said. Did my voice sound a little breathless? Glancing down, I watched in fascination as my nipples puckered to tight peaks. Had I been so overwhelmed deep inside that I'd missed when this whole situation turned erotic? Or was it this guard's touch making me lose my sanity? I should be fighting him, but what he'd said made a certain sick kind of sense. Besides, everyone knew the Outlands had spies inside the city. If they sent negative information about the new exile, I'd be fair game. Probably would be anyway. But if word got out I was smart enough to pick my battles and to turn what was clearly supposed to be a punishment into an unexpected perk, they might think twice before fucking with me.

Deciding to live in the moment, I relaxed, molding my body into the big man at my back. He grunted his approval before sliding his hands to my hips and up my body to cup my breasts. I moaned and arched into him, giving my breasts a little back-and-forth shake to rub them over his palms.

He sucked in a breath. "Witch," he bit out before pinching my nipples and tugging them a bit roughly.

I cried out, letting my head fall against his chest and closing my eyes. I tried to pretend it was only the two of us there, but the sounds of the gathering crowd made that impossible. Besides, I found the extra stimulation more than a little arousing.

With my eyes closed, it seemed like I could hear every conversation going on around me. Even over the animalistic growls and groans of the guards, I could hear people expressing their lust over my body. Wanting this man to fuck me hard. Wanting to watch as he pounded his length into me. A few even tried to worm their way closer, telling him they'd help teach me a lesson.

"Come on, Dak," one said. "It will be worse on her if we both fuck her."

Dak only growled. I imagined him baring his teeth. He pulled me closer as if to say, *Mine! Back the fuck off!*

"I'll punish her as I see fit," Dak said, giving my nipples another firm tug. "If I need help, it will be from someone I know can get the job done."

Intense male!

I couldn't help giving a little smirk. Why I trusted this Dak -- especially given the fact he was the main reason for my current situation -- was beyond me. I knew he wouldn't do anything I didn't want -- or couldn't convince me to try. Couple that with how sexy I found dominant, Alpha males, and I was a bit more reckless than I should have been.

"Sounds like Dak knows what he's about," I purred. "I doubt a little man like you could handle me anyway."

The other man wasn't exactly little. He was only slightly smaller than Dak in height and musculature, but I knew the barb would get an aggressive reaction from both men.

Dak's hand flew to my throat, his grip punishing, all but cutting off my air. Still, I only grinned. "Watch your tongue!" he snarled, "or I'll let them all fuck you!"

I thrust my bare tits out as if to display them now that he wasn't covering them with those rough hands. I even rolled my hips, drawing attention to my bared sex. I knew my dark curls glistened with my arousal. I wondered how wet Dak had me, and if everyone watching could see how much this turned me on.

With another growl, Dak abandoned my breast and cupped my pussy possessively. His fingers delved between my lips to find the dip of my entrance and teased me. My aching clit rubbed against his hand, and I cried out at the sensation. My hands flew to his thick wrist where his hand still circled my throat. He loosened his grip, but didn't release me. Which delighted me. I loved this show of dominion over me! Was I losing my mind completely? Shouldn't I be showing strength? Fighting him at least a little?

I thrust my hips at Dak's fingers, taking them just inside my cunt. He snarled, his grip on my throat tightening once again. Seeming to catch himself, he relaxed his fingers, but his breath came in harsh rasps, as if he were on the verge of losing all control. Dak's cock was a pulsing thing at my back, growing even larger. He was going to fuck me with it soon. At the thought, I grew wetter in a rush.

"Greedy little female," he growled. "She wants my dick in here, I'll wager."

I did. Instead of answering, I moved my hips with little snaps, fucking myself with his fingers. His grunt of approval was my permission to continue. The voices around us grew louder, but I couldn't process them. The only thing that mattered was his fingers so deep in my pussy. The heel of his hand continued to put much-needed friction on my clit.

"So fucking close…" I whispered.

With a yell, he pulled his fingers out of me, leaving me empty and yearning. "Noooo!" I wailed.

He let me go, so I spun around just in time to see him rip his shirt off, revealing more of that muscled, scarred torso. I couldn't help myself. My hands darted out, my nails sinking into his skin as I explored all that muscled expanse.

"Wicked thief," he bit out. "Release my cock."

I did. Unlacing his trousers, I shoved them down his hips, freeing that huge dick. I'd just registered his size when he fisted my hair in his hands, forcing me to my knees in front of him. His intent was clear. Too far gone at this point to even think about resisting, I opened my mouth, sucking him deep without preamble.

"Fuck!" Dak roared. Looking up at him, I could see his eyes were closed in bliss, his face turned skyward as if looking to the heavens for whatever deity had blessed him with this pleasure. His cock pulsed in my mouth, leaking little salty drops of pre-come with every pull. Muscles rippled and flexed, that intriguing Adonis belt making me wet just looking at it. I nuzzled the crisp hair below his navel before engulfing his cock once again. God, the man was magnificent! I gripped his strong thighs, the hair dusting them abrading my palms deliciously. I wanted his rough body wrapped around mine as he fucked me to oblivion. Probably wouldn't happen like that, but he would be fucking me with this magnificent cock. Soon.

While I continued to suck, he tossed his shirt to another guard, grating, "Tie her hands behind her back. It's time to fuck this little thief before she's given to the Outlands."

A whimper escaped from me as the other guard bound my hands. Though I continued to suck Dak's cock greedily, I was anticipating the coming display and my own pleasure. How would he take me? Doubtless from behind. Would he bend me over or take me standing upright so everyone could see my body quivering for him? Would he come inside me?

Instead of immediately taking charge of me, he let me continue to suck him. I took him as deep as I could, fucking him with my mouth as I desperately wanted him to do to my pussy. Not likely he would, though. He'd said he'd give me pleasure, but I seriously doubt he'd offer to do so with his mouth. After I'd wrung several more startled yells from him, Dak lifted me by my upper arms. I thought he'd spin me around and plunge ruthlessly into me; however, he knelt before me.

"Steady her," he growled to the guard. Another warm torso pressed against my back, large hands going around me to cover my tits once again. Dak frowned up at the man, but said nothing. Another grunt, and he'd lifted my leg over his shoulder. There was a moment for me to process what he was about to do before his head darted between my legs.

I screamed when his tongue flicked my clit. Screamed again when it thrust into my opening. Had the other guard not been behind me, I'd have fallen.

No doubt about that. As it was, my leg buckled. Fortunately, the burly guard had no trouble supporting my slight weight.

"So fucking hot," he muttered at my ear. "I want a turn, Dak," he rumbled.

"Do as I say!" Dak snarled back. "Do not let her fall! If I have to stop my feast because of your clumsy handling I'll castrate you on the fucking spot!" The intensity in his voiced said Dak wasn't kidding.

The other guard simply grinned back, apparently not intimidated by Dak, but not defiant either. "I'm not sure you've ever volunteered to punish an outcast before."

"She has fire," Dak said. "I want a taste of it before the Outlands consume her."

"I can see the appeal," the guard murmured. "I'll wager her nipples are as spicy as fireberries."

How was I supposed to appreciate the danger to follow when the pleasure now was so great? I didn't really want to be the meat in this sandwich, but I might not protest if Dak suggested it. The guard's running dialogue kept me on the edge without seeming threatening. I was in danger. I knew this. Yet I couldn't seem to find it in me to fight. Just like Dak had said, if I was going to die after this, I'd at least have pleasure before I met my fate.

Throwing caution to the wind, I raised my other leg to curl around Dak's neck. Instead of being put out with me, however, he simply stood, gripping my ass as he continued to eat me. Ragged snarls came from between my legs as he shook his head violently, burying himself deeper in against my cunt. I screamed, humping against his mouth, needing more of his wicked kiss, needing to come so badly I was nearly sobbing. Dak smacked my ass, digging his fingers into the fleshy globes. Then again. Finally, he untangled my legs and set me on the ground.

Spinning me around, Dak kicked my legs apart. He'd threaded one of his arms behind mine, pulling me up against him with all the leverage on my body he wanted. His big dick bobbed between my legs, smacking my clit with his every movement. Was he going to fuck me now? My breath stuttered at the thought. I glanced down. That big cock slid between my legs, glistening from my moisture as Dak moved back and forth through my swollen lips.

"Ah, God!" I hadn't meant to scream, but there it was. I wanted this. Desperately.

"The little thief is hot-blooded," Dak observed, sounding a bit more in control than he had been when eating my cunt. "Consider this a taste of what's to come. Assuming you survive long enough out there for it to happen again." With that, he rammed his cock inside me in one brutal thrust.

I cried out in both pain and pleasure. The pain was fleeting and only magnified the pleasure. Dak's strokes were long and brutal. Our flesh slapped together in a loud staccato rhythm even over my cries. He used his hold on my arms to pull me into his thrusts, fucking me that much harder. With each surge inside me, his dick hit the top of my sex, the sensation so intense I knew I'd never last long. I needed this orgasm. I wanted to grab hold of him, but with my hands bound it was impossible. There was no way I wanted him to go without finishing me. One of his arms circled my upper arms, the other my forearms, giving him leverage he needed to fuck me hard. I needed more.

"That's it, little thief," he whispered at my ear. "Show these fucks how passionate and wanton you are. Show them how good you fuck. Show them what they'll never have."

Why was he encouraging me? Wouldn't this simply invite others to take what he was taking? Not that it mattered. I was too far gone to restrain myself. I pushed back against him as much as I was able, screaming, "Harder! Fuck me harder!"

With a brutal roar, Dak pistoned inside me, indeed giving me the fucking I'd asked for. My tits bounced hard. My backside would doubtless be red where his body slapped against it. I would definitely go to the Outlands with his marks all over my body.

Just as I was about to close my eyes and ride him out, rough hands gripped my hips. My eyes snapped open, and my gaze focused on the man kneeling in front of me. This must have been the guard who'd tied me. The one who'd talked filth to me as he held me while Dak ate his fill.

Digging his fingers into my flesh, the guard gave me a wicked grin as he found my clit with his tongue. Instantly, my orgasm detonated. I heard myself scream, but the roaring in my ears prevented clarity of anything else around me. I tried to thrash, to slam myself back onto Dak's cock even more forcefully, but the guardsman's grip prevented it. With rapid flicks of the man's tongue on my clit, my orgasm seemed to go on and on, the intensity of it rocking me to my core. Dak gave a bellow just as the guard pulled back. The next thing I knew, I was on my knees before Dak, his big cock shooting jet after scorching jet of cum over my tits, the guardsman having maneuvered me where I needed to be. When Dak roared his release, the other man released my hands as a creamy line splashed my chin. I scooped it up with my forefinger, sticking the digit in my mouth even as I reached for Dak's cock with my other hand.

Not waiting for an invitation, I engulfed his still-spurting cock, swallowing the remainder of his creamy cum as it jumped from him. Dak shuddered in my grasp, making me feel powerful even though I was the one naked on my knees in front of him, waiting to be exiled to the Outlands. He'd been right. I was glad I'd gotten to have this pleasure before what might be impending doom. Because I was still lust-high, I knew I couldn't fully appreciate the extent of the danger awaiting me, but hell. Why would I want to? I could do nothing about it. I'd either live or I wouldn't.

Dak pulled me to my feet. Which was when I finally realized the crowd we'd drawn. Guards and nobles stood all around the court, the dais filled with encouraging onlookers. Most of them were cruel and crude in their comments, taunting me with how they suspected my new life would be. They called me a whore, offered Dak money to give me to the mob before my exile. Instead of responding, Dak merely wiped his cum from my chest, raising an eyebrow at me. As I lifted my chin, refusing to let the mob -- or him -- cow me, he slipped the hilt of a wicked, serrated blade into my palm so the blade was flat against my forearm. If I was careful, I could get it out of the city without anyone noticing. He didn't say a word. Glancing around me at the lust-mad mob, I knew I should probably be embarrassed, but all I could manage was a cocky grin. Yeah. Dak might have fucked me, but I'd fucked him right back, and we'd both come our brains out. Besides, I now had the means to protect myself in the Outlands. God have mercy on anyone crossing my path.

Chapter Two

Dak's parting words to me? "If anyone crosses you, fight them to the death. Don't let up no matter what. If you do what I tell you, all will be well."

Right. I was naked with one knife. I didn't even have fucking shoes. If there had never been an old reality show made for times like this, there should have been.

The Outlands were simply that. Outside the city's influence. Each city was walled off, separating it from the wilds. The Outlands. Inside, each city was like a small country. There were laws, and everyone living there was expected to support the city's government. Those who didn't were banished.

Cities were expected to protect and care for those within their walls. If they didn't they risked uprisings. Even those cities that had absolute control over their citizens were careful not to wall off more than they could reasonably handle. Armies cost money, and there would always be more citizens than hired killers. That wasn't to say governors didn't push the limits of control. In the Outlands, there was no law. No moral creed. Survival of the fittest ruled everyone. Only the strong survived unless the strong took you under their protection. If I was going to survive, Dak was right. I had to be strong.

Using my knife, I cut a path through the foliage, looking for shelter as long as the light would allow. Ideally, I'd get as far from the city as I could. If I was attacked tonight, I damned sure didn't want anyone from my former home to witness my downfall. Especially after the show I'd put on.

Maybe an hour before sunset, I found two small overhangings separated by a stream of cold, clear water running between the rocky outcroppings. Wind from the spring blew through a cave that connected the overhangings through the rock separating them, exiting in a cool gush of air. It would be cold, but if I used the side opposite rushing air, my scent wouldn't be discernible to anyone downwind. Which was my first mistake. I should have figured such a place was too good to be true. No sooner did I step under the shelter than I sprung a trap.

There was a loud snap and the rustling of leaves. Just as I tensed to spring from the overhang, a heavy metal grate came crashing down flush against the rocks. It fit too perfectly to have been anything but designed that way. Great. Not only was I trapped, I had nothing to keep me warm. God only knew how long I'd be here.

I clenched my teeth in frustration. So much for lasting in the Outlands. I hadn't even made it one whole night before I fucked up.

Examining the tiny space, I noticed what I might have had it been full light outside when I decided to camp for the night. Little niches had been cut into the rocky face to accommodate the grate. *Fuck!* Yeah. I'd walked right into that one. I wanted to scream in frustration. As night fell, moonlight gleamed off the metal on the bars as if even the cage itself were laughing at me.

"Well, well, well," came a Cockney-accented voice. "What 'ave we 'ere?"

"Lor' luv a duck! Looks like a lit'el bird caught in a cage. Know what I mean?" came another male voice as he laughed at my predicament.

"What's doin', Dove? You lost?"

I wasn't sure if I should answer them or not so I crouched down in my prison, concealing my knife under the pretense of hiding my naked body from them.

When I didn't answer, the first one asked, "Cat got yur tongue?"

The other laughed, looking eager to open the cage to get to me. "Thee're not shy are you? Lit'el girl should wear clothes if she don't wan' attenshun. 'Nuff said, yeah?" They both laughed, obviously expecting to have easy prey. "Please us good an' we might let you go, Dove."

"Let 'er out uf 'er cage so we can pay aaahr respects proper. Know what I mean?"

Another round of laughter as one of them hefted a rope, raising the grate to prop it up with a thick bar. The second he'd propped the heavy steel securely, I sprang, launching myself at the closest one. He caught my body reflexively, which occupied his hands. Which left his throat exposed to my knife.

I stabbed him in the side of the neck with both hands, the serrated edge sawing through the anatomy with little trouble. Dak had given me a sound, sharp weapon. Hot blood sprayed across my chest and face, clouding my vision.

With a startled yelp, the other guy backed away a couple of steps. Swinging my head in the direction of his cry, I swiped my hand over my eyes to clear them as best I could. If he figured out I couldn't see, he'd attack. When I made out his form in the dark, I gave a battle cry and sprinted the three steps to him, tackling him to the ground. He got his arms up in time to catch my knife. The blade went through one side, scraped bone, then came out the other side. He gave a high-pitched scream, trying to push me off him, but only managed to wedge my knife tighter in his arm so that one of the teeth stuck on the bone.

He turned over, trying to scramble away from me on all fours, but I pinned him down, slight though I was. Grabbing his head in one hand, his chin in the other, I gave a yell as I twisted with all my might. The satisfying sound of his neck snapping echoed in the night.

"Fucker," I muttered, kicking his body for good measure when I got to my feet. I pulled my knife from his forearm, wiping the blade on his pants. I was surprised I was as calm as I was. When I'd fought the guardsman in the city, I'd been calm as well. Until Dak had showed up. There had been something about the whole situation up until that point that made me believe I would be victorious. I suppose that was my talent. I knew when I was fighting a losing battle. In those instances, my first instinct was always to flee.

The first guy had blood everywhere from my less-than-finessed kill so I was glad I'd been able to take out this guy cleanly. I now had a shirt, smelly though it might be. The guy wasn't overly big, but he was still quite a bit taller than me. Getting his shirt off took some doing, but I managed. Just as I was getting ready to slip into it, two big arms closed around my body from behind.

Fear seized me as tightly as those arms did. Whoever had me was stronger than me and meant business. Thank God I still had my arms free.

With a cry I stabbed at him with my knife, first going low, then high. Both times he managed to dodge cleanly. I hadn't even scratched him. He let me go with one arm, his other easily holding me against a body hard as granite. With the other hand, he struck my knife hand twice until I dropped it with a cry. I wasn't sure, but I thought something crunched in my wrist. The guy hadn't made a sound as he easily disarmed me.

I had no weapon. My feet were bare, making kicking him worse than useless, but I wasn't giving up without a fight. He'd either kill me or decide I was too much trouble and let me go, but no way was I simply letting him have me.

Harsh breaths sounded beside my ear -- was the guy smelling me? -- so I snapped my head back, catching his face. My first blow landed. He gave a pained grunt before simply spinning me around and tossing me over one massive shoulder. I landed so hard it knocked the wind out of me, and for precious seconds I was too stunned to fight.

When I was finally able to do more than suck in breath after breath, I pounded his back, kicking and squirming wildly. I tried to sink my teeth into his skin, but there didn't seem to be a spare ounce of flesh on him. When I did manage to bite a chunk off his back, he growled and swatted my upturned ass. Hard.

Through it all, the barbarian never said a word. Nor did he hurt me. Well, except for my now aching wrist.

I continued to struggle, trying to twist my body so I could either slide down his front or fall headfirst onto the ground down his back. Which earned me another swat to my ass. Apparently the big guy had infinite patience as long as my ass was in the air where he could chastise me.

Bracing one hand on his back, I wiped the back of my hand over my mouth and face. Now the immediate fight was over, I was aware of how much blood I was splattered with. The coppery taste of it was heavy in my mouth where I'd bitten this guy.

He didn't appear to be in any hurry, just strolling through the darkened woods with a naked woman over his shoulder. I probably should have been more concerned about that, but I figured if the guy had wanted to hurt me, he'd have done so long before now. And I didn't count the injury to my wrist because I *was* trying to stab him.

"I can walk, you know," I said, trying to sound reasonable. No response. "It's really hard to breathe like this. I promise I won't try to get away." Again, he said nothing. But he did swat my ass lightly. As if he knew I was lying? "Oww! Stop doing that!" Which earned me yet another swat. This time, he lingered, rubbing my abused flesh with one rough palm.

With a sigh, I resigned myself to an uncomfortable journey. Surly wherever he was taking me couldn't be far away. Sure enough, in the distance I heard boisterous laughter and music filtering through the trees. Straining to look around him earned me another swat, but when he lingered again, kneading my ass, I suspected he'd simply wanted an excuse to touch me. So I merely hissed in a breath in protest as I continued to try to see what lay ahead. Firelight illuminated the distance leaving no doubt we were headed toward a large gathering.

"Where are you taking me?" As expected, I got nothing. "You know, it might be a good idea for you to put some clothes on me if we're going to be visiting other people." Nothing, though he gave my ass one last squeeze and seemed to take a deep breath, squaring his shoulders before stepping from the shadows into the firelight.

His long strides sped up as he meandered through the edge of what looked like a small village. Men and women in various stages of undress danced around a huge bonfire. Others -- again, mostly undressed -- watched from the edges. Still others fucked in full view of anyone who cared to watch. Meat cooked on spits in a couple of different places, making tantalizing scents waft through the air. My stomach chose that moment to growl. Right next to the big guy's ear. He stiffened and stopped walking. Which finally garnered some attention from the raucous crowd.

"Talon! I see you had good hunting!" The voice was female and a pleasing contralto. I twisted around, trying to get a look at her, but fucking Talon just swatted my ass. Again. Still, I managed to get a glimpse of a tall, proud-looking woman dressed in a fur-lined halter-top that accentuated her muscled, scarred abdomen. Fur-lined panties and fur-lined boots showed off her muscular thighs that were, again, crisscrossed with scars, and a fur cape rounded out the ensemble dedicated to wholesale animal slaughter. She looked like something straight out of an old-world barbarian fantasy film. Only this chick was anything but a virgin sacrifice. In fact, trailing behind her were two naked males with collars. She held the chain leashes in one hand. One man was tall and lean, though muscled proportionate to his height, and oiled to show off his body to perfection. The other was shorter but stockier and heavily muscled. Though also oiled, he didn't seem as proud as the other one.

At first, I wasn't sure if she was talking to my guy. After all, dude was a man of few words. Then he sighed, his shoulders falling slightly as if in resignation. Unfortunately, acknowledging her meant turning to put my ass on full display for the other female. And her pets. Still the man -- Talon? -- didn't say a word.

I heard her footfalls moving closer seconds before a hand squeezed first one ass cheek, then the other.

"Hey!" I screeched my outrage. Naturally, Talon gave me another swat. If I didn't know better, I'd swear he'd squeezed my ass just to get me to protest so he'd have a reason to swat me again. When I got down from here, I was going to do some spanking of my own. "Fucker!"

"Your pet has need of manners," she remarked, sounding amused. "Then again, you're not exactly one to want a docile pet."

Without warning, Talon pulled me from his shoulder to set me on my feet. He glanced at me before giving a smirk and turning me to face the woman.

Her lips parted in surprise. "She's killed?"

He laid a big, rough hand on my shoulder as if proud of something that seemed to shock his acquaintance.

"I was going to offer you the use of Zeus," she indicated the short, stocky male with her, "to break her in for you, but I'll not have one of my favorite pets maimed. That one --" she pointed at me "-- looks feral."

I glanced back at Talon, who merely shrugged as if to say *Danger good... ugh...*

I rolled my eyes. "You know, I'm right here," I said. "I do know how to speak." Glancing back at Talon, I muttered, "Unlike some people."

Talon immediately clamped his hand on the back of my neck as if to say *Shut up, bitch!*

"Perhaps she needs a lesson from me," the woman said. "Give her to me for the night, and I'll see she shows you proper respect."

This time, Talon looked calculating. He pulled

me back against his larger body possessively, but I could see a gleam of excitement in his eyes. Then I knew what he wanted.

"I'm willing to bet Talon is considering taking you up on your offer," I said, glancing up at my man. *My man?* When the fuck had I started thinking in those terms?

At my words he stiffened, his grip on my neck tightening, but I didn't think it was to keep me quiet. He hadn't squeezed me as hard this time. A warning to keep silent or one to tread carefully on the negotiations? I was pretending he meant the latter. "But I'm also willing to bet he wants me as is. Not beaten down." This time, Talon relaxed. The smug look on his face said I'd read him correctly. It also meant this could turn into a bit of fun, if I were careful.

She glanced at me. "Your pet seems to know your mind fairly well. How newly acquired is she?"

"He stopped me from dressing in the shirt of one of the guys I'd just killed. Then he took away my weapon, slung me over his shoulder, and marched through the Outlands to bring me here. I've been in his presence for a couple of hours."

Hard as I tried, I couldn't get the woman to more than glance at me. If nothing else, I was going to have that satisfaction before the night was over. Talon nodded his agreement of my explanation of our time together, smirking as he did so, which seemed to vex the woman even more.

"What did you have in mind?" She continued to look at Talon, as if he were the one talking. Behind my back, Talon's cock pulsed against me. Oh yeah. This male was definitely thinking in terms of two women getting it on. I had no idea if he intended to participate, but I couldn't imagine a male who wouldn't.

"*We* propose the three of us working off a little steam," I said. I knew I'd scored when his cock pulsed at my back again, swelling even larger than before.

"I will not allow another Alpha to fuck me," she said without hesitation, her expression at once haughty and distasteful. "While I have no problem sharing mutual pleasure with you, Talon, I will not allow penetration of any kind." He grunted. Approval? "So I'll want my own pets with me." Again, Talon grunted. Could the guy not speak at all? Her brows drew together in vexation. "I'll also expect your little pet to entertain me. I'm sure my pets would like a reward for pleasuring me well, so I'll expect your little bitch to be their plaything. And I like variety," she said before I could respond. Though she did glance at me this time. Score one for the feral bitch.

"We'll agree to that," I said. Was that a fine shudder that ran through Talon? "But I'll warn you now. If you think I will let them hurt me, think again. I only cut out the throat of the last man who thought to hurt me. Any *pets* of yours getting that close to me will be minus their cock and balls."

She seemed to grind her teeth, staring straight at Talon, obviously making a point not to look at me. When Talon merely raised an eyebrow she lost her temper.

"How can you let that little bitch talk to me that way, Talon? I will do what I want to her. She's a *pet!*"

In a surprising move, Talon moved me behind him. Naturally, I positioned myself to see his expressive face. I wanted to see how he handled this woman. Would he finally talk? He stood a head taller than her but got up in her face, leaning down to look straight into her eyes. This was the Alpha the woman had spoken of. I had no idea if she were one or not, though she claimed to be, but she took a step back before realizing her mistake. Apparently satisfied she understood she was not to allow her pets to harm me, Talon nodded.

"I'll think about it. If I decide the two of you are worthy of my time I'll be at your lodging after the evening meal."

Talon straightened, reaching for me. I expected he'd pick me up. Maybe sling me over his shoulder caveman-style again. Instead, he merely snagged my upper arm, his hand completely wrapping around it. He walked the rest of the way to his home with his shoulders back as if he were proud to have such a "pet" as I.

"If you think I'm just going to sit back and accept your ownership of me, wild man, think again."

He grunted, as if saying, "I'd expect nothing less."

God! I was carrying on a conversation with a man who wouldn't -- or couldn't -- talk and assuming I understood his every grunt and growl? If I got out of this with my sanity intact I'd be surprised.

Chapter Three

Inside his dwelling, the furnishings were exactly what I'd expect from a barbarian from the movies. *Everything* was covered in fur except the stone fireplace. Thankfully, the furs were a safe distance away from the snapping logs.

"Not that I don't like your place -- it's definitely better than a fucking cave -- but I'm covered in blood."

Taking my arm, he led me to the back of the room. Behind a wall was a large, round sunken tub with steam rising gently from the surface of the water.

"Wow," I managed. "How did you get this?"

He shrugged as if it was no big deal, but I could tell he was pleased by my reaction. With a wave of his hand, he indicated I should get in the water. As suspected, the barbarian undressed, intending to follow me in. I shrugged to myself. I was getting ready to do more than merely bathe with him. Why not use this time to familiarize myself with his body and let him explore mine?

I watched him now, enjoying such a magnificent male stripping for me. OK, so technically, he wasn't doing it for me, but I could imagine what I wanted. Other than a few spankings, which I was pretty sure were more for his benefit than any real show of punishing me, the guy hadn't treated me like an inferior. In fact, he'd paraded me through his village with me sporting the blood from my kill as if I were his most prized possession. Primitive, but not altogether unflattering.

As he stood, boldly meeting my gaze with such a proud arrogance, I took in everything he had to offer me. He was heavily muscled. Strong, as I'd found out earlier tonight. He sported several scars over his body, just like the woman had, enhancing his masculine beauty. I suspected he was as proud of his scars as he was of my viciousness. Like both were something he'd earned by right of his strength.

Dark hair dusted his chest and down to his navel and below as well as his arms and legs. In a nest of crisp, black hair, his cock bobbed with his every movement. If I weren't careful, I'd get lost in the exquisite way it swayed. He was large. No doubt about it. Maybe even larger than Dak had been. The head was an angry purple, as if it were fed up with all this teasing and wanted to get to the fucking portion of tonight's activities. The hair on his head was also a deep black. He wore it braided at the temples back along his head, probably to keep the stuff out of his face during battle. He picked up a leather tie and gathered his hair at the back of his neck to tie it back. I frowned. I'd love to run my fingers through the thick mass. Or thread my fingers through it to guide him where I wanted him.

With a questioning look, Talon lowered his hands. Did what I want matter to him? When I smiled and nodded he set the tie down, a satisfaction lighting his eyes as he climbed into the water with me.

I moved to give him room, but he simply reached for me, urging me to straddle him. His calloused hands slid up my sides and back down to rub my ass gently. His heavy-lidded gaze was fixed on my breasts, not seeming to mind that they were covered in dried blood. If ever there was a male who looked smug and satisfied, it was this one.

"What are you so happy about, barbarian?" I asked. "I'm not yours. I'm only staying here until I can figure out how to escape you."

His grin said, "Right. Let me know how that works out for you."

Scooping up two handfuls of water, Talon let it stream over my breasts. Blood ran down my body in dark red rivulets. Meeting my gaze, he nodded at me, then looked at my breasts.

"You want me to do it?"

At his sharp nod, I mimicked his action, letting water run down my torso. He grunted then reached for a block of soap on the wooden ledge. He started to use the bar to soap me up, then grunted and ducked his hand under the water. Rubbing the soap between his own hands, he made a rich lather then went straight for my tits. I couldn't help but grin.

The big barbarian took his time, cleansing every inch of my skin until I was certain there was no lingering blood. Hell, there probably wasn't a speck of grime on my skin anywhere.

Apparently satisfied with the job he'd done, Talon lingered on my breasts, scissoring my nipples between his fingers. I loved the feel of his rough hands lathered in the soap. It was such a contrast. Erotic. I found myself smiling and enjoying him. Talon seemed in no hurry to finish, just kneaded my breasts. Pinched my nipples. His cock pulsed between us though he made no move to relieve any ache he felt. Didn't even press my body close in order to mash that magnificent erection tightly against my belly.

Finally, he sighed as he turned me to lie across his lap with my hair in the water. As gently as he'd washed my body, he washed my hair, making sure to get all the blood out. He massaged my scalp until I was a big puddle of goo in his arms. I moaned, and he grinned. Apparently, he'd hoped to elicit that exact response from me.

"What can I say, big guy? I like to be petted."

As I lay in the water, he massaged my arms and hands, letting me float like a dreamy, erotic trip. He gave the same treatment to my legs and feet before urging me to straddle him once again.

This time, I slid my arms around his neck, wanting to thank him for the massage. For giving me these moments with him. Not just in the tub or what was to come with him and the she-barbarian. But for everything. His being proud to parade me around covered in blood because he saw my viciousness against the two goons as a strength. For treating me as an equal when he obviously didn't have to. I had no idea what this man was or what he did, but he was a good man. I knew this without a doubt.

I was just about to press my lips to his when he jerked back. Brows drawn in confusion, he looked at me as if my trying to kiss him completely confounded him.

"Did I do something wrong?" He continued to give me a baffled look but -- surprise! -- said nothing. "I was only wanting to thank you. Kissing can be quite pleasurable."

He nodded his head slowly but didn't make a move to kiss me. Carefully, as I might when trying to tame a wild animal, I brought my palm to his cheek, brushing his bottom lip with my thumb. His gaze darted to my lips and back as if he was tempted, but stiffly shook his head with a heavy shudder.

"Is it me you object to or some facet of your culture I don't understand?" I could understand the latter, but the thought of the former kind of didn't sit well with me. I didn't want him to not want to kiss me.

He nodded, touching his finger to my lips then

his own before placing a hand over my heart then his.

"Kissing is only for mates?" When he nodded, I added, "Not pets."

He shrugged, as if to say, "It is what it is."

"Well, that's certainly understandable. Do you keep pets after you're mated then?"

Shrug.

"I suppose there has to be an intimate act that is left for mates alone." Though it still stung a little. He was proud to have me as a pet, but didn't want me as his woman.

"Oh, well," I said, trying to blow it off. It was probably good I got a dose of reality because I could totally see myself liking this guy to the point of *liking him* liking him. Which wouldn't do at all given we'd known each other only a few scant hours and the extent of our relationship included him parading me naked around his village and making a date with another woman to share for mutual pleasure. "It's just that one little thing. It's probably a good thing I made this blunder with you now rather than after your fellow Alpha gets here. Is there anything else that's off limits?"

His brows drew together again. He studied my expression intently, obviously trying to decide how to proceed. Again, he pressed a finger to his lips then to mine then pointed to the door with a questioning look.

"Do I want to kiss that woman?"

Nod.

"Do I want to be her mate?"

He nodded again, this time more vigorously, as if I were understanding exactly what he meant. If the look on his face was any indication, thinking I might want her for a permanent lover didn't sit well with him.

"My culture doesn't place the same significance on kissing as yours does. But then, we don't keep sexual pets. While I'd have no problem kissing a woman, I'd prefer my mate be a male."

Again, he pointed at the door. What could he be getting at? Oh, wait!

"Would I want to be mated to one of her pets?" When he nodded again, I shook my head. "No, Talon. They're not my preference."

He swallowed, though I knew what he would ask next, and I think I might have lost a little piece of my heart. When he hiked his thumb at himself, I smiled.

"I don't know. I haven't known you that long, but I can tell you this. If I had to base that decision on only our time together so far, I would definitely want you for my own." At his questioning look I settled myself closer to him. My pussy rubbed against that big dick enticingly, and it pulsed against my lips. "You treat me well. Not that people here don't treat their pets well or anything, but I don't feel like your 'pet.' You treat me like an equal. Intentional or not." When he again pointed to the door I shook my head. "I don't think you're treating me like barbarian girl treats her pets. I *agreed* to spend tonight in pleasure with her and her men mostly because I knew you wanted it, but also because I wanted it. Today, I was banished from the city. It was supposed to be a death sentence. If I'm going to die tonight or tomorrow or anytime in the near future, I want to live as much as I can before then. I want to experience pleasure in all its forms." Again, I laid my hand on his cheek. "And I'd like to know the love of a good man, or whatever emotion is as close as I'm likely to get. I never thought I'd experience that particular pleasure, but I think I could come close with you."

Talon's chest expanded, and his chin went up proudly. Once again, he slowly pressed a finger to my lips. Then to his.

"I'd love to kiss you, Talon. I just don't know what you'd expect if I did."

He tilted his head, his eyes narrowing. He didn't look angry, only puzzled.

"I mean, would you expect us to be mates if I kissed you? Because I can't commit my life to anyone while it's so uncertain."

He sat up straighter, pounding his chest and grunting fiercely.

Then it hit me. "You'd protect me," I said. Not making it a question. "Would you want me for your mate? You don't know me, but you'd tie your life to mine? Is that what being mates means to you?"

He nodded. Then put his finger in my chest, stabbing lightly. Making a fist with the same hand, he squeezed it tightly, the muscles in his arm bulging, the veins swelling.

"I'm strong because I had to be, Talon. If you could explain things to me, maybe we could work something out." I shrugged. "I have nothing to offer you. Nowhere else to go unless you show me where. Would you want that kind of mate? It doesn't sound like the type of woman you deserve."

He ran his hands over my body, molding my curves with a gentle caress before pointing to himself. Then rested his hand over my lower belly before putting his hand over my chest, then his.

"OK. I'll give you that. I'm young and could give you children we would both cherish. But aren't there other women who would please you better? Be a better match for you? Despite what it looked like when you found me, I'm not a warrior."

Talon shook his head decisively, pointing to me with a sharp stab of his finger.

Why was I even questioning this? I meant it when I told him I had nowhere to go. I should consider this a turn of good fortune, but Talon was a good man. I didn't want to take advantage of his kindness. Looking at his sigh-worthy body, though, I admitted I was tempted.

He framed my face in his big hands, forcing me to meet his gaze. Looking straight into my eyes, he did something that started the fuck out of me.

"Mine," he rumbled in a deep, husky voice. "My. Woman."

Despite not wanting to take advantage of this gentle giant's generosity and obvious infatuation with me, a thrill coursed through my body at his proclamation. Did I want to be his mate? I wasn't sure. I certainly wasn't averse to the idea. It just hadn't been on my radar before now. I definitely had few other options, the best of which was to venture out on my own until I ran into someone else. Like Igg and Ook I'd killed. If that happened, I probably wouldn't be lucky enough to both defeat them *and* run into someone I could trust not to maim me in my sleep. At least with Talon I knew he could have done so already if he'd wanted.

Before I could look at it from all angles, Talon's grip on my face tightened. Giving me a little shake he repeated, "Mine." Then, "Yours."

My breath caught at that. "Are you saying I'm yours… and you're mine?"

He nodded slowly, then rested his forehead against mine. "Yours," he breathed. His voice was pleasing, but rusty. As if it had been a very long time since he'd used it. Though I had no idea why he hadn't spoken before, I found it endearing he did so now.

I didn't have time to process any more because Talon leaned in to kiss me. Big hands still framing my face, his lips met mine in a gentle, tentative caress.

God, his mouth on mine felt good! He seemed to test how best to go about kissing me instead of simply taking what he wanted. When I moaned, he deepened the contact, licking at my lips as if seeking entrance. I gladly let him explore, enjoying the feel of such a big, dominant man mastering my body with tenderness.

His tongue swept inside with bold, shallow strokes as if he were afraid I'd reject him yet was unable to deny his dominant nature. I flicked his tongue with mine, and his big body shuddered. The taste of him was exquisite, like rich tobacco and wine, darkly sensual and exotic.

When I threaded my fingers through his hair and thrust my own tongue deep, he seemed to snap. Growling, he plunged into me, licking and sucking at my tongue, flicking it with bold, greedy strokes. I grew lightheaded with the need he built effortlessly. All because he seemed to be inexperienced yet had a need to dominate. The contradiction was heady since I was on the receiving end of his exploration. The thought of him exploring this pleasure with another woman sent a spike of jealousy through me I had never experienced before.

I pulled back, baring my teeth at him. He gave me a confused, questioning look as if to say, "Did I do something wrong?"

"If you ever do this to another female, I will gut you," I said with as much conviction and jealousy as I felt. At first he tilted his head back as if he weren't sure he'd heard me right. Then he grinned broadly, chuckling at my nonsense. I thumped his chest. "I mean it! If you ever kiss another woman I'll kill you!"

"My female," he grated, his voice still rusty. We really needed to work on that. "Your male." Then again, that rasp was sexy as hell. Maybe he could just not talk unless it was to say filthy things to me.

Then he stood. Reflexively I wrapped my legs around his waist. Water sloshed over us, and he snagged a linen sheet as he stepped out of the tub. Without putting me down, he wrapped the sheet around me, rubbing dry as much of the water as he could before giving himself a cursory rubdown.

His cock pulsed against my wet pussy lips, and I couldn't help but slide against it to put friction on my clit. Talon hissed in a breath, gripping my ass in one big palm before swatting it smartly. I yelped, but slid over him again just to see what he'd do. As expected, he swatted my ass again, harder this time. The sting only fueled my lust, making me crazed to have him. To fuck him long and hard until we were both spent.

Firelight crackled next to us as he laid me on the soft fur before the hearth. Talon pressed me into the fur, his body hard and hot over mine. I loved his weight pinning me. Forearms beside my head, he leaned in to kiss me again. His lips were hard and aggressive this time as he grew more confident. Over and over he plunged his tongue inside my mouth. I loved every second of it, never wanting it to end.

When he trailed licks and nips down the side of my neck, I arched into him, turning my head to offer him better access. He could have anything from me he wanted if only he'd continue creating these sensations inside me. Never had sex felt like this. In the city, Dak had made the act pleasurable for me, but this was on a whole different level. And Talon hadn't even penetrated me yet.

He kissed over my chest, the valley between my breasts, then sat up before bending over me again, pushing my breasts together to lap at the nipples until I squirmed and whimpered continually.

I was losing my mind, I was sure of it. Everywhere he touched seemed to send pleasure zinging straight to my clit.

"Talon," I gasped. "My God! It's so good!"

He grunted, taking one tit into his mouth. The whole thing. I screamed, arching my back, gripping his hair to hold him to me. That wicked tongue swirled around my nipple several times before actually making contact with the pebbled peak. When he let my breast go, it was with a loud popping sound and only long enough for him to give the same treatment to the other one.

I spread my legs, raising my knees to open myself wide to him. Anything he wanted was his. As long as he didn't stop, all would be well.

Continuing his journey south, he licked my belly, my navel, until he got to the downy hair at my mound. Once there, he paused, looking up at me before closing his eyes and inhaling deeply. He let his breath out on a loud, satisfied groan.

"So good," he rasped. "Aroused for me."

"Yes, Talon," I gasped. "You've made me this way. Done this to me."

"You love it." It wasn't a question.

"I do."

With another deep breath in, he held my gaze as he lowered his face to my cunt and took one long, wet lick.

I jerked. So did he. It was like lightning spearing me in the chest. I shuddered violently with every stroke of his strong tongue, which he seemed to delight in. With every swipe, he grew more aggressive, growling and snarling into my pussy. He sucked my lips, my clit. Then his big fingers penetrated me, and I thought I'd lose my mind.

"Talon!"

"Uhhhg."

He slid a third finger inside me, thrusting them over and over. Just as I was about to come, he pulled them out and dove between my legs. His mouth covered my pussy as his tongue penetrated me. I screamed again, and then Talon was the one losing his mind. He shook his head, growling savagely as he worked my flesh. My clit throbbed and pulsed with my heart. It was almost too much. I could feel an orgasm building, the intensity staggering, but could do nothing to temper it. I tried to push him away, but that only seemed to make him more aggressive. He shook me off only to dive back in without so much as pausing.

"Talon," I gasped. "Fuck me."

He didn't stop. Instead, he redoubled his efforts, snarling into my cunt and pressing his face closer. The orgasm inside me continued to build. I continued to fight it, beginning to fear the intensity of it.

"Please! Oh, God, please, please, please!"

"When. I. Say." That was the dominant male I knew him to be. The Alpha.

I screamed again, this time in fear. When my orgasm finally hit, I might not survive it.

Just when I was afraid I couldn't take anymore, he sat back to give my pussy a sharp slap. Before I had time to more than gasp at the unexpected pain, Talon had covered me with that big, brawny body. Forehead to mine, he probed my entrance until the head pressed inside.

"There are... issues," he said, seeming to have trouble putting into words what he needed to say, but it was obviously important he get it out. Though his voice wasn't as rough as it had been -- it seemed to grow stronger every time he used it -- he still seemed as if the whole experience was new to him. As if he were having to relearn how to speak. "Know I will... protect. Always." Each word was enunciated carefully, as if he were trying very hard to get it right. To make me understand.

I had no idea what he meant, but I did trust him to take care of me. He'd latched onto me for some reason, and he was a man who would protect what he considered his. Knowing I could have landed in much, much worse hands, I was grateful. If the big barbarian wanted to keep me, I was willing to give myself to him.

He didn't give me time to respond. I sucked in a breath, and he surged inside me.

Bliss!

Immediately, that orgasm I'd feared crashed over me with all the subtlety of a raging bull. My screams rang out loudly in Talon's dwelling. Likely the whole village could hear me, but I couldn't give a fuck. Never had I experienced such mind-numbing pleasure. All I could do was feel. And cling with all my might to Talon.

He fucked me hard, hissing as I came around his dick. Thick and pulsing inside me, his cock filled me completely, stretched me so that I burned. Once he settled into a steady rhythm, he wrapped his arms around me tightly. Only his hips moved as he moved inside me with staggering intensity.

Though I tried to hold on, I knew there was no stopping my next orgasm. No holding back. No stopping my screams as I clawed his back mercilessly.

Finally, he swelled inside me, his breaths coming in ragged gasps as he continued to fuck me. His heavy balls smacked my ass with every stroke, which only added to the sensations. I was about to scream once again when he covered my mouth with his and roared his own completion.

Our cries mingled, each catching the other's, taking them inside. I treasured this time with him even as I tried to get my bearings. I'd never been so caught up in the moment as I was with this experience. The harsh reality of my new existence would probably break my heart if I weren't careful.

We tried to catch our breath. When he would have rolled off me, I gripped him harder, whimpering to get him to stay where he was. I loved his solid weight on me. He lifted his head enough to catch my gaze and smiled tenderly at me, then kissed me.

"You own... my heart," he rasped against my lips.

My breath caught. He groaned before kissing me languidly again. I could feel the longing and determination in his touch. This man wanted me with all the fierceness in his mighty body. More. I truly believed he wanted me to want him back.

There was a knock at the door. Talon's head whipped in that direction, and he snarled, baring his teeth. I still couldn't help but notice his cock twitching like crazy. I grinned.

"You know, this is for your benefit. We don't have to let the she-barbarian do a goddamned thing you don't want her to do. *Or* her pets. I can tell them to leave if it makes you more comfortable."

He raised an eyebrow, but I saw a fleeting look of disappointment in his amazing blue eyes. I couldn't help but grin.

"I take it, deep down, you're still a guy. Seeing me and another woman pleasuring each other would still turn you on."

He gave me a sheepish grin. "I need to know your limits, Talon. I don't want to accidentally do something to hurt you."

"No. Kissing," he said.

"No kissing," I repeated. "Do you want the guys to fuck me?" His cock pulsed at the mention, and I grinned. "I guess I have my answer there."

He leaned in to kiss me again as another knock came, more impatient this time. "Issues," he said again, his brows coming together as if he were trying to get out something important wasn't sure how to word it. "There are… issues."

"You mentioned that before. Can you tell me?"

He shook his head. "This will… help you. Later." As he spoke more and more, I noticed a sexy accent. I was growing as infatuated with him as he was with me. There was obviously more going on that he couldn't put into words. Or maybe he just didn't want to scare me off?

"What will?"

"This," he nodded at the door.

I know I looked confused, but he would offer no more. Maybe he couldn't figure out how to word it. He'd told me I was his and he was mine. That I owned his heart. If he kept that promise, if it meant the same thing to me as it did to him, everything else would work itself out. Besides, it was obvious this culture was steeped in all things sexual. I loved my pleasures. I could adapt.

He got off me, helping me to my feet as he reached for the linen to clean between my legs gently. He turned to go to the door, and I remembered one thing I needed to know before he let in our guests.

"Talon. What is the she-barbarian's name?"

He started, then gave me that embarrassed grin again. "Magenta."

"You know there was no way she was going to tell me. She'd insist I call her Mistress or some shit. I'd refuse. The situation would devolve into a battle or something."

He inclined his head, a satisfied look on his face as if to say, "I'd expect nothing less."

Chapter Four

Talon didn't bother to cover his erection as he opened the door to admit Magenta and her pets. I remembered one's name was Zeus, but had no idea what the other was called. Talon snarled at Magenta when I knew he was anything but angry.

"I told you after the evening meal," she said, looking down her nose at me, already sizing me up. "We just finished eating."

"Well, we haven't," I said, jumping on the only thing I could think of that would make Talon express displeasure. I also suspected he wanted to establish dominance before we began this.

Magenta rolled her eyes. "I suspected as much when the whole village heard both of you rutting like animals." She turned slightly. "Luca." The tall male entered with a platter laden with fruits and cheeses. "You can feed your pet while mine look her over. They'll want to make sure they know how she moves. I won't have her disfiguring my own pets."

I took a step forward. "I will eat in peace. If the three of you wish to start without us, I'll be happy to watch, and I'm sure I'll be appropriately aroused. As to disfiguring them, as long as they don't try to do something to me I expressly refuse to allow, there will be no problems."

Magenta refused to look at me or acknowledge my presence in any way. Instead she motioned for Luca to set the tray of food on the hearth. Obviously she expected I'd eat my food on the floor. Like a *pet*. I raised my chin, knowing I'd refuse even if Talon asked me to.

Talon scowled at Magenta, stomping over to the hearth to retrieve the platter. With his long strides, he carried it to the table and waved me over. That was as far as he went though. He sat in a chair and snagged me around the waist when I tried to sit in another chair. Lifting me to sit on his lap, he turned me to face away from him, but spread my legs so that my thighs were spread wide, my knees resting over his own powerful thighs. Like this, I was open to any who wished to view me.

I glanced over my shoulder at Talon. "Really, barbarian?"

He shrugged, the grin never wavering from his ruggedly handsome face. I almost forgave him when he wrapped one muscled arm around my chest, covering my tits, and cupped my pussy possessively with the other hand. Almost.

"I still don't like you in this moment, Talon," I said with no real conviction. He chuckled against my ear, kissing my neck as he squeezed a breast. He lazily grazed my neck up and down, which sent shivers up over my body. I knew the other men couldn't tell how turned on I was getting because Talon's big hands effectively blocked my nipples -- which I was sure were pebble hard -- and my pussy -- which was probably soaking wet.

I let my head fall back against his chest. The deep rumble coming from him told me he was pleased by my easy acceptance. I wasn't sure if this was his way of keeping both women in his home happy, or if it was simply his way of playing with me, but I couldn't really stay mad at him.

Then I felt something at my lips. I opened my eyes, and Zeus was on one knee in front of me with a piece of cheese grazing my lips. "It has a sharp bite."

He grinned. "Like you."

OK. I liked Zeus.

Magenta scowled at her pet but said nothing, undressing without a word. Luca helped her with the fastenings through all the fur in her outfit. Knowing Magenta didn't like that *her* pet was giving *me* attention eased my anger further. I opened my mouth to accept the cheese bite from Zeus. He smiled and offered me a slice of fruit next. By degrees, I relaxed.

Talon rumbled a masculine purr beside my ear, rubbing his face against mine as Zeus fed me one delicious bite after another. He offered me a cup of sweet water, which I drank with an appreciative moan.

"What's your name, mistress?" Zeus was charming and polite, but there was a cunning intelligence in his eyes. I wouldn't be surprised if there was more to him than a simple "pet."

"Mia," I said without hesitation.

"Mistress Mia," he said offering me another bite of cheese.

"No. Just Mia," I wasn't going there.

He smiled. "Mia, then."

Just as I thought *I could get used to this*, Zeus gave me another bite of fruit. This one was dripping with juice. He didn't make an effort to catch the drops. Instead, they fell on Talon's arm. Which Talon moved as he nipped my ear. The next few drops landed on one tit. When I bit into the fruit, a steady stream ran down my chin to my chest. Zeus glanced at Talon -- who nodded -- before leaning in to lick the sticky juice from my skin.

I stiffened, before crying out when his tongue rasped over one nipple. This was wonderful! Talon's big dick pulsed against my backside with every swipe of Zeus's tongue and every cry the other man milked from my throat. The stubble on Talon's jaw abraded the side of my face in an erotic scrape as he rested his chin on my shoulder. My every sense was on fire, loving the lavish attention.

I glanced at Magenta and Luca. The man had finished undressing her and was massaging her shoulders. He was attending her, but his eyes were fixed squarely on me. Magenta stood proudly naked, her breasts large but high and firm. Muscle made her body ripple with her every movement. Had she not been such a bitch, I'd have found her extraordinarily attractive.

OK, so I still found her attractive even though she was a bitch. Her long hair was braided in an intricate style that was at once functional and exotic. The silky-looking chestnut strands were threaded through with gold, probably from the sun. Her skin was lightly tanned except where her outfit covered her, the tan lines standing out like an erotic invitation for a man -- or woman -- to trace them with his tongue.

Talon grunted, nipping my earlobe sharply before sucking the little bit of skin between his lips and licking away the sting.

"What?"

He nodded in Magenta's direction. Did I like looking at her?

"Well, she's a beautiful woman," I admitted. "Of course I like looking at her. Don't you?" I purposely talked about the other woman as if she weren't in the room to fuck with her. As expected, she bristled.

"As if I care what you think, *pet*."

I shrugged, a little smile tugging at my lips. "Got you to speak directly to me, didn't I?"

That got a snicker from Zeus around a mouthful of nipple. The... *pet* didn't even try to hide his amusement.

Magenta's face and neck flushed scarlet. "I will turn you over to the warriors," she hissed to Zeus. "Do you think they'll go as easy on your ass as Luca does? They'll abuse you until you beg them for mercy, but they will show you none!"

That got a "whatever" shrug from Zeus, but, interestingly, a deadly frown from Luca. I said nothing. Magenta obviously had no idea the byplay going on there. Who was I to enlighten her? None of my business.

"In any case," I said as if nothing had happened, "the thought of the two of us writhing on the fur in front of the hearth isn't *un*appealing. I imagine the guys would enjoy the sight as well."

"I'm not here for *their* pleasure." She glanced at Talon before stiffening and focusing on Zeus still licking and sucking at my tits. "The pleasure of pets matters to me not at all. I'm interested in my *own* pleasure." Again, she glanced at Talon. My eyes narrowed as the truth hit me. This woman wanted Talon! Badly. What would she say if she knew what had truly transpired between me and Talon?

We'd agreed to enjoy this, but could I actually watch him fuck this woman knowing she wanted him for her own? True, I had no doubt he held no interest in Magenta. At least, not for anything other than mutual pleasure for him and me. And he was obviously willing to let Zeus and Luca fuck me. So, what did I do about this? She'd said she would never allow another Alpha to actually penetrate her, but how much of that was bluster?

"No," Talon murmured in my ear. "Not for me."

I stiffened. Zeus glanced up at Talon, who merely nodded for him to continue. The wicked man twirled his tongue in my navel before nipping at my belly with his white teeth. I sucked in a breath. That man certainly knew his way around a woman's body. Had I not been a little concerned about the rest of the evening and how it might affect my budding relationship (of sorts) with Talon, my eyes would have rolled back at the sinful pleasure he created within me.

"But we agreed we were doing this." I didn't want him to think I had a double standard. If he wanted to fuck another woman, I wanted him to feel comfortable doing it even though I was feeling so possessive right now I could pluck Magenta's eyes out just for looking at my male. Which dampened my own pleasure in a huge way. I'd never felt this level of jealousy toward anyone. And Lord knew I had no real reason to be possessive of Talon. I'd met him mere hours ago. What did I really know about his culture and how they viewed permanent partners, anyway?

"Do this for me." He was getting better at voicing his thoughts out loud. "That one holds no interest for me." His voice was soft beside my ear but still held that rough edge to it as if here were still getting used to using his voice again.

"So, you don't think me a hypocrite?" I looked over my shoulder and caught his smug expression before he could mask it.

"My female wants her male all to herself."

I tried to act put out, huffing as I turned back to the tantalizing things Zeus was doing to my belly. The man seemed to know he would have to start over in order to build my pleasure back to where it had been, but didn't seem to care. Talon's deep rumbling chuckle made me blush. He sounded so wicked when he did that! Like he was enjoying my responses way more than was healthy for my sanity and knew it.

"My pleasure is in yours," Talon said at my ear. Then took my nipples between his fingers and tugged gently until I squirmed.

Zeus groaned appreciatively, his gaze fixed on my tits where Talon stretched them out before letting them go. I knew they jiggled before settling. When Talon didn't immediately grab them again, Zeus took one peak into his mouth, suckling strongly. His other hand found my other tit, pinching the nipple and twisting lightly before turning it into a rougher motion. I moaned my enjoyment, arching to him. I threaded my fingers through his short, nut-brown hair, holding him to me. His tongue on my fevered skin felt amazing.

Zeus looked up at Talon. "I will pleasure your woman well, Master Talon." He whispered his words, apparently wanting no one but the three of us to hear. He glanced back at Magenta and Luca. The barbarian woman's eyes were closed in bliss as Luca knelt before her. One of her legs was over his shoulder, and Luca's face was firmly between Magenta's legs. She threaded her fingers through his hair, holding him to her. Occasionally, she seemed to glance our way, but her concentration was on her own pleasure.

As if to draw my attention back to my own delights -- and to remind me who I belonged to -- Talon stroked between my legs, circling my clit with lazy circles. I kind of liked that he didn't want me to forget he was there, no matter how much he wanted me to feel good. I still wondered how I would react to see him pleasuring the stunning Magenta. Perversely, now that he'd assured me watching me fuck Magenta's two pets would bring him pleasure, I realized maybe I was just a little deranged. Because I kind of wanted to see what he'd do to Magenta if he chose to give her pleasure.

Would he simply finger her? Play with her tits? Would he want to eat her pussy? Fuck her? How much of it could I stand? Even though she'd said no penetration from Talon, I had the distinct feeling that wasn't what she really wanted. If I were betting, I'd say she wanted to be dominated by him in every way possible. Which I would never let happen because I wasn't certain I didn't want it myself.

Fuck. Just thinking about it now got me wet. Maybe I could watch him playing with her. Maybe?

"She's dripping wet," Zeus said, awe lacing his voice. "Fucking dripping..." He trailed his fingers through my cunt lips, bringing my cream to his lips to taste. I shivered. "Shall I paint her nipples for Luca to lick off? Or perhaps Mistress Magenta?" Zeus gave a sideways glance at his master with a wicked gleam in his eyes. That man was up to something. Something naughty.

Talon grunted, giving a half shrug as if to say, "Whatever you like."

Zeus trailed his fingers through my soaked flesh again. He sucked my cream from his fingers before trailing them through my cunt again. I whimpered at the contact. His actions were so fucking sexy! Petting me. Tasting me. Before me was a man who lived in the moment and took his pleasure where he found it. He rubbed one nipple, smearing my juices over the peak. Without a word, Luca left Magenta to lick my nipple. Zeus scooped more of my moisture to his mouth. When Luca let my tit go with a loud *pop*, Zeus cupped Luca's jaw in one hand and kissed the other man, thrusting his tongue wickedly. Luca groaned as he sucked on Zeus's tongue. Did he taste me?

"Looks like you've enamored my pets," Magenta said, speaking to me voluntarily for the first time.

There was still resentment in her voice, but she seemed riveted to the sight of the four of us -- her pets on the floor pleasuring me and kissing each other, Talon and I sitting in the chair, me spread over his legs with my pussy open to anyone sitting in front of me. "Makes me wonder what you taste like."

"It's not like I'm moving."

She looked at me with her head tilted. Like she might look at a dessert she'd like to try. It didn't take long for Magenta to make her decision. "Move her to the table, Talon," she commanded. "I'll not kneel for a pet."

Talon growled at her but didn't hesitate to lift me. Luca snagged a fur to lie over the wood before Talon set me upon it. I scooted so my ass was at the edge, my feet resting flat with my legs spread wide. Talon leaned down to take a swipe. When his tongue made contact, he jerked like he'd been hit. Then dove in, snarling at my flesh as he sucked and licked. There was no way I could prevent the sharp cry. Before I could thread my fingers through his hair, however, Magenta pulled him away to take his place.

"Greedy Talon," she chastised. "You've had your turn." Her hands were rough on my thighs -- like Talon's -- but smaller. The bite of her nails as she held me open to her perusal was also different, but not unwelcome.

"I must say," she continued, "she has a pretty little pussy. So pink and puffy. Wet." How could her words turn me on when I knew she still saw me as a possession and not a person? Probably because Talon grunted in assent while licking his lips to get more of my taste.

I found his gaze with my own. The intent, brows-drawn way he watched Magenta as she dipped her face to my sex made me clench. It wasn't the anticipation of the woman's touch, but of Talon's reaction. Already, his dick pulsed and bobbed. Arms crossed over his muscled chest, he swallowed as Magenta stuck out her tongue and took a tentative lick. Had the woman never tasted another female before? If she considered herself an Alpha, it made sense she hadn't. She would consider it beneath her, just as an Alpha male wouldn't want to suck another man's dick.

Magenta lapped at my pussy, her tongue fluttering lazily over my clit several times before she took one fold of my flesh between her lips and sucked. With a little slurping sound, she let it go only to suck on the other one. Raising her face, she still looked as if she couldn't decide if she liked this or not. Then Luca came to her side.

"Try this," he said as he dipped his fingers inside me to gather moisture on the pads. "Paint her nipples like Zeus did. Then lick the peaks until they pucker under your tongue."

Luca demonstrated, coating one of my nipples in my own juice before licking it with the flat of his tongue in a slow, sensual lick. When he pulled away, my nipple stood out hard and proud. Magenta mimicked Luca's action. When my nipple pebbled under her tongue, she jerked as if startled.

With a look of wonder she took my tit into her mouth more fully, drawing on it strongly as she pulled away until it slipped from her mouth with a loud *pop*. Over and over she did this, exploring my tits. Occasionally, Luca or Zeus would paint the peak with my juices, and she even started to moan around my tit.

Until Zeus slipped his hand between her legs to gather her own moisture. And painted my lips with it.

Chapter Five

I grinned at Zeus, who winked at me. I let him trail his finger over my lips several times before I opened my mouth to suck the digits. Magenta's flavor burst over my tongue a split second before her strangled cry of surrender. The next thing I knew, Magenta covered my body with her own even as she covered my lips with hers. This was forbidden! Not what was supposed to happen. I pushed away with a cry, turning my head.

Talon was staring at us, transfixed. His eyes were wide in disbelief, but he didn't look angry. "I didn't do that," I said, afraid he'd take exception. Even that he might discard me. "I didn't kiss her."

He seemed to weigh a decision, not knowing what to do, then he looked from me to Magenta and back. Luca had coaxed her from me back to the table and had buried his face between her legs to feast, distracting her. Two fingers slid in and out of her cunt while he tongued her greedily. She was nearly mindless with lust. Doubtless she had no idea what she was doing. Talon's dick pulsed like mad. Clearly, he was turned on, but torn as to what to do.

"You're mine," he repeated. "Yes." It wasn't a question.

"Only yours, Talon," I said, looking into his eyes. Magenta was clawing like mad to get to me even as Luca spread the other woman's moisture over my mouth again. She tasted so sweet it was hard for me to resist, but I turned my head. Luca looked at Talon questioningly.

"Only mates kiss each other," I said. "I don't

want her like that."

"Tonight," Talon said, his eyes alight with desire. Lust. "Only tonight. Only her."

"Not the men," I said. They at least seemed to have their wits about them. In fact, unless I missed my guess, they had something greater planned they were working toward.

"My thanks," Luca said to Talon.

Talon narrowed his eyes, the full implication of what had just transpired hitting him. His lips curled as if he'd finally gotten the joke. I wished I had.

"She kissed what she considered to be the pet of another Alpha," Zeus whispered in my ear. "Something she will remember at a later time and know how mindless she was for the touch of another's pet."

I looked at Luca, who was now kissing Magenta over and over, making her even more mindless. She whimpered, clutching at Luca, who happily fingered her pussy and fed her her own juices even as he continued to kiss her.

"She kisses the two of you."

"It's not the same thing. She owns us and has no one she claims as a mate. You, she considers the pet of another. By surrendering herself to such lusts, she has proven she's no Alpha. A fact that will somehow be well known beyond this dwelling before the night is over." He winked at me. These two had set her up? Talk about intrigues.

Again, I looked to Talon. He nodded as he stroked himself. "Only tonight," he repeated.

"I'm yours?" I questioned, needing to be sure. "Only yours?"

"For now," he said. Was that resignation in his voice?

"Talon? I don't --"

"Later," he said, gently. He moved to my side and kissed me lovingly. "I'll always be yours, but you will also belong to another."

I looked up at him in bafflement. "But I don't want to belong to another."

"Trust me," he said against my lips. "Protect you. Always."

Was that Talon's way of reassuring me? Then he reached a hand to Magenta's pussy and coated my lips at the same time Luca coated Magenta's lips with my juice. When he let Magenta up, the woman found me again, pinning my body with her own, fusing her mouth to mine.

Her tongue twined with mine, stroking and delving. Several times, I felt fingers probe my entrance only to have one of the males slip those fingers between our lips for us to share. I tasted Magenta as well so they were playing with both of us equally, seeing how high they could drive us. It was pleasant enough for me, but Magenta seemed to lose her ever-loving shit.

She straddled my leg. Knowing what she needed, I raised my knee to contact her pussy so she could grind her clit. Magenta had no trouble figuring out what to do. She snapped her hips wickedly as she kissed me. Her excitement fueled my own.

I scooted down and rolled to one side, bring our pussies in line. At the first contact between our wet, swollen pussies, both of us gasped. *Now* we were getting somewhere. The silken glide of her lips over mine, her clit over mine, pushed us both dangerously close to orgasm. Magenta adjusted her position to sit up on her knees, my leg thrown over her shoulder, her arm clamped around my thigh in a death grip.

With a snarl, she ground her pussy against mine, her teeth bared at me as if to dare me to take this pleasure away from her. With a grin, I reached for her tits. She eagerly leaned in to allow me to pinch her nipples. They were large and long as they stiffened in my grasp. I loved seeing the peaks jutting out and flipped them with the backs of my fingernails. Impatient to taste her, I sat up on my elbows, then pushed up to my hands. My leg was still over her shoulder, but I managed to find one nipple with my tongue, fluttering it over and over until she moaned.

Luca moved my leg to lock around Magenta's waist. Our cunts were still grinding with each move of our hips, but I was able to sit up fully. To take her other breast between my lips and suck her nipple to a hard, pouting peak.

"That's it," came Luca's soft, deep voice. "Make her come like this." I had no idea if he was talking to Magenta or me, but it was sexy as fuck. I was getting more and more turned on by the minute.

Then Talon was behind me, dipping his hand between Magenta and me to separate our clits. Magenta sobbed a broken denial, but stopped just short of begging him to stop. We both moved on him, coating his fingers in our moisture as we looked into one another's eyes. No longer was Magenta the Alpha she'd pretended to be. Now she was as helpless as I was in the face of her denied pleasure.

"Talon," I breathed, prompting him to remove his hand. He held it between us, an offering. I sucked one finger into my mouth while Magenta took another. The two of us cleaned him, both of us moaning our pleasure at tasting the other on Talon's hand. I was totally getting into this! Woman or not, bitch or not, Magenta was turning out to be a seriously hot fuck.

Just as I was about to find my orgasm, Zeus pulled me away from Magenta. "Hey!" I protested, but soon realized what he had planned. Luca kissed Magenta fervently, urging her to lie back on the fur-covered table. Surprisingly, the woman didn't resist, allowing him to lay her fully down and spread her thighs wide for his probing fingers.

"You like fucking another woman?" Luca's question caught me off guard. For a moment I thought he was talking to me, but Zeus silenced me with a finger over my mouth when I would have answered.

"Say nothing," he whispered for my ears alone, his lips grazing my ear. Then my neck.

"I --" Magenta started, but Zeus cut her off.

"I know you do. Admit it."

"Zeus!" Magenta's cry was broken.

"Now!" Zeus had seemed to be the easy-going one, but now, he was all authoritarian, demanding she yield to him.

"Yes!" Magenta screamed. "I do! I love it!"

"You *need* it! *Crave* it!"

She looked at me, the bitch from before gone. In her place was a wanton sex kitten. Well, a sex tiger. She was still an intimidating woman. All muscle and strength. But now, she looked almost… desperate.

I had nothing to give her. At this point, I might have surrendered to her, given her anything she demanded of me. Mostly for my own continued pleasure, but also because I wanted to see what would happen when this was over.

Zeus gave her pussy a decisive slap, the sound echoing in the room. I groaned, rolling my hips. Talon was at my side immediately. Instead of kissing me or petting my pussy, he gave my mound an identical slap. Which made me gasp in surprise. The resulting sting…

made me scream.

So he did it again. And again.

Before I knew it, I had canted my hips to his slaps, spreading my legs wide so he had all the access he wanted. Talon growled with every swat and my resulting whimpers. Luca loomed over me, jacking his big dick slowly as he watched my quivering body.

"So beautiful," Luca murmured. He glanced at Talon. "Lucky."

"Yes," Talon agreed.

Then I lost the train of the conversation because Talon plunged three fingers inside me while circling my clit with his thumb. It was over for me. I screamed, fucking his hand as I reached for Luca. I pulled the other man to my chest, arching at him so there was no mistake what I needed from him. He didn't hesitate, didn't try to master me as Zeus was Magenta. He simply gave me the pleasure I needed.

"Look at her," Zeus commanded Magenta. "Her male and your pet pleasure her so well. Wouldn't you love to be the one finger-fucking her? The one eating her sweet pussy? The one making her come all over your tongue?"

With a sob, she nodded. Zeus picked her up. As he sat in a chair, he turned her away from him and had her straddle him as I had Talon earlier. Her legs were spread, resting on the outside of his so that she was open for all to see. I gazed at her bare pussy. Her lips were puffy and glistening. Moisture dripped in shining drops from her sex to Zeus's balls.

"Magenta," I breathed.

Talon rumbled approval between my legs.

Luka murmured, "Good girl."

I was turned on beyond belief. I knew Luca and Zeus wanted to trap Magenta in her own lust -- which was likely well deserved -- but I just wanted to get off.

"Your pussy looks yummy all spread open like that. Don't you ache to be filled with something?" Luca taunted Magenta with what we all knew she wanted.

"I do," she all but sobbed.

"Zeus could ram his cock inside you right there," He said. As I watched her pussy avidly, another pearled drop slid from her slit to land on Zeus's balls. He shifted her so that his cock slid through her lips and over her clit, sandwiched between her wet folds.

Magenta moaned. "Not like this," she gasped. "I have to --"

"You have to what? Be in control?" Zeus picked up the thread, speaking as he teased Magenta.

"Yes!" she wailed. "I'm in control!"

"Does it feel like you're in control?" Zeus's tone was harsh, almost disgusted, but he winked at me over Magenta's shoulder.

"I'm --" She gasped. "-- the Alpha --" Another gasp as she tilted her hips to rub over his cock, trying to get friction over her clit. "-- in this group."

"Are you?" he sneered. Instead of thrusting inside her or fingering her, Zeus reached between her legs to push his cock away from her. She screamed in frustration, reaching between them to bat his hand away and get his cock back against her.

Zeus nodded to Luca, who stood, taking his mouth from my tit. I nearly screeched in outrage, but Talon chuckled before lifting me and carrying me to the rug before the hearth. I could still see the trio, but Talon covered me with his big body, sliding his cock deep inside me.

"We only have a few minutes before they have you again," he said, surprising me by the full sentence. He must be getting used to speaking.

"Talon," I breathed.

"I am... proud," he said, kissing me with long licks as he fucked me. He pulled my leg over his hip and shifted his weight slightly to one side. The man might be of few words, but he knew his way around a woman's body. The pleasure was instantaneous. "Few mates to a warrior would give him this gift."

"I doubt many warriors would let his woman have this pleasure. Thank you."

"You are comfortable?"

"With where this is leading? I'm good for myself, but I have a feeling they are getting ready to change Magenta's life forever." I grinned. "Not that she doesn't deserve it. Is this all right with you?"

His cock pulsed inside me. "Fucking hot," he murmured. "Magenta is nothing," he said as he surged inside me. "But you..." he shuddered as he wrapped himself around me ever tighter. *You are everything.*"

I loved the way he fucked me. His lips found my neck and he sucked, marking me once. Then again. "Talon!" I screamed his name as his hard body pushed me over the edge. "Oh, God! Yes! *AAHHHHH*!" My orgasm hit me hard, fast, and intense. I clung to Talon as I moved on him, taking my pleasure. I'd thought he would come inside me, but instead, he pulled out and gave my pussy one more wicked smack.

"She comes so beautifully," Zeus said. "I know you'd like to be there with Mia as she peaks. I bet her tongue and fingers are magic." His tone was soft but devilish instead of harsh as he had been before. With a sigh, I turned my head to look at the trio. And gasped.

Zeus still had Magenta in his lap, but Luka was tying her hands together at the wrist and securing them to a lead. When he finished, he looped her arms around Zeus's head while she squirmed and shrieked.

When she kicked out, Luca said, "Do I need to bind your ankles too? I'd hate for you to miss the pleasure we had planned for you."

"Let me go!" she yelled, but she stilled. "Please," she whispered. I was surprised to see tears leaking from her eyes. "Please," she said, her voice breaking.

"They nearly have her," Talon whispered in my ear. He'd moved so that he knelt next to me. He turned my head, smoothing my hair from my face, and offered me his cock. I opened my mouth without hesitation, taking him deep. I moaned in bliss as his salty essence exploded on my tongue. Precum beaded from the head steadily so I sucked harder and harder, working for my reward. "Once they make her submit to them, they'll come back to us..." I stuck my tongue into the slit on his cock head and his breath hitched. "Fuck!"

"You like that," I said. It wasn't a question. I knew he did, but I gave him a saucy grin.

"Fuck!" he repeated, his eyes wide, his breath hitching. When I did it again he gasped. "Greedy little female," he breathed. "You can't even wait for me to come. Taking it... taking it from me!"

I sucked him as I flicked my tongue several times. He pulled back, trying to take my new toy away. So I grasped him by the balls and pulled him back. His shaft slid down my throat, hitting the back. I nearly gagged, but managed to relax my muscles so that he could freely fuck my mouth. Once he started moving like I wanted him to -- hard and deep -- I relaxed and let him use me for his pleasure. Oddly, looking up at his big body lathered with sweat, his face a mask of desperate lust, was freeing in the extreme. To think I had this much effect on a man like Talon made me feel more powerful than I ever had.

It wasn't long before he was grunting with every

surge of his hips, sweat dripping from him to land on my quivering tits. Just as I heard Magenta scream a defeated surrender, Talon bellowed my name. His cum hit me hard before I could relax again and swallow all he had to give. Some of the pearly liquid spilled from the corner of my mouth, and I scooped it up with a finger. Gaze holding his, I licked my finger, grinning as he gasped for breath above me.

Talon gave me a crooked grin. "My female," he said, breathing heavily. "Loath to share you."

I chuckled. "Yet your cock is stirring again at the mere mention of it."

He gave me a sheepish look. "Watching you and Magenta is… arousing."

"That sounds like an understatement. If Zeus and Luca want to fuck me, are you going to be good with it?"

"Tonight, yes. I want your pleasure tonight."

I sat up, framing his face with my hands. "If that's all you want, Talon, *you* give me pleasure. I don't need anyone else."

"Yes," he said, holding my gaze intently. "You do. You will."

"I don't understand. Does this have to do with what you were talking about before?"

"Yes. This will help you later." Then he glanced at the trio across the room before rubbing the back of his neck. "And it will bring me pleasure to watch."

I laughed. "You're the most incredible man I've ever met, Talon. But you're still a guy."

"Indeed."

Chapter Six

I stretched on the fur, arms over my head, letting my legs fall wide. I was opening myself for anyone. For Talon's pleasure. He wanted me to feel good, but I knew he got just as much enjoyment from watching me as I did from participating. I'd have to grill him about whatever he had planned for me later because I had the feeling my future depended on it.

My future happiness. My future with Talon.

Turning my head, I glanced at Zeus, Luca, and Magenta. The three seemed to have come to an understanding, that being their positions were going to be reversed. Whether or not that worked out well for Magenta remained to be seen, but I was willing to do my part. I grinned at the trio. Luca met my gaze. When I nodded, he did as well, catching Zeus's attention and jerking his head in my direction.

My heart pounded inside my chest. Despite the uncertainty of what lay ahead for me, I was excited. I found I wanted this experience. Earlier, I'd mused that if I was fated to die because of my exile, I was going to experience pleasure in all its forms. Now I realized how right I'd been. What Talon had in store for me made my stomach clench, but I trusted him. If he said he'd protect me then he would. He said I'd still be his woman. I'd hold on to those things and give him the benefit of the doubt.

I turned my head to watch as Zeus carried Magenta over to me. He walked with her long, tanned legs hooked over his powerful arms so that she was spread wide. His cock bobbed as he walked, hitting her clit with every step. Finely honed muscles played beneath her skin, but, naked as she was, she looked like the pleasure pet more than the powerfully built Zeus or even the leanly muscled Luca. There was a look of something like intoxication on her face. Whatever had been going on among the three of them had her in such a state of lust she had no control over herself. I knew how she felt. Talon had done that to me with effortless ease.

Talon reached for me, pulling me from the furs and into his arms. Kissing me deeply, he groaned against my mouth. "Fucking hot! You will do this for me, love?" His speech seemed to be coming easier, but his voice still had that husky rasp that drove me crazy. I'd only known this man a few hours. How could he affect me so much?

Then he was laying me atop Magenta, my legs straddling her face. On straightened arms, I gazed at her swollen flesh. Moisture glistened from her bare pussy, and I found myself actually licking my lips. Was I looking forward to this as much as Talon was?

Magenta wrapped her arms around my legs and pulled me down to her waiting mouth. Immediately, the sensation of her tongue lashing my clit hit me with a punch of lust. I cried out, grinding my pussy against her mouth before I could stop myself. Then I caught Talon's hungry gaze as I descended to Magenta's luscious cunt.

The salty essence of her sex made me groan. She raised her knees, spreading herself wider for me. Finally dropping my gaze from Talon's, I laid my body flush against Magenta's and buried my face between her legs and licked.

Magenta screamed into my cunt, vibrating my clit so that I shuddered with need. Had I thought I might not enjoy this? With renewed vigor, I sucked her lips, letting them each go with a little "pop" before I curled my tongue around her clit. In response, she rocked her hips against my face and moaned into my flesh. The feel was different than when a man ate me out, but it wasn't in the least unpleasant. I found that I liked wringing gasps and cries from her as well.

Thrusting my tongue into her cunt, I groaned. She rolled her hips for more of my touch. This was a far cry from the way she'd been with me earlier. Whatever Zeus and Luca had done or said to her had completely changed her. Perhaps this was Magenta as she really was. Maybe the men knew this from the beginning and had been waiting for the right time to push her in this direction. Either way, she was embracing her new role with open arms. The same as she was going down on my cunt.

"Good girl, Magenta," Luca's deep voice sounded above us. "Can you make her come? Can you eat her that good?"

She grunted. And thrust her tongue deep. Her clever fingers found my clit, and my orgasm crashed over me unexpectedly. I screamed sharply as my body convulsed with every lash of her tongue. I caught sight of Talon at the corner of my vision jacking his big cock. The thought of him watching me as he masturbated sent another spike of heat curling through me. Another quick, hard orgasm swept me up, and I screamed again, this time burying my face between Magenta's legs, eating her with all the passion erupting through me. I was rewarded when her body beaded with sweat and she shrieked her own pleasure.

"Ah, my little *pet* certainly loves her pleasures," Zeus said. I could tell he was behind me. Probably at Magenta's ear. As she continued to lick, I felt Zeus's blunt fingertip circle my pussy opening, coating his finger in my cum. "Suck her for me, *pet*." Magenta's mouth left my clit, I assume to suck Zeus's fingers. The thought of this powerful warrior woman being made so lust-drunk that she surrendered to men she considered inferior to her was hard to wrap my mind around. If there was one thing I knew absolutely about the Outlands, it was that one never showed weakness to another. To do so would invite certain death. It was survival of the fittest out here. I think that was why Talon was so proud of my show of violence earlier. He had a pet -- now a mate -- who could protect herself. Who could have his back. This reaction in Magenta must have been building for a very long time. Apparently, Zeus and Luca were the perfect men for her. The only question was, what would they do with her now?

Luca moved in front of me, offering his cock. I glanced at Talon, who nodded eagerly. With a grin, I opened my mouth, taking his length as deep as I could. Though not as big as Talon, he was long and deliciously thick. I tasted Magenta on him and moaned around his length.

After several minutes of my ministrations, Luca pulled from my grasp. I whimpered until I realized what he'd planned. Fisting his cock, Luca placed the head at Magenta's entrance beneath me. I watched, fascinated, as he slid slowly inside her and began to fuck with a slow, leisurely motion.

When I turned to look at Talon in lust-filled wonder, I found he was standing beside me. Leaning down to give me a hard, fervent kiss, he thrust his tongue inside my mouth. I tongue-fucked him back, which clearly delighted him. I knew he tasted Magenta on my lips and couldn't help the fine shudder that ran through me. Especially since the woman still sucked and tongued my pussy with abandon. If she minded that she was literally the "bottom" in this situation, she didn't show it.

Releasing my lips, Talon gently turned my head and pressed me toward Magenta's cunt. I smiled as I licked her clit, testing my positioning so I didn't get in Luca's way. It took some doing, but we finally found a rhythm that suited both of us. Magenta didn't seem to mind either.

Talon growled, leaning down to lick beside me, his tongue grazing my own tongue, Magenta's clit, and possibly Luca's dick. Not that anyone seemed to mind. I shifted so I could wrap my lips around Luca's dick from the side, so that with each thrust inside Magenta, my lips slid the length of him. Both Luca and Talon groaned, Luca's dick pulsing against my lips.

"Fuck!" Luca bit out. "Fucking hot!"

With a grunt Talon kissed me again before moving behind me. It wasn't long before I felt him probing my entrance with the head of his cock. I rocked back, enticing him to enter me. Magenta's tongue continued to flutter against my clit. Occasionally, she'd whimper, her tongue leaving me.

"That's it," Zeus hissed, sounding as excited as I felt. "Lick his shaft as he enters her. Lick him when he withdraws. Lick her juices off Luca's dick!" With a defeated moan, she did. Her lips seemed to be everywhere. I could tell when she licked Talon, but she managed to keep at least some of her mouth on me. My clit was swollen painfully, pulsing under her tongue as Talon fucked me. His shaft was harder than I'd felt it yet as he enjoyed the sight all of us made.

Luca swatted Magenta's ass, and she jumped. For a couple of seconds she stopped moving altogether, as if he'd startled her. Then she moaned, settling back in to tongue my pussy with a vengeance. My orgasm seared through me as Talon pounded into me. He smacked my ass when my cunt contracted around him. Then again. And again. I knew my ass would be red, but, unlike the first time he'd done it when bringing me here, I found myself arching up to meet his swats.

"Oh, fuck!" I cried. "Do it again!"

He did. Several times. Then he gripped my hips and pounded me, fucking me in abandon. I glanced back over my shoulder at him. Tendons in his neck stood out in stark relief as did the muscles of his chest and arms. Sweat glistened on his tanned skin, and my mouth watered to lick each drop from him.

With a shout, Talon pounded into me twice more before ejaculating inside me in a powerful surge. His dick pulsed inside me over and over as he roared his satisfaction. When his grip on my ass loosened, Magenta pulled him out of my cunt, taking him in her mouth. I started to roll over but Magenta gripped my ass to stay me. It wasn't long before I felt her mouth on me again, licking the mixture of mine and Talon's cum. Which pushed me over the edge one last time. My clit was super sensitive, and I shuddered with every stroke of her tongue before finally rolling off her to catch my breath.

Luca's movements sped up, his muscles bulging as he surged inside Magenta, his orgasm finally overtaking him. "Fucking hot! Fucking hot!"

Talon sat back on his heels, taking his cock from Magenta when she tried to suck him down again. His chest heaved as he recovered from his orgasm, but his dick was still semi-hard as he watched Luca fuck Magenta with all his might. Zeus took Luca's place, Magenta sucking him with fast, hard strokes.

She cried out, her arms over her head in surrender, eyes squeezed shut as her muscles clenched. Moments later, Zeus growled, "Come, Magenta! Come on my cock!"

She did. I was sure her screams could be heard all over the village. As mine probably had. Zeus soon followed her with his own bellow of satisfaction, emptying himself into her until his cock slipped from her folds in a wet rush.

Zeus looked to Talon. "You're welcome to use our pet if you wish. Her treatment of your woman would justify anything you wanted."

Talon shook his head. "Her last word was no. I respect the lesson you taught her, but I won't go against her wishes in this."

He nodded. "Which is why you're respected the Outlands over."

"What the holy fuck are you doing, Talon?"

A spike of dread came over me as I recognized that voice.

Luca scooped up a spent and whimpering Magenta, who wound her arms around him and clung as he carried her out. "My thanks, Talon. We appreciate you and your woman's help in this."

"Your woman?" The newcomer stepped full into the dwelling, allowing Zeus and Luca to pass with Magenta. He shut the door behind them. "I leave you for half a day, and you go and have a fucking orgy. With the woman we picked out for Zar!"

I scrambled to pull a fur over my used body. Not that this particular male hadn't already seen -- and fucked -- everything I had to show. In the door, looking equal parts confused, angry, and disbelieving, stood Dak.

"Now wait just a goddamned minute," I said, my

ire rising with every second. "It's not like you haven't fucked me. And in front of an audience, too. At least Talon gave me a choice I could live with: do it or don't. My choice with you was to either accept you or the other guards would have their turn."

Before I could blink, Talon was on Dak. He tackled the other man, pummeling him with every ounce of force in his mighty body. It happened so fast and so furiously I only had time to gasp. Surprisingly, Dak took it. He blocked what he could but didn't strike back. Which was probably the only reason Talon let up on the beating.

Gasping as he spit blood, Dak said, "It was the only option."

"Talon, no! I was only trying to get him to back off you!" I was horrified! Angry as I was at Dak for trying to make Talon feel guilty, I didn't want him hurt. At least, not badly.

"He… misused you!" he snarled, then roared, "Death!"

"No! Talon, NO!" I physically grabbed his arm, putting myself between him and Dak. Not because I felt particularly sorry for Dak, but because I didn't want Talon to murder a man who obviously meant much to him when I'd made something out to be worse than it actually had been.

"Look at me," I said, pushing Talon back so he could focus on me instead of continuing to pummel Dak. "Look at me!" I took his face between my hands. "Dak didn't hurt me. He *helped* me. Had he not taken matters into his own hands, I probably would have been gang raped. And you know how I react to danger. I'd have fought to the death and likely lost."

When Talon hesitated but still looked unconvinced I continued. "He made it pleasurable for me. Allowed me to freely show my passion and, in a way, my fierceness. I have no doubt the display we put on kept more than one male from trying to take me." I gave him a saucy grin I hoped would put him at ease. "You know I'm a handful during sex. I doubt the average male could handle me."

Talon raised his chin, straightening to his full, considerable height in all his naked glory. His cock bobbed in front him enticingly, almost as if the fight with Dak had turned him on. Despite the situation, my sex clenched for it, already readying my body to receive him. How had I become so completely his in only a few hours?

"Mine," Talon said. His voice sounded stronger than it had thus far. He'd nearly lost that gruff, raspy timbre that made me cream for him. Now, it was deep and rich. Full. Not at all unpleasant but not what I'd grown used to the past few hours.

Dak started as he struggled to his feet, astonishment clearly etched on his face. "You're... talking?"

Talon shrugged. "Have reason to."

With a glance at me, Dak said, "Her?"

"Told you... mine." Though he'd spoken more and more throughout the night, Talon seemed to be reverting, his sentences short, no longer complete, as if the stress of the situation were getting to him.

"All right, all right," Dak said, raising his hands in surrender. "I understand. But what if Zar doesn't agree?"

"Then I leave. With her. She's not a pet. Not even to Zar."

"I get that, but are you sure you want her as your mate? You've already lost one. I won't lose you if she bolts on you or decides she wants another. You nearly lost your mind the last time. If she can't... adjust to our lifestyle, or if Zar doesn't want her... Talon, understand me. I *won't* lose you a second time."

Talon leveled Dak with an intense gaze. "It is done."

"Fuck," Dak swore, stabbing his fingers through his hair. "You were supposed to observe her. Maybe protect her if she needed it. Not fucking *mate* with her! What the fuck were you thinking?"

"Wait a minute," I said, standing as I wrapped the fur around me. "What exactly is going on here?"

Dak sighed. "Talon... goddamn it. Just... goddamn it!" There was no rancor in his expletive. Just tired resignation. He sank into a nearby chair and propped his head in his hand, one elbow resting on the table. "Do you have any idea how bloody difficult you can be?"

"Hello?" I said. "I asked you guys a question."

Dak turned to me. "Talon was supposed to follow and observe you. If you proved to be a woman he believed could stand with our king, Zar, he was to secure you and wait for me."

I grinned. "Well, he did half of what you asked. He just didn't wait on you. Also, I have to tell you, I really like Talon. I made a decision to stay with him. I'll admit I made that decision with the understanding that being exiled was pretty much a death sentence. If I was going to live I needed a strong partner working with me."

"Well, you certainly have that in Talon," Dak said dryly. "But does that mean you intend to run the first time you realize you'll be safe on your own? Perhaps when we pass the first city where you can start over?"

Talon stiffened where he stood, obviously not

having thought of that particular angle. The man was so infatuated with me it wasn't even funny. Which made me fall just a little more for him.

"If Talon keeps treating me like he has since he found me, he has nothing to worry about. The man has been nothing but good and kind to me." I tapped my finger against my chin as though contemplating. "Though he *did* swat my ass in front of Magenta when he first brought me into the village." When Talon looked stricken, I laughed. "I suspect, however, it was more because he wanted an excuse to touch my ass than to show any real dominance. I also suspect he liked hearing my outraged squawk. So I'll forgive him. Especially in light of how much it turns me on during sex."

Talon gave me a relieved, if annoyed, look before crossing to me and taking me in his arms for a fierce hug.

"So, the question becomes, what do we do now?" Dak looked at Talon. "Does she know what is supposed to happen?"

Talon shook his head. It seemed like that might be all he'd do, but instead he nodded to the door. "That was supposed to help prepare her."

"You said that before. Prepare me for what?"

"Talon and I are part of the Triad in our part of the Outlands. Our king, Zar, is the head. Most territories have triads or duos. It's a way of spreading the power so one leader doesn't have too much. It also means more than one man or woman is offering insight to decisions. Still, we are… different. We've always been together, even before we were the Triad. The three of us. We are…" Dak trailed off and looked to Talon for help.

"We are together in all things. Including bed

play." As curious as I was about what Talon was saying, I couldn't help but notice the look of awe on Dak's face. It was as if hearing Talon speak was the most amazing thing he'd ever heard in his life.

Dak blinked several times before turning his attention back to me. Then he looked back to Talon as if the man were a creature he'd never seen before. "You've mated her." It sounded like he was musing to himself. "My god, Talon. Zar will go his own way regardless, but I can't let you leave." He looked at Talon as fiercely as if they were headed into battle. "Understand me. I *won't!*"

Talon blinked several times before bowing his head in acknowledgement, his grip on me tightening. He buried his face in my hair, and I melted a little. This big man needed me to comfort him?

I glanced up at Dak from Talon's brawny arms. The man looked just as lost as I suspected Talon was. Surprisingly, my heart went out to him. Was it because of the sex we'd shared earlier? Or because of the feelings he obviously had for Talon?

Giving Talon a squeeze, I pushed away from him to approach Dak. The man sat at the table, head in his hands as if defeated. "Fuck," he swore softly.

"Tell me what I need to do to make this better," I said softly. I threaded my fingers through Dak's hair, gently urging him to look at me. As I'd suspected, there was a defeated glint in his eyes.

His gaze raked me from head to toe. The scrutiny wasn't unpleasant. In fact, he looked at me as if seeing me for the first time, not as a woman he'd used and discarded. If he'd done the latter, I would have had to gut him.

"You need to impress Zar. Make him desire you above all his pets."

"Explain this triad to me." I had to have information if I was going to figure this out. "I get the feeling it's more than a ruling body."

He nodded slowly, a different interest shining in his eyes. This time, he looked as if I'd surprised him. "While we are the final say in everything in our territory, our Triad is different from most. Other territories and villages have triads or duos who share power equally, but we do not. As I said, we've been together all our lives. We were groomed for this from birth. Zar is the eldest and therefore the leader. Talon and I are close to the same age. Talon is the better warrior. I'm the better mediator. Together we discuss and come to a consensus on all matters. But ultimately, the decision is Zar's. While he has always been able to compromise with us alone, he will go his own way if he deems it necessary."

My eyes narrowed as a suspicion crept into my mind. "Does he know what you're doing now? Is he expecting you to bring back a woman he's supposed to mate with?"

Dak sighed. "If I told you yes would you be more inclined to attempt this?"

"Fuck," I swore, turning from them. "Way to set a girl up."

Talon was at my side, his hand on my shoulder. "Don't worry."

I whirled around. "I *do* worry. Talon, I'm willing to bet the three of you are the same as a mated unit. I will *not* see you torn from your family. No matter what my future holds, that isn't happening."

"Mine!" he growled. "Stay."

"Talon, just... stop. Let me think."

He growled again. This time it sounded wounded. Instantly, Dak was at his side. "We will figure this out, brother," he murmured softly. "I'm not losing you or Zar."

"Not losing her." He pulled me close again.

"OK, just stop. No one is losing anybody." The second I'd uttered the statement, I knew it was true. Dak and I hadn't formed the bond Talon and I had managed to, but seeing the way they obviously cared for each other -- it wasn't one-sided -- made me know I had to fix this some way. "Did you guys even plan this through? Dak, you said Talon was supposed to observe me, see if I was a fitting woman for Zar, then take me and wait for you. What did you expect would happen if you agreed Zar would like me?"

He shrugged. "We'd take you home."

"And then?"

He blinked. "Zar would take you for his mate." As if he really meant *Duh*.

I pinched the bridge of my nose. "Fuck." It was turning into my favorite word. "And what would have happened if Zar didn't agree to your plan?"

"He will," Dak said, straightening. "He will!"

I wanted to smack the dumbass. "You were just lamenting the fact that he might not! What the fuck are you doing?" Before I thought, I smacked the back of his head. Hard. "In the words of a very old, very good film... *snap out of it!*"

Of all the things I'd expected, Talon's deep, rumbling laughter wasn't one. He gathered me into his arms and carried me to the furs, chuckling all the way. "Perfect," he said, still shaking with laughter. "She will be perfect."

Dak followed Talon, kneeling beside me. "Can't argue with that. Just do that"-- he hiked his thumb over his shoulder to where we'd all stood moments ago --"and all will be well." He leaned forward to run his hands from my waist to my breasts. I was tempted to bat his hands away, but it felt good, and I didn't want to. "I do have a question for the two of you though," he continued. "If those three were supposed to help prepare Mia for sex with the two of us and Zar, is that what actually happened? Because it didn't look that way when I walked in."

I glanced at Talon. "Yeah," I mused. "That's right. I didn't fuck Zeus or Luca. I didn't do more than suck either of them."

Talon rubbed his hand over the back of his neck, giving me a sheepish look. "Changed my mind."

I grinned. "You didn't want to share me with any man outside your Triad."

"Maybe," he replied with a shrug.

"It didn't bother you when I tasted Magenta's pussy and gave her pleasure."

Dak groaned, his hands stopping their exploration. "You didn't." He sounded pained. Like he'd just acquired the biggest case of blue balls ever.

"Didn't what?" I asked, raising my eyebrows. "Didn't eat her until she screamed? Didn't lick her clit while her men fucked her?" No way I could miss the way his cock swelled behind his pants in an instant. "I did. And I'll tell you something else. *I loved every fucking second of it.*"

Chapter Seven

Dak looked at me as if he were about to eat me up. And I wasn't at all broken up about that. Talon lifted his chin, smirk in place as if to say "I told you so," but he said nothing.

Swiping a hand over his mouth, Dak took a step back from me. The look on his face said he wasn't sure what to do with me. Naturally I smirked at him. I imagine Talon and I were wearing identical looks.

"I knew she would be the closest we'd ever find to satisfying Zar, but I had no idea she could be this aggressive."

"If you talk about me like I'm not in the room one more time..." It earned me another astonished look from Dak. "Let's get one thing straight," I said, rising up on my knees before them. "I'm not a pet. I refuse to act like a pet. And I damned sure won't let you treat me like a pet. I will make this work with Zar, but if that's what he expects, we *will* butt heads. Is this going to be a problem?"

"Not if you keep your promise to do your best to make this work," Dak said. "Zar is... difficult... on the best of days."

"But I know you can convince him you are the right woman for us." Talon added the last with a prideful look. No pressure there.

Then I realized the current situation. I was on the floor. On my knees. While Dak sat back, Talon was standing to his full height, looking down at me in delight. Oh yeah. Our minds were working in the same direction. Dak, on the other hand, looked so shell-shocked I wanted to laugh.

"It's not like you thought I was a virgin," I said, raising an eyebrow at Dak. "You fucked me hard before you turned me loose in the Outlands. Did you think I'd suddenly reverted or something?"

"I -- no! I just wasn't expecting you to take to any of this without some kind of persuasion."

"And you don't think pleasure is its own persuasion?"

Now, he gave me a lopsided grin as he stood. "Depends on the one providing the pleasure. You offering?"

In answer, I grasped Talon's cock. Never taking my eyes from Dak, I eased Talon's cock into my mouth until the head hit the back of my throat.

"Fuck," Dak whispered, jerking his pants down and moving beside Talon to offer me his cock.

I sucked him several strokes before I let him slide from my mouth. "What makes you think I'm going to suck you too?" I asked, grinning at him. "You doubt my sexual mojo even after sampling me. Why should I reward your doubt with another taste?" Before he could answer, I sat back, tapping my finger on my chin. "Maybe I'm just not your type."

Talon growled and guided me back to his waiting dick. With a grin, I enveloped him again, my eyes on Dak. Talon's fingers tunneled through my hair, guiding me as he moved. "So fucking good..." he rasped. "Hot. Wet."

Dak growled, his expression changing from bemusement to determination. "I saw her first," he muttered. "Hand picked her." He batted Talon's hands from my hair. Thankfully, Talon didn't try to use me as an instrument of tug-of-war and released me. Even if it was with a snarl at Dak.

I chuckled as I swallowed Dak's member, his

salty essence mingling with Talon's. I had to admit, this was not at all unpleasant. Two men who acted as if they had to have me was heady in the extreme. It had been fun with Magenta, but the three of them had been working out issues among themselves. I was merely a useful tool in their arsenal.

Now I had two men -- one I was totally infatuated with, one I'd fucked my way to ecstasy with not half a day ago. I knew both men loved what I could do with -- and to -- them and knew they'd see to it I enjoyed myself as well. It all combined to make the act that much more enjoyable. Hotter.

"Mmmm," I hummed around Dak's cock, moving my mouth on him as I jacked him with my hand. I still pumped Talon with my other hand, not letting him go. Despite Dak's hold on my hair, I pulled away to give Talon another suck, licking and slurping as I went.

"Delicious," I groaned as I switched back to Dak.

Over and over I did this. Until finally, Dak got impatient. "Here," he offered me his cock while Talon was still deep in my throat. "Lick us both." Talon hissed in a breath, but grunted his assent, his cock twitching like a son of a bitch as he pulled out of my mouth.

I opened my mouth wide, sticking out my tongue for them to lay their dicks where they would. No way I could take them both, but I loved this experimenting and teasing. Both cocks resting side by side on my wet tongue was such a sight. Both large and veined, Talon's slightly darker and wider than Dak's. Dak's thinner but longer. Both men urged me to continue stroking, their cock heads directly on my tongue.

I could make them come like this. I knew I could.

Already, Dak was on the verge. I could tell by the way his balls drew up tight and sweat dotted his skin. He'd removed his shirt and unlaced his breeches to push them halfway down his thighs. I itched to explore his body like I had Talon's. I itched to explore Talon's once more. Two powerful males with powerful bodies. All for my pleasure.

Or theirs.

Whatever.

With a wicked gleam in my eye, I enveloped the tips of both of them, one cock resting on top of the other. Both men groaned. Talon thrust slightly, gliding over Dak and deeper into my mouth. I pulled back, knowing I'd end up hurting one or both of them if we continued.

"I want you both," I said, sitting back. "Inside my pussy." With a grin, I added, "Now."

I didn't even get the last word out before Dak plucked me from the floor before them and moved to lay me on the bed. I sucked at the skin of his neck while he gently settled me down. I suspected he took extra time just to keep me touching him. His heart pounded nearly as hard as my own. Two men I was deeply attracted to were about to do wicked things to my body. If I'd known this was what had been in store for me when I'd been sentenced to exile, I'd have gladly stripped and paraded myself around the whole goddamned city with a smile and a fucking princess wave.

It took little effort for Dak to maneuver me on top of him, my back to his chest. His deep groan was music to my ears. I felt his shaft prodding my entrance before sinking inside me with a wet glide and wonderful stretch. I was about to be pretty stuffed, and I couldn't be happier about it.

Dak spread my legs, pulling my knees high so that I was completely exposed to Talon's avid gaze. Talon's brows knitted together as he watched Dak sliding in and out of me as he absently stroked himself.

"Lovely," Talon whispered in a broken groan. "Fucking beautiful…"

"Are you going to join him?" I asked a little breathlessly. "Because I'd really like you to."

Talon grunted but didn't immediately move to position himself to enter me alongside Dak. Instead, he dipped his head to my pussy and tongued my clit while Dak fucked me with slow, measured strokes.

"Ahhh!" It had been good before, but this was Talon *and* Dak. *My men*! Besides, that put Talon's tongue dangerously close to Dak's cock, and the images flooding my mind just then nearly set me off. "Gods! Do that again!"

He did. Only this time, I suspect he got a taste of Dak's cock because Talon groaned and Dak stiffened.

"What the fuck?" Dak growled, raising up on one elbow. One arm wrapped around my middle while he peered over my shoulder. His tone sounded indignant, but his movements told the real story.

At first, he held still, imbedded deeply inside me. Gradually, however, he slid out until just the head of his dick was inside me. Gazing up at both of us intently, Talon lowered his head, licking Dak's cock from the base to where our bodies joined and over my clit, all with the flat of his tongue.

For several seconds, none of us moved. I don't think we breathed. Then Dak stroked inside me. Back out.

"Do that again," he commanded in a lust-roughened voice. His body quaked around me as Talon repeated the erotic motion.

"Fuck!" Dak groaned as he pumped inside me a couple of times before pausing again for Talon. This time, Talon turned his head to the side to wrap Dak's cock with his lips. When he reached my clit, he sucked it gently, flicking it with his tongue. I shuddered, spearing my fingers through his hair.

Dak moved in and out of me slowly, letting Talon keep doing what he was doing. The moments seemed dreamlike, laden with sexual tension. I held my breath, afraid to move lest I break the spell. Finally, Talon grasped Dak's cock and slipped him out of me. Exhaling a shaking breath, Talon enveloped Dak all the way to the base before releasing his suck and guiding him back inside me.

"Fuck!" Dak bit out, seeming to have lost the ability to say anything but that one word. I knew the feeling. Hell, all I could do was whimper out my need. I'd known there was more to this Triad than was on the surface. Apparently, this sexual attraction wasn't something they were prepared for either. So what would that mean when we met up with this Zar?

Later. I'd deal with it all later. Not only could I not wrap my mind around those dynamics, my mind was rapidly turning into one lust-induced pile of mush.

"Inside," Talon muttered, his voice nearly unrecognizable. "Need inside."

He crawled up my body and positioned his cock beside Dak's. Sweat from Talon's brow dripped onto my breasts as he moved. He was on his knees, one hand gripping his dick, the other gripping my hip. Carefully, he rolled the head around my opening beside Dak until he was able to slip inside.

Immediately, the full, stretching sensation burned through me. It was incredible!

"Damn, damn, damn!" Dak chanted. His arm around my waist tightened as Talon seated himself fully inside me.

"Steady," Talon muttered before kissing me lightly. "Adjust yourself."

Adjust… Was he fucking kidding?

"Talon, I'm *dying*! Please! *Move*!"

With a sharp nod, he did. They kept a slow, steady pace for a while, letting us all adjust to the sensations. I was beyond caring. I simply spread my legs wide and let them fuck me however they wished. It wasn't long before they were surging into me with ease.

"So fucking tight," Talon ground out. "I can feel you, Dak. Feel you against my cock, and it's fucking amazing!"

Dak groaned, his movements speeding up as they both took in the new sensations. "We're both fucking her so good," he said, his voice raspy. "Fucking her… together!"

"Yes!" I cried out my pleasure as they took me over and over. The fullness was a nearly unbearable delight. One I knew I'd never get enough of. Nothing in my life -- not even the kink of the orgy earlier -- had prepared me for the intimacy of this moment. The pure eroticism was more than I could readily comprehend. All I wanted to do was feel this for the rest of my life. As my men caressed my body with their big, rough hands, they took their own pleasure. I knew they'd never explored this side of carnal delights before and was proud to have been a part of their discovery. The question was, how would their reaction to each other affect my place in their lives? Maybe this was what they'd been leading up to with their Triad. Maybe they were a trio of mated males who simply hadn't acknowledged it yet. If all they needed was each other, then where did that leave me?

All my worries and musings were quickly pushed to the side when an orgasm the likes of which I'd never even imagined began building inside me. Dak plunged into me from beneath, his strong arms holding me tightly. His muscled chest slipped against my back in a sweat-soaked lather. Talon surged into me on top. He braced himself with one hand while he buried his other in my hair to bring me to him for a soul-searing kiss. My clit caught friction with every surge of his big body, and it didn't take long for everything to detonate inside me in one massive climax.

I screamed into Talon's mouth, letting him lick the inside of my mouth as I screamed. He sucked my lips, bucking inside me. I could feel my pussy milking them both, trying to coax seed from their rigid cocks. Within moments, both of them followed me. I was so full I actually felt each of their ejaculations. First one, then a second later, the other began. Both spurted inside me several times, hot semen rushing inside me with each pulse. Both men roared their release with ear-splitting war cries. I was certain there would be an investigation from the villagers, but couldn't be bothered to care.

Talon and Dak lay there with me sandwiched between them, both still inside me. Our mingled cum leaked from my pussy, punctuating the pleasure we'd just shared. Finally, Talon rose, his chest heaving. Sweat made his skin shimmer, and my pussy wept for him. I couldn't help the shudder of desire coursing through me from the sheer masculine beauty he displayed.

He grinned, looking supremely satisfied and

pleased with himself. I couldn't help an answering smile.

"Well," Dak said, still not making a move to roll me off him. Instead, he lay with his dick still firmly inside my pussy, and it felt for all the world like he was readying for another round. "That was certainly... enlightening."

Talon actually flushed, turning from us.

"Go to him," I whispered to Dak. I needn't have worried. Dak carefully set me aside and went to the big man, clamping his shoulder with one big hand.

"Talon," he murmured. "That was an incredible experience. Don't doubt yourself."

Talon raised his chin as he looked at one of the two men in the world who knew him better than he knew himself. "You. Zar. Mia. You are..." He seemed to struggle for words. "My... world." He shook his head then looked at me, a fierce expression on his face. "My *life*."

He was including me in this. Which was what I wanted, but Dak looked troubled. "I suppose the physical manifestation of our Triad was inevitable, but I don't know about Mia."

Talon got a stubborn look on his face. "She is mine. Same as the Triad is mine. Always."

"I know, but you know Zar won't accept this readily. He'd come nearer accepting the three of us as a mated unit than he would accepting Mia into our union. Remember how he reacted after we found you? When Jaina left?"

"Do not talk about it!"

"Talon, I have to." Dak looked weary now. "I nearly lost you. *We* nearly lost you. It caused chaos within the Triad, and our enemies nearly bested us. As much as I believe Zar needs a fitting mate to soothe him, to fight by his side, maybe we were wrong. Maybe we just need each other."

"And Mia," Talon added stubbornly.

Dak sighed. "I agree she would be perfect for us, but I will follow Zar. You know this."

"I do."

"Then you understand why I can't claim her in front of Zar as you do. You live with your heart. Zar lives for the people. I have to live for the Triad. For balance."

"It is your nature." Talon didn't back down, but he truly didn't seem to hold any ill feelings for Dak for disagreeing with him. Not for the first time, I began to wonder if there was more to the big guy than met the eye. He didn't communicate outwardly overly much, but it was easy to overlook the keen intelligence inside him because of his unwillingness to talk. He was obviously a battle-hardened warrior, but inside he had a heart that craved love and tenderness.

Yep. I was a total goner for him.

Chapter Eight

I could not remember being so exhausted in my life. Not only had the orgy I'd participated in with Talon drained me both physically and emotionally, but the guys both taking me with such fierce tenderness had done me in. Before I'd drifted off, I was certain I'd simply pass out. Not so much. Though my body was pleasantly sore and spent, my mind was a whirlwind. How the fuck was I supposed to convince Zar to prefer me over all his pets? Why the fuck had I promised Talon and Dak I'd even try?

Why, indeed? I wanted this. Wanted them. I was totally in love with Talon. I'd give him up if it were in his best interests, but not without a fight. The only problem was, the fight wouldn't be to take him from his Triad. It would be to have the Triad accept me into their lives.

Right. I wished myself all the best with that.

Sometime during the night, I finally managed to pass out, but my sleep was restless. Not only that, but the guys woke me more than once for sex. Which I craved. I felt like this was my only chance at such pleasure. I feared once this trek was over so was my life with these men.

When dawn finally broke, I was pleasantly exhausted but determined to make this work somehow. My mind was still in turmoil. I wanted Talon and Dak to convince Zar on their own to accept me, but I had the feeling it would ultimately fall to me. If I failed, I'd have to leave. As much as I loved Talon, I couldn't take him away from his family, nor could I compromise my own self-worth.

I'd have to work it out. I *would* work it out.

The trek deeper into the Outlands wasn't unpleasant, though it took four days. During that time, I got to explore my men at my leisure. The nights were always filled with more pleasure than I'd thought possible. Every now and then I made them take a break in the middle of the day. Or morning. Or knock off early -- midday -- and say "fuck it" to more walking and just fuck. Which was why it took four days instead of a little more than a day. But none of us cared. The extra time together gave us a chance to learn each other both physically and personally.

While both men were dominant to the core, they were both surprisingly... insecure?... with my position in their life. The closer we got to our destination, the more desperate the sex became. I did all I could to reassure them, but I was beginning to wonder what I was in for. I also recognized that they were pinning all their hopes on me. Honestly, I couldn't help but wonder what kind of man Zar was. If these two fierce warriors -- and unless they were greatly exaggerating, they were beyond fierce -- deferred to Zar, either the man was seriously scary or they simply had too much respect for him to do otherwise.

The night before we were due to arrive in the village I didn't sleep much. Not only did we make love most of the night, but I worried I couldn't make good on my promise to keep us all together. I had the feeling I was getting ready to have a contest of wills with a man as stubborn as I was. If he didn't want me, could I quell my first instinct -- which would be to cut off his balls before sashaying my sweet ass out the fucking door -- and set to convincing him I was a good match for his Triad? If there was one thing I knew it was myself. Meek and submissive I was not.

Cheers greeted the men at the entrance to the city. Flower petals rained down on us, sticking in my hair as I walked between the two men. Dak waved and smiled, obviously enjoying the attention. Talon looked uncomfortable, eking out a smile only when he thought it was necessary. I couldn't help myself. The pull to comfort him and ease his discomfort was too strong to resist.

I eased closer to Talon, who immediately took my hand in a tight, possessive grip, pulling me closer to his side. Dak glanced at us, raising his eyebrows at Talon, who merely lifted his chin. With a grin, Dak moved closer to my other side, taking my hand as well. He continued to wave and greet onlookers.

The only tension came when we reached the steps to the palace. A harem of naked and nearly naked women converged on *my* men, all but shoving me out of the way. Needless to say, that didn't go over very goddamned well with me.

Dak let go of my hand to catch one female, who literally launched herself at him with an excited squeal, peppering his face with kisses, her boobs mashed against his chest, which she rubbed over him shamelessly. Talon actually stepped back. The look on his face said he was debating tugging me in front of him. Clearly that didn't sit well with him, so he dropped my hand and braced himself. Three women leapt into his arms, all of them kissing and rubbing all over him. One actually sank to her knees and nuzzled his crotch with her face, hands going to his hips like she might if she were sucking him off.

Dak glanced back as he pried arms from around his neck, trying to set the woman on him away only to be assailed by another. One of the women on Dak knelt before him as well, her intent clear when she began unlacing his breeches. Obviously, she had more on her mind than simply nuzzling him through his pants as the woman on Talon was doing.

What was a woman to do?

I snagged a handful of silky golden locks and yanked the woman at Talon's feet back so hard I had more than a few strands of her hair in my fist when I slung her backward. Punting Dak behind the knee, I kicked out when he went down and caught one of his women in the shoulder to send her flying. Dak groaned, but, wisely, said nothing.

Talon closed his eyes and braced himself, clearly expecting a blow from me. Had it not been for the fact that he'd looked miserable from the outset, I might have. Not out of any belief he'd enjoyed their attentions, but a girl had to set boundaries as much for her men as for other women. Instead, I snagged the arm of one of the women climbing him like a tree and twisted it behind her, wrenching up so that her shoulder had to be screaming. The bitch cried out, letting go of Talon reflexively. Well, reflexively because I dragged her ass back until I was pulling her up the steps. I let her go when she screamed, which was a very satisfying sound. No permanent damage done, but I was pretty sure the message was received when the rest of the women let go of both him and Dak to gather round their injured companions.

"Talon?" One of the women looked up at him, eyes confused and pleading.

The big man looked miserable. His nature wasn't to hurt women, and these females clearly expected his protection.

"Take Iris and Rose and go to your rooms," Dak said in a strained voice, still struggling to put weight on his knee. "We will send the healer and someone to talk to you."

"What's going on? Does she not know her place? I've been with you the longest!"

"Iris…" Dak said, his tone stern. "Do as you're told."

"And *that woman*?"

"Is my mate," Talon said without hesitation. And there went another little piece of my heart. "You are *not*."

Iris gasped, looking from Talon to me and back again before turning to Dak. "And you?"

Dak moved closer to me, but wasn't as forthcoming as Talon. "I'm leaving it up to Zar, but I want her to be mine as well." Which kind of pissed me off, but I couldn't say it was unexpected. Dak was trying not to get too involved with me, to keep his distance as it were, until Zar gave the go ahead. Probably because Dak didn't want his loyalty divided. It made me angry, but also softened me toward him just a little more. The man was loyal to the end. Which couldn't be a bad thing. Which also meant there was more going on with this Triad than they were willing to let me in on.

"If the Triad is mated, the territories are vulnerable," Iris said. "Every other union will be readying to take us all as slaves." She sounded equal parts pissed, terrified, and resentful as her gaze slid back to mine.

"We will protect our territory," Dak assured. "Above all."

"Blackheart will disagree. He'll believe you'll protect your mate above all. It was always understood the Triad would *never* mate, which is the reason for all your pets. Otherwise, I know you would have chosen one of us long before now, and I've always been Zar's favorite." Which, I figured, was the *real* reason for her protests.

"Zar likes that thing you do with your mouth," Talon interrupted harshly. "He holds no affection beyond shared pleasure for any pet he's ever owned."

Iris narrowed her eyes at Dak. "You may be close to Zar, but I doubt you know his mind."

Talon leveled her with a steady gaze. "I know my brothers better than I know myself. It's my nature." He let that sink in. The second Iris showed a flicker of doubt he continued. "Zar holds no affection for any female and very little toward anyone other than me and Dak. Even that is secondary to his people. It's wishful thinking if you believe you're the single exception."

It was the most I'd heard Talon speak since I'd met him. Apparently, the sheer volume of words was enough to convince the women, because all of them but Iris bowed respectfully and left. Iris, however, wasn't done.

"You know he won't accept her. You've said as much. Then what will you do, Talon?"

"Watch yourself, Iris," Dak murmured. "This is a volatile situation. You don't want to get caught up in it, because I doubt any of us will regret the collateral damage."

"You're saying that" -- she adjusted her stance as she took several deep breaths --"to *me*? I've been with your Triad since you took over from the old ones. If anyone is to be your mate, it should be me!"

Dak tilted his head, his eyes squinting in something between anger and annoyance. "You're part of a harem of women with a specific purpose. Everyone there is. You were each chosen because of your sexual and physical gifts." I raised my eyebrows.

Dak shifted his gaze, seeming to feel my disapproval. "We never intended to take a mate. Finding one woman who could fulfill all of our sexual needs seemed be impossible as well as uncomfortable for the woman in question. We always acknowledged this." The way he said it sounded like the understatement of all time. "But things have changed. I have no idea what will happen when we talk to Zar, but I know I'm going to try. Because..." Dak glanced at Talon, who gave a subtle shake of his head. "Because Talon has made up his mind, and I nearly lost him when he lost Jaina." There was something more there. With Talon?

"Yet another reason to stop this, Dak," she beseeched, finally moving close enough to clutch his arm. "I was here when Jaina fled. I remember how hard it was on all of you. You can't let this pet come between the three of you. She has to go!"

"She's my mate," Talon reiterated. "Where she goes, I go."

Iris gasped. "You'd leave the Triad? Leave us all vulnerable? As the warrior, you're the strongest and the most able to defend us. I won't allow this!"

Which was when I hit my limit.

"Look," I said, moving away from Talon and closer to Iris, each step a slow, measured movement. "I appreciate how you might become attached to one or all of them, but this isn't your goddamned decision to make."

She bared her teeth at me. "You will not be mated to the Triad! *I won't let you!*"

Iris struck fast, swinging a fist at me before kicking out. Apparently the woman was a lover. Because she was one piss-poor fighter. I ducked her blow, caught her ankle, and flipped her back on her ass. She scrambled back, looking first to Talon then

Dak for help. What ever she saw in their faces had hers turning pale.

"Stop."

The voice came from the top of the stair in front of the massive stone structure. We'd been at the foot of the steps when the women had waylaid my men. Though this new man didn't yell, there was a wealth of menace and censure laced liberally through the word. As much as I really didn't give a fuck, the clear reprimand nearly had me hanging my head in embarrassment.

The man, who I presumed was Zar, was *massive*. As big as Dak was, this man was three or four inches taller and more heavily muscled. His legs stretched the leather of his breeches taut. As tall as Talon was, this guy had three or four inches on him and probably fifty or more pounds of muscle. He wore dark brown leather breeches that hugged powerful, bulging thighs. Thick boots laced up his calves to his knees were lined in a dark fur sprinkled through with gray, similar to his hair. A cape of the same color fur was draped over his shoulders, fastened to a dark leather harness strapped over his powerful chest and shoulders. I noticed several different loops where various blades of different sizes were stored on the vest. While the cape might be a bit much, it was probably more for show. *And* to conceal all his blades. No doubt about it. The man before me was more than a ruler. He was a conqueror.

He looked from Talon to Dak. Then to me. Had I not distinctly remembered putting on clothing before we entered the city, I'd have looked down to make sure my boobs weren't hanging out, his scrutiny was so intense. As it was, I had to fight to keep from fidgeting.

"We have no need for another pet," he said blandly. "Sell her or give her to someone." He turned to go, but Talon growled loudly, stepping in front of me.

"Zar," Dak began. "We have some things to discuss."

That had Zar turning back to us, the movement slow and menacing before his gaze landed squarely on Talon. That piercing gaze boring down on him with a vengeance. At length he muttered, "Son of a bitch," before stalking inside the building, not waiting for the others to follow. But follow they did. Talon snagged my hand firmly in his before marching up the steps, head held high.

"This is going to be rough," Dak muttered. "Let us do the talking."

"Yeah. Cause you've done such a great job so far," I shot back. There was no way these two men could hold sway over this Zar if he didn't want to be swayed. I knew it would fall to me, but I hadn't realized until now how much hope I'd held out that they'd somehow be able to work this out among themselves.

The hall was vast. Cavernous. A great dais sat with three stone chairs, the center one slightly higher than the others. Lit sconces were placed at various places around the room and the dais, creating an eerie, flickering mass of shadows on the bare walls. This was a place of judgment, reminding me of the Judgment Hall I'd seen in the city less than a week ago.

We continued on behind the dais through a thick, solid door into a smaller set of rooms. The main area was surprisingly warm and inviting but still decidedly masculine. Again, there were fur rugs all over the stone floor. In another area through an arched doorway, a massive four-poster bed sat in the center of the room. Trophies hung on the walls in several places -- all large animals. Taking a closer look at Zar, I noticed several claws hanging from a chain strung from one shoulder to the other on his cape. Yep. Definitely a show of strength on his part.

He stood facing a low-burning fire, one big hand resting on the stone of the fireplace. Long moments passed before he said anything, making me fidget. Which was likely his intent all along. I glanced at Dak and Talon and saw the other two men were just as anxious as I was.

Let Dak do the talking. Right. It didn't take a genius to know I didn't fit in here in any form or fashion. Sure, the sex was fantastic, and Talon was grasping at me so hard it was nearly painful, but I knew when I met their gazes I was going to fight for this. I just had no idea how.

"When you said you were taking extended time in the city, I understood you had duties there to keep your position as Captain of the Guard secured. We need that front in order to keep as many of their exiles safe as possible." He pinned Dak with a lethal look. "Obviously, you had other… motives."

"I did," Dak said, not trying to deny it. Which made him go up a notch in my estimation. "This wasn't for me, or even Talon. You need her. She's what you've been looking for."

Zar looked me up and down for several long moments. "No. She's nothing like what I need. At all."

"You can tell that from the non-existent time you've been around me?" Even as Dak growled at me and Talon tried to keep himself between me and Zar, I was rapidly reaching a point where I could no longer contain my reactions. I'd never had a filter on my best day, and this was shaping up to be far from my best moment.

Zar narrowed his eyes. "I don't need to spend time to know you'd never survive in our world. Hell, I doubt you'd survive your first stiff fucking with the three of us." He gestured to himself. "You might be able to take Dak or even Talon, but I'm a very big man with voracious appetites. I'd likely break you in half."

"You have no idea what I'm capable of." I bared my teeth at him. "And you obviously don't think Dak and Talon know you -- or themselves -- well enough to know what you *all* need."

"Whatever you think I need, I guarantee you a woman is not it," he said with a sneer. "Least of all one as weak and fragile as you."

I snagged the knife Dak had given me from its sheath at my hip and threw it at him end over end. "You have no idea what I'm capable of!" I shouted at him. He caught the dagger by the blade with little effort, looking as if he'd been expecting my show of temper and was amused by it. A single drop of blood fell from his palm to land at his feet but he didn't seem to notice his injury. Zar looked as if I'd just proven his point for him. Probably because I'd failed to draw blood through my efforts. His hand didn't count because he'd obviously intended it as an intimidation tactic. "I may not know your Triad as well as you think you do, but I know Talon is hurting. I know Dak is conflicted. And you? I've been in your presence all of five minutes, and the one thing I absolutely know for sure is that you're *terrified* of even entertaining the idea of a permanent relationship with a woman. You don't want a mate, not because you don't feel the need to have one. You don't want one because you're afraid she can't handle you physically!"

He snarled. "What if you're right? Do you honestly think I want to hurt a woman? Not only that, but if we took a mate, she'd have to be our first priority. Am I supposed to tell my people I've found something more important to safeguard?" As he spoke he got louder and louder until he was yelling at me. "I cannot let the whole of our territory go unprotected because you're too weak to take care of yourself." He punched the stone of the hearth in his anger. "*Fuck!* Dak, I should kill you where you stand!" He all but roared the last at Dak. "You bring a woman into our home, one Talon is clearly smitten with, then use my feelings for him to attempt to sway me on a decision we *all* made after Jaina left!" He took a menacing step toward Dak. "*It will. Not. Happen*! She can't take care of herself, and I can't protect her and everyone else as well! None of us can if we are to put the needs of our people first!"

"*Enough!*" I waited until Zar turned his furious gaze on me before I attacked. When I was done, there would be no mistaking I could handle myself against any threat. Including the men around me if necessary.

I charged the three steps toward him with a battle cry as shrill and chilling as any jungle cat. His body stance said he expected me to go high, to launch myself at him and go for his face or neck. He was right. Just not how he expected it to unfold.

When I reached him, I slid between his legs where he'd widened his stance in anticipation of my weight hitting him full force. Once behind him, I leapt up onto his back, wrapping my legs around his waist and one arm around his neck. I snagged one of the many hidden blades tucked into his harness.

"Does this feel like I'm a weak and helpless female?" I snarled my question beside his ear... as I brought my blade across his throat in a swift, decisive cut, drawing blood.

"Mia!" Talon barked, but it was too late. Blood dripped from the thin line I'd cut from ear to ear on Zar's neck.

I dropped down and rolled to one side, keeping all three of them in front of me in case Dak or Talon took exception to what I'd done. Zar clamped a hand over his neck to stem the flow. All of them waited several heartbeats before anyone moved. They probably expected blood to bubble through Zar's hands, but they were wrong.

"What?" I said, still crouching. Just in case I needed to spring again. "You didn't honestly think I'd kill the prick, did you?"

Zar lowered his hand, looking at his palm to assess his blood loss, then touched the scratch running the width of his neck. He now watched me with new interest, his keen eyes zeroing in on me as if he were only now considering me worthy of his attention.

"You didn't honestly expect I'd draw blood, did you." It wasn't a question. "I bet you didn't think I was capable of landing a blow against you."

"That was... surprising." He said it like it was a vast understatement.

"Was it?" I tilted my head, fingering the other two round blades in my hands. "Then you'll really be surprised by this." I tossed one with a flick of my wrist. He dodged -- just like I knew he would -- but not quickly enough. Though he moved fast, I anticipated his move and compensated for it so there was no way my blade would miss.

I nicked his ear. I'd telegraphed my throw so I knew a seasoned warrior like himself couldn't possibly miss what I was doing. When I released the blade, had he not moved, it would likely have struck him between the eyes. A second, immediate flick of the same wrist nicked his other ear as he shifted out of the path of the first blade. It was a move I'd learned on the streets of the city. One I'd practiced over and over. Now, I realized that by learning a trick that had saved my life on more than one occasion, I might have won the big barbarian's respect. Any time I'd attacked someone in this fashion, they'd automatically assumed I was a blade master. Hopefully, Zar would be no different.

To his credit, his attention was focused solely on me. He didn't bother to touch his damaged ears. Only looked me over, eyes darting over my form. Likely looking for more weapons.

"Don't worry, barbarian. The only blade I brought with me was the one tossed to you. The other two were yours." I buffed my nails, doing my best to look smug when I was more nervous than I'd ever been. If this didn't go right, Talon would be crushed. *I* would be crushed. Because, though I hadn't yet been able to get to know Zar, I was already falling for Talon and Dak. There were issues. Deep seated ones. But I knew I could help all of us *if* I could prove I was as strong of character and will as Zar. With that in mind, I hardened my features. "Consider my letting you live a parting gift."

Talon roared in protest, making a move toward me, but I bared my teeth at him. "I told you I wouldn't be a pet, Talon. You need to be with your Triad, and Zar will never see me as anything else." Dak had grabbed Talon's arm while Talon looked like his heart was being ripped from his chest. He bellowed again, thrashing to free himself from Dak. I'd never seen such pain in a human before. The sight nearly brought me to my knees. Before I could stop them, tears welled.

I couldn't help the softening of my expression. It broke my heart to see him like this. I wanted to go him, to embrace him as fiercely as I realized I loved him. If I did, thought, he'd never let me go. I knew it from the stark look in his eyes. I knew that look mirrored my own. "Goodbye, my love," I said, meaning the endearment. I was betting everything Zar wouldn't let me get far. He'd have to have time to process this, but I had to be away from his lodge, and he had to come after me publicly.

With those parting words to Talon, I fled the room, sprinting through the great hall and out the door. At the foot of the steps, I noticed all but one or two of the men's harem gone from the hall. The two who remained were gesturing furiously with two guards at the bottom of the stairs. My instinct told me to find out the problem, but my focus had to be on winning my men. If not, my future was lost.

Growling in frustration, I fled into the encampment and out the gates. If I was right, if I had shown my potential and my strength to Zar, he'd soon be after me. If not, then I was fighting a losing battle because I'd given him all I had in my arsenal. I was a scrappy fighter, but I wasn't a warrior.

Chapter Nine

Talon's roars carried even outside the encampment. He sounded equal parts furious and in despair. Once outside the wall, I slipped into the forest, taking care not to leave a noticeable trail. I suspected all the men were excellent trackers, but I wanted them to work for it. Any notion they were being led down a path would cause Zar to do the opposite. Which meant the going was slow.

A heavy, warm rain began to fall. Had I not been in a fight for the future of myself and three men I was beginning to care too much for, I would have enjoyed the feel of the water on my skin. Mud quickly formed in places away from the trees in the forest and splashed up to cover my legs to the knees. The fur they'd dressed me in was surprisingly resistant to the water and didn't make me as miserable as I was afraid it might. Which was good. Because the rain came in torrents.

I swiped my arm over my face, trying to clear my vision of tears as well as rain. I could barely see a few feet in front of me. Not knowing the terrain, I knew it was foolish to continue. They'd know it too. Would they come after me or wait until the rain stopped? *Would they come after me at all*? I was convinced Talon would. The other two…

A strong arm snaked around my torso. Another circled my neck so that my chin rested in his elbow. The grip wasn't tight, but definitely discouraged me from trying to get away. Then the scent of warm, rain-wet man hit me. The smell was intoxicating, hitting me like a drug. How could anyone smell so good when I knew he was likely as covered in mud as I was?

"You didn't truly expect to get away from us, did you?" The deep rumble of Zar's voice whispered across my ear, his breath tickling the fine hair at my nape. I tried not to shiver, but wasn't sure I pulled it off. Oh well. Maybe he'd think the rain had chilled me.

"Of course I did. I'm not as unskilled as you'd believe. I'm capable of much more than I let on."

"Really? Then how did I catch you so easily?"

"I don't see Talon and Dak. With three of you searching, one was surely to stumble across me. You'll have to do some convincing to make me believe otherwise."

He seemed to mull this over, his chin resting on my shoulder. "Perhaps. Why not come back with me now that I have you? We can talk this out by the fire while we dry."

I had him. I knew it. I just had to push a little harder. He had to make a show of bringing me back after I'd run. "Or, you can go back alone and just let me go. I'm obviously beneath your notice, and I refuse to be a pet. There's no reason for you to take on the responsibility of someone who will only run at the first opportunity."

"There's no reason for you to run," he said, using my own words. "Why would you want to? You know Dak and Talon would never treat you as anything other than the wife they want you to be for them."

"Because you've already written me off for anything other than a pet. As much as I feel a lasting connection to Talon -- and Dak, to a lesser extent -- I won't compromise my self-worth. Not for him, or you, or anyone else. My suggestion? Take Iris to bed. She'd better fulfill your needs in that area." I shrugged. "Maybe."

"And what of the rest of my Triad? Do you think she would suit them as well?"

"That's not my problem," I answered immediately, leaving no room for doubt as to my feelings. "I made it very clear to both of them I would not be seen as inferior to anyone. If they choose to stay with you, they will abide by your wishes, and you've made your wishes clear."

He rubbed his face against me, inhaling in the sweet spot between my neck and shoulder. His damp skin smelled wonderful. A temptation. A drug. When he pulled me harder against him, there was no way to miss his throbbing erection against my lower back.

"So, you enjoyed the chase," I quipped. "Don't get used to it. I'm leaving today."

"And go where? You'll be better off staying with us where you'll be protected."

"Which is exactly my point." I snapped my head back, catching his chin. With a grunt, he loosened his hold enough that I was able to drop to the ground before rolling away from him. Getting to my feet, I lifted my chin, giving him my most defiant look. "I don't *need* protection. I may get into scrapes, but I will *always* figure my way out of them."

He sized me up now. That was twice I'd gotten the drop on him. The first time could have been lethal. This time, I could have dashed into the woods just a few seconds ahead of him while he shook off the effects of my blow. He circled me slowly, so I matched his movements, not letting him get behind me. I suspected either Talon or Dak -- or both -- were nearby so I scouted several possible escape routes out of the corner of my eye.

"You don't know the area," Zar said matter-of-factly. "We do. If you flee, we will catch you."

"Why would you want to?"

He shrugged. "I could care less, but Talon seems to have... bonded to you. While I don't agree he made a good choice for a mate, what's done is done."

I narrowed my eyes. "Then we have no reason to continue. I won't live where I'm not wanted, and I refuse to influence Talon to leave a family unit who both needs and wants him."

"You'd give him up that easily?"

"There's nothing easy about it!" I wanted to stab the guy in the throat instead of merely scratching his skin. "Talon is a remarkable man. He's a fabulous lover and so protective and caring it hurts! Any woman would be crazy to let him get away from her! But I'd be a selfish bitch if I took him away from his family. I can't do that to him. Dak would probably follow him if for no other reason than to be there if Talon needed him should anything happen to me, but *both* of them belong with their Triad. Unfortunately, you happen to be their leader, and you don't care for them as much as they obviously care for you." My words were angry. *I* was angry. As far as I could tell, they were wasted on the big oaf, though.

He regarded me for a long time. I refused to lower my gaze or break the silence first. I'd made my decision as much for myself as for Talon and Dak. It was time for Zar to make his own decision.

"Oh, for fuck's sake," he growled, lunging for me. Much as Talon had so many nights before, Zar hefted me over his shoulder and swatted my ass. Hard. Then he headed back to the village.

I struggled, lashing out with my fists, but his back was hard as a tree trunk. He clamped his arm over the backs of my knees, ensuring I couldn't get away. Oh, I could have just stabbed him in the kidney or something, but I didn't *really* want him dead.

"You might haul my ass back to Talon and Dak, but I guarantee you I will get free and when I do, I'll be gone!"

He grunted, swatting my ass again.

"What *is* it with you guys and swatting my ass?"

"When a woman needs it, it's best to simply do it rather than risk her bolting at the first opportunity."

"I already said I was going to do just that, you ape!"

He swatted me again, this time lingering to rub my bottom through the leather over the back of my fur "panties" before giving me a firm squeeze. He grunted. "Nice."

I elbowed him in the back of the head as I wiggled, earning me another swat. "I'm not a piece of fucking meat!" He said nothing, just grunted and kept walking. Every time I struck him, he swatted me. By the time he strolled into the village my ass hurt like a son of a bitch, but he was grunting every time I struck a blow.

As if they'd planned it that way, Dak and Talon moved out of the woods on either side and behind Zar. None of them said a word. Talon kept his eyes on me, pride flaring in them. Pride and possessiveness. Dak grinned, winking at me. When I opened my mouth, he gave a shake of his head for me to keep silent. Rolling my eyes, I braced myself on Zar's back and let him carry me in a most undignified fashion through the village.

Everyone we met stopped, looking curiously at the four of us. They'd been curious the first time I'd entered the village as well, but not like this. It was like they expected something to happen and couldn't look away. Whether it was good or bad, I had no idea.

When we reached the top of the steps to the stone keep, Zar let me slide down his body. I kicked his shin, which only made the motherfucker grin. Neither Dak nor Talon gave any sign for me to stop, so I did it again. Zar kept his hands gripping my hips firmly, allowing me to move but not to get away. The only move he made to stop me was when I attempted to hike my knee into his balls. He twisted slightly then so his thigh took the impact. Which was when I noticed he was still hard. Even more so than he'd been when he'd caught me after the chase through the woods.

I stopped fighting, instead glaring at him. "Fucker," I muttered. He grunted. Then Zar did something that completely caught me off guard. One hand went to the back of my head while the other slid around my waist to pull me to him. Before I could do more than gasp, his mouth descended to mine. His tongue swept into my mouth, taking me with a fierce kiss of possession. Of claiming.

Several people from the crowd gasped before a steady hum of surprised murmuring broke out. My head started to spin with the sensations Zar created in my body with his fierce kiss. I remember thinking Talon's kiss was the sweetest I'd ever imagined. I'd loved the way he seemed uncertain what to do, his obvious need to please me. Zar, on the other hand, had no hesitation in him as he kissed me. He was out to take what he wanted. Which was when the whole situation hit me.

Zar was kissing me! In front of the entire village!

When he finally let me go, Dak was there to take his place. Then Talon. Talon hugged me fiercely, like he'd truly never expected to see me again. "Mine," he rumbled next to my ear. "Mine forever."

There were so many questions running around in

my head, I didn't know where to begin. Though this was the outcome I'd hoped for, I still had to figure out Zar's intentions. Had he truly changed his mind? Did he see me as an equal? Or at least not as a liability? I had to get to the bottom of this, but when Talon scooped me up, holding me tightly against his big, broad chest, all I could do was sigh like a sap. For whatever reason, this was happening. Somehow, I'd deal with Zar. Just not until we were in private.

Once Talon had me securely with him, he looked out to the crowd, a wild gleam in his eyes, and roared in triumph. The gathered people cheered with him. It seemed like Zar's fears weren't shared by everyone. Dak joined him as he gripped his shoulder. Zar was hard to read. But he looked… proud?

Whirling around, Talon carried me inside, back to their rooms. Right back to where all this started. My knife was still in the corner where it had clattered to the floor when Zar had tossed it aside after catching it. The blades I'd tossed at him were there as well, one imbedded in the wood trimming a door, the other on the floor where it had bounced off the stone wall.

My mind spinning, I asked, "You going to enlighten me about this turnaround?" Talon set me on my feet but wrapped his arms around me, holding me close. I couldn't help but smile up at him and rest a hand on his magnificent chest.

Zar simply looked at me. He leaned against the doorframe a moment before straightening and shutting the door. "I may have… misjudged you."

I snorted. "Oh, really."

"Zar doesn't apologize often," Dak said, clearly still not certain where all this was headed. "And only to Talon or me. Just hear him out."

"Still hasn't," I snapped. "But I'm not interested

in an apology."

"What are you interested in?" Zar approached me, his gate slow and steady. A predator stalking prey.

"I'm still the small, weak woman you had here a couple of hours ago. Nothing has changed."

"No. It hasn't. You may be small, but I misjudged the weak part apparently." His tone was dry as if he knew the joke was on him and was willing to take the ribbing.

I freed myself from Talon and advanced on Zar. "Best you remember that, too. If you don't, I'll always have you by the balls."

His lips quirked. "Understood... *wife*."

* * *

I couldn't help it. I giggled. Apparently, Dak and Talon found the situation just as amusing as I did because they both chuckled.

"Just so we understand each other," I said, approaching him slowly. When I reached him, I slid my arms around his neck. "You kissed me like you meant to keep me."

"So I did." His big hands pressed against my back, pulling me to him. He bent down to cover my lips with his. The hungry, masculine growl that rumbled through his chest thrilled me, making me melt for him. "So sweet," he murmured against my lips before lapping at them again. His tongue slid inside my mouth in a sensual thrust.

With no effort at all, he lifted me, urging my legs around his waist. "Time to sample what my brothers already have."

My stomach fluttered in anticipation, my pussy wetting for him. With one hand, he held me, the other he used to tear away my top and bottom, leaving me in only knee-high, fur-trimmed leather boots. The second he'd ripped away my bottoms, his big hand came down on my ass in a hard smack. Then he dipped between my cheeks to find my weeping cunt and trail gentle fingers through my folds. "Fuck," he swore. "You're a needy little wench, aren't you?"

"I can be," I gasped. "With the right motivation."

I loved his chuckle. Against my lips, it vibrated through me straight to my clit, driving me wild. I reached between us to find the rigid outline of his massive cock. It stretched the confines of his trews, pointing straight at my pussy as if it needed to be inside me as much as I needed it there.

With a frustrated grunt, I finally freed the laces and pulled him out, stroking him as I rubbed my pussy against the length. Now was definitely not the time to be shy. The slick head coated my hand with precum where I touched him. Resisting licking him from my palm was more than I was capable of. I looked him in the eye as I drew a long, slow lick across my hand. Zar promptly growled and fisted my hair in his hand to pull me back for a kiss.

"My filthy little girl," he growled. "Can you take my lusts and make them your own?"

"You'll have to try me to find out," I said a little breathlessly. "I might surprise you like I have since you met me."

I continued to slip my folds up and down him while I mashed his dick against them.

"My little mate is nothing if not surprising." God, I loved his voice! And this big, hard body of his. As if he'd simply decided enough was enough, he reached between us to grasp my hand around his cock. "Now, little wife, I claim you for my Triad… and for my *own*!"

When Zar shoved inside me, I wasn't sure if I

was going to come instantly or pass out. I think the events of the past week had finally caught up with me. All I knew was I craved this! Even all the kinky sex and all the group sex and all the *everything* I'd experienced over the past day hadn't been enough to truly give me what I needed because all I could think of was taking everything from this man I could before I gave *all* of them everything I had.

My head fell back on my shoulders as I clutched Zar's shoulders. He gripped my ass almost painfully as he situated himself inside me. I thought he might start fucking me right then, taking me standing up at his leisure simply to prove he could. He was, after all, much larger than me and had he not made a point to tell me how small I was? It was all about power dynamics. Wasn't it? Instead, he walked the few feet from where he'd stood to the bed and laid me down on it, following me to cover my body with his much larger one.

I loved his weight pressing me down. When he would have taken his weight on his arms, levering himself above me, I dug my nails into the muscles of his back and tightened my legs around his waist. He still tried to shift so that he wasn't on top of me completely, but I sank my teeth into his shoulder until he grunted, simply wrapping his arms around me.

"Are you sure, little warrior? I don't want to crush you." Despite the need I saw in his eyes, despite his callous personality, he stroked my hair gently with one hand while holding me tightly with the other arm.

In answer, I rocked my hips at him, digging my heels into his back. Zar gave one shuddering sigh. Then Zar set in to fuck.

With a bone-jarring thrust, Zar took his pleasure from me, sinking into my pussy over and over again.

Each time he surged forward, he hit as deep as he could go, the added sensation to my sensitive clit and the walls of my cunt only making the pleasure that much greater. It wasn't a warm-and-fuzzy kind of pleasure. It was almost painful. The only thing that kept it from actually hurting was how turned on I was. Instead, it was a brutal pleasure, devastating in its intensity.

I gasped, clinging to Zar as if my life depended on it. In some ways, it felt like it did. He'd taken me as his mate in front of the village. Kissed me for all to witness. He'd even called me "wife." But did that really mean he'd accepted me in the way I needed? Or was this merely to appease Talon?

"Focus on me!" Zar's sharp command broke me from my dark musings, bringing me back to the moment. "You doubt your mate?"

I gasped. Could he read me so well already? I'd known him only an hour! I don't know why I was surprised. Hadn't I read him within minutes of meeting him? Lying to him was an option, but it felt wrong. If I expected him to be truthful with me regarding anything, I had to extend him the same courtesy.

"I doubt you see me as someone who can stand with you instead of someone in need of your protection."

He grunted even as he continued surging inside me. Though he'd let up on the strength of his fucking, he didn't stop. Rather, he slowed his pace to something we could both sustain for a long while without coming.

"You're right. But I'm willing to let you prove yourself, and I swear I'll never treat you as anything less than my beloved mate."

"Then we're doubting each other."

"We are," he agreed. If he had approached this any other way, I'd never have believed we had any chance. Instead of trying to gloss over the reality, he simply gave it to me straight. "Give us time, Mia. I have no doubt we'll surprise each other in our acceptance."

"Are you saying that to ease my mind?" I had to know what he was thinking. As much as I needed what was best for Talon and Dak, I knew Zar needed it too. It was the reason both of us were in this position to begin with. Well, that and a healthy dose of good old-fashioned lust.

"I'm saying it because it's the truth. I doubt you take anything at face value. I don't either. I'll learn your capabilities, and you'll learn mine. While I'm looking for physical ability from you, you'll be looking for emotional ability from me." He shrugged. "Both are quite powerful. Yes?"

Zar truly saw the problem the same as I did. Or, at least, recognized there was a problem to begin with. It was more than I expected. He wasn't the kind of man to give in easily or to admit he was wrong about a given situation. He made a decision. He stuck to it. By allowing me time to insert myself into the lives of his Triad, Zar was saying that maybe I could be more to them than merely a warm body for their bed.

He must have seen what he needed to in my eyes because he gave me a half-grin and a grunt before picking up our earlier intensity again. It didn't take long for me to be desperate for him, needing to come like I needed to breathe.

I clawed at his shoulders and back. When I needed more, I found his ass and dug my fingernails into the flesh there. Zar growled loudly, shifting his weight for better leverage, and pounded into me with all his considerable strength. I screamed my pleasure, letting my legs fall wide so as not to get in his way. I needed this. Needed his violent fucking because I knew it was what he needed. What my men needed, I provided.

With a roar, Zar rose to his knees, flipping me to my belly in one smooth motion. One hand pressed heavily between my shoulders, the other grasped my hip with bruising strength. Head on the fur-covered bed, ass in the air, I whimpered, wanting him desperately.

"Back inside me," I pleaded, rolling my hips. Zar responded by smacking my ass a couple of times before doing as I'd asked.

"Fuck!" he bit out.

Then he did. Hard.

Zar set up a driving rhythm that shook me to my core. His strokes were long and full, filling me with each brutal thrust. Again, the intensity bordered on pain, but the little bite only added to the eroticism.

Some innate sense made me glance up. Talon was focused on me like a predator, his expression unreadable. I met his gaze with what I was sure was a dazed look. Apparently, that was what he'd been waiting on.

"Zar," he snapped. "Ease up."

"No!" I screamed.

At the same time Zar roared at Talon. "My mate! Take her as I need to!"

"Need more!" I cried. "Don't stop!"

Talon clearly looked undecided as well as worried.

"Don't worry, brother," Dak murmured. "He won't harm what we've been given." When Talon still looked anxious, he continued. "Look at her face. As she gazes at us, her eyes are glazed in pleasure, her lips parted as she gasps. You know she's a strong woman. Do you honestly think she'd not fight Zar if he were hurting her?" At that, Talon relaxed a fraction. I wanted to reassure him, but I finally understood what Magenta had experienced. Zar was giving me so much pleasure, such… intensity, I couldn't focus on anything other than Zar pounding into me.

As his speed increased, so did the force of his thrusts. Sweat erupted over my body. It must have his too because I felt droplets landing on my bare back as they were jarred loose from him with his fucking. His cock swelled inside me, letting me know he was as close to coming as I was.

Zar lowered himself over me, wrapping one arm tightly around my chest. The other found the place where his dick surged inside my weeping cunt. When he found my clit with his clever fingers, it was over.

I screamed. Loudly. My hips bucked as Zar surged into me with bruising intensity. His big cock swelled and swelled until he finally… released. He was hot inside me. Insistent. As if his seed were determined to plant inside me to tie me to him. I gasped in a desperate breath before I screamed again. As he continued to pump into me, he pulled me upright so that I was on my knees, his chest to my back, his arms wrapped around me… his cock still pumping me full of seed.

"Our mate," he rasped at my ear, his breathing ragged, his chest heaving behind me. I was limp as a rag doll, but his strength held me upright. "Strong. Cunning." His voice was soft but held an unmistakable note of pride. Perhaps he was truly seeing me as an asset rather than a liability.

"She is," Dak agreed. "She'll protect our people

as fiercely as we do." He sounded as though he truly believed what he said instead of merely reassuring Zar he'd made a good choice in accepting me.

"I believe she will," Zar said, nuzzling my neck. Kissing me tenderly. Praising my body's responses to his fierce lovemaking. His fingers were still stroking where our bodies joined, spreading the combination of my cum and his own over my clit and his dick. He was still semi-hard inside me, thrusting slowly. Contentedly. I wondered if he'd positioned us thusly to show the other two the evidence of our consummation.

Talon's gaze slid the length of my body then locked to where Zar and I were joined. I knew what was coming next but was unable to warn Zar in time. The next thing I knew, Talon was in front of us licking my clit, Zar's dick, and any cum dripping from my body like a starving man after a feast.

"What the... FUUUUCK!"

At first, Zar sounded shocked. Maybe even a little angry. Then, probably as the sensations hit him, he sounded as stunned as Dak had that first time.

"Yeah," Dak said, amusement coloring his words. "That's what I said. Well, close anyway. Same difference."

Instantly, Zar was hard inside me, his cock surging to life. "What is this?"

"Tell him you don't want it and he'll stop," I said, turning to look over my shoulder. I nipped his chin. "Or stop being a pussy and let Talon show you how he feels."

"How he... ah!" Zar let his head fall back. His whole body trembled around me. Apparently, he wasn't so averse to the situation once I explained it. The whole thing made me giggle. At least, until Talon flicked my clit with his tongue.

"The two of you…" Zar said, his voice catching. He swallowed heavily.

"Oh yeah," Dak said, grinning at the befuddled Zar. "I was about as prepared as you."

Zar looked up at Dak helplessly, but, like Dak had before, his hips rocked back, allowing Talon access to his length. Had the situation been any different, I'd have enjoyed his discomfort. As it was, I was just as uncomfortable, though from lust instead of the unfamiliar situation.

"Just go with it," I said. "While you're at it, think about your Triad. You're bond is non-conventional, no one tying you to anyone else other than those two men. Perhaps this is the first step in admitting you can grow deeper feelings for Dak and Talon?" When he said nothing, I added. "Or maybe you should simply accept pleasure in all its forms when it happens."

Zar nodded, still looking at Talon in dumbfounded fascination. The affection in the other man's eyes was plain for anyone to see. Evan as hardheaded as Zar was, he noticed it. When Talon took another lick, Zar barked out a yell. When Talon fisted Zar's cock and pulled him out of my wet flesh to give one long, hard suck down his length, it was over.

With a fucking war bellow, Zar spilled his seed. Instead of pulling away, Talon took him deep again, swallowing everything Zar had to give. Zar's arms tightened around me as if I were his lifeline in an impossible, unpredictable sea.

"Bleeding gods!" Zar sounded stunned. When Talon rose and pulled me into his arms, I kissed him eagerly, tasting Zar on his lips. "Dak, what have you brought into our lives?" Zar the unflappable was completely off balance.

"To be honest," Dak said, "I'm not sure. I can tell you I better understand myself and my relationship with the Triad. We were raised together, but not as brothers. We were trained to always have each other's backs. I can't tell you I'd have taken this particular step without Mia's encouragement, but I can tell you I'll do it again as many times as I'm allowed. Not necessarily because I have a romantic love for the two of you -- no offense, but you're not my type. I'll do it because it feels fucking good."

"Good point," Zar muttered as he moved behind me once more. When Talon released me, Zar turned me gently to face him. "Little witch. Perhaps you've cast a spell over me."

I grinned. "Perhaps. Tell me you hate it or --"

"I know, I know. Or stop being a pussy."

Chapter Ten

Zar didn't tell us to stop. Instead, he took me with Talon with a ferocity I'd only ever dreamed about. Both men surged inside my pussy greedily. Sandwiched between them, I clung to Talon while Zar fit his big cock beside Talon's and fucked me as hard as Talon did. When they were done, Dak took me alone. He covered me with his big body and kissed me like he… almost like maybe he… loved me.

Just before we both came, he looked at me with me with wonder in his eyes and pride right there for me to see. It had gone on most of the night. My men didn't actually fuck each other, but all of them sampled a bit of a blow job from one or the other more than once. When they did, they took me even more vigorously.

After that, we all collapsed in a heap on the big bed and passed out. At least I did. The last thing I remember was all of them somehow wrapped around me, praising me for the pleasure I'd given them. I'm sure I mumbled some kind of response but I have no idea what it was.

I woke to the sounds of swords ringing out in the great hall outside our rooms. None of the men were with me, but I could hear them shouting through the heavy wooden door.

Panic seized me. What was going on? They were fighting? Inside the great hall? That couldn't be good.

Not bothering with clothes, I grabbed a short sword from a weapons rack, testing its weight and balance by giving a few practice swings. I'd noticed Dak placing his sword there the first time I was here, though now it was now conspicuously absent. Since he kept his sword there, I had no doubt the other swords were in good condition and would stand me well in a fight. Assuming I could manage. Agile with a large weapon I was not. I was more at home with a knife. From a bit of a distance. Or from behind.

All's fair in love and war. Right?

I opened the door to the sight of several large warriors teaming up on my men. Their armor was similar to that worn by Zar and Dak, but the design was obviously of a different tribe or something. Talon had on breeches and boots but fought bare-chested and was paying the price with several cuts and gashes over his torso. That sight more than anything else put me into a fighting rage.

Two big men were locked in deadly combat with Zar. Dak and Talon seemed to be keeping the leader of their Triad in the back away from as many attackers as they could manage. Unfortunately, Zar, being the proud, fearsome warrior he was, took exception to their protection, cursing them as much as he did the men he was battling.

While Zar had two attackers to contend with, the other two had three or four. Beside the door, Iris stood with a group of women watching the battle rage before them. The pets seemed anxious, but Iris looked smug. Obviously, the woman had something to do with this attack inside the heart of the village. I decided in that moment the woman had to die. First, however, I had to rescue my men.

Snagging a flaming torch from the wall sconce in my free hand, I ran to the nearest warrior. He didn't see me and wouldn't likely have glanced twice at me if he had. Well, OK. That's not entirely true. He probably *would* have, but he'd have stopped and stared at the naked chick running at him with a battle cry, a flaming torch, and a sword. Either way, I knew it would give Zar the opening he needed to make short work of him so we could help Dak and Talon.

As it turned out, the guy kept his back to me, even through my yelling, and got a sword in the back for his trouble. Zar finished him with a sword swipe to his neck, taking the guy's head before turning to focus entirely on the second warrior.

I ducked around to the next closest man and gave him the same treatment as the first. The third guy met me with a vicious swing of his own sword. Ducking, I went low, cutting at his legs. I used my torch to brush along the fur-lined pants and boots, setting his clothing aflame in seconds.

"What the fuck are you doing?" Zar yelled, snagging my arm and pulling me behind him protectively. I simply turned around, putting my back to his as I yelled back over my shoulder.

"Saving your asses!"

"We've got this! Get back in our rooms and get some fucking clothes on!"

A warrior who'd managed to get through Dak and Talon's defenses gave a vicious swing. Even glancing behind me as I was, I could still see the near miss to Zar's chest. He had on his leather, but no heavy armor. The slice would have opened a deadly gash had Zar not managed to block it.

The guy came in close with a yell, head-butting Zar. He would have knocked me down with his much larger body but I sidestepped, spinning and slicing the attacking warrior in the backs of the legs. He crumpled to his knees with a cry just before Zar took his head with a vicious back swing.

Again, I found Talon and Dak, worried for them

even though they seemed to have no permanent damage. They'd both fought off or killed all their assailants but one. Now, they had that warrior pined, his back against the wall. The guy might be as good as dead, but he knew it, and that made him dangerous.

Blood was everywhere, even painting my bare skin where I'd ducked under an arterial spray... only to have to jump a sword to keep from getting my legs chopped off. Blood had arched like a fountain from my forehead to my belly. I swiped my arm over my face to clear my vision. The stench of both sweat and blood hung heavy in the air.

As I studied the room, I found Iris and the other pets in a corner of the great hall. All the women were huddled together looking more afraid now than they had before the Triad had killed their enemies. Even Iris looked a little shell-shocked, as if she couldn't believe her eyes.

I stalked toward the group of women, sword and torch still in hand. Blood dripped from the tip of my weapon, and the stench of burning flesh began to overshadow the metallic scent of blood. I must have looked like a demoness from hell because all of them -- even Iris -- whimpered in fear.

"Dak!" Iris called, her gaze darting from him to me. "She's blood-mad! Rabid!"

"Or maybe," I said through clenched teeth, "I simply smell a fucking rat in the cat house!"

"Don't cats eat rats?" One of the girls whispered her question to another one of the girls.

I hissed.

"Explain," Zar snapped at me, ignoring the byplay.

"They were in here during the fighting. Came in through the fucking door *after* you were already engaged. Why would they do that? Why not get help? Why not run for their fucking lives?"

Zar turned his stony gaze to the group of women. Iris had stepped closer to the door but nothing missed the warrior's keen eyes. Again, he only said, "Explain." Though his voice was gentle, his eyes told the true story. Not only did he not believe Iris was there by accident or with good intent, he was not going to tolerate lies on her part. Menace was there for all to hear. Judging by the look on her face, Iris hadn't missed it. Also, he hadn't held back his true feelings in the way he addressed me. With Iris, he'd softened his tone to something less threatening. Did he see me as an equal?

Equal or not, he'd addressed me as he might have Talon or Dak. Not as he addressed Iris now.

"We wanted to help, but they were too well armed. Once we got inside, we were afraid to make for the door for fear of being cut in two by the brutes!"

Oh, she was good.

"I wouldn't bet on that," came a voice from the doorway. Magenta stood there, bloody sword in hand, her men flanking her. Zeus brandished a great-sword -- covered in blood -- while Luca wielded two katana-type swords -- also stained with blood.

Instead of addressing Zar or either of the other two, Magenta spoke to me. "The village guard is in an uproar. Apparently, some of them got the impression the Triad had been compromised in some way."

"Why does everyone automatically assume I'll be a liability?" I groused, wanting to punch something.

Magenta shrugged. "I tried to tell them you were a feral little thing, but some of them took matters into their own hands."

"Those men aren't part of our guard," Dak

commented. "I don't know any of them."

"That's because they're Blackheart's men," Luca supplied softly.

"So..." I turned my gaze to Iris, narrowing my eyes. "Someone teamed up with your enemy to take the village and dismantle -- or kill -- the Triad?"

Surprisingly, Iris lifted her chin. "I did what was best for the community and our neighbors in the outlands. If the Triad is weak, we'll all be enslaved!"

"And what do you think will happen to these people if you aid a coup?" Zar said, stepping closer to Iris in a totally menacing way. All pretense at gentleness gone now. "Blackheart knows the vast majority of our people back us solidly because we treat them fairly. He will lay waste to this village because people see it as the center of our power. If he does, it will ensure the others pledge their loyalty for fear of the same."

"No he wouldn't," Iris scoffed. "He said he only wanted to see us all prosper."

"What did he promise you personally, Iris?" Dak asked. His voice was soft, but I detected the edge of anger underneath.

Iris shrugged. "I'm to take my place at his side as his mate."

Talon raised an eyebrow, glancing at Dak and Zar before speaking. "You didn't know Blackheart is already mated?"

"He is not! There is no woman at his side! No woman he claims above his pets!"

"No *woman*, no," Zar agreed. "His general is his mate. They make up that region's Duo. Rumor is Blackheart will take on a second mate to make a Triad, but he doesn't prefer females. Even his pets are male."

Iris just stood there, a confused look on her face.

"But, he told me --"

"He told you whatever you needed to hear to betray your village and the Triad," Dak finished. "He's looked to our lands for years. Even approached Zar once to join our regions, with Zar making the third male in their union. Zar refused. Blackheart didn't take it well."

"More because he couldn't accept the relationship rejection than any real need for more territory," Zar muttered.

"Then what did he have planned for me?" Iris questioned, though I could tell by the look on her face she knew.

"Probably to kill you with the rest of the village," I supplied.

She turned at hissed at me. "Bitch! This is all your fault! If you'd have just stayed gone when you ran off instead of letting Zar drag you back none of this would have happened!"

I laughed. Like, *really* laughed. "Like I could stop him! He's nearly a foot taller than me and probably has a good hundred and fifty pounds on me! What exactly was I supposed to do?" With each word, I crossed the room closer to her, still holding my sword. I pointed it at her when I continued. "*Don't fuck with me!* You made your own decisions. Now live with them."

Real fear glistened in Iris's eyes then. She dove for Zar, who stood only a few feet from us, wrapping her arms around one of his legs. "Please forgive me!" she pleaded. "You have to know I was only acting for the good of the people! Just like any good ruler would do!"

Zar's fist clenched, the muscle in his jaw working overtime. Obviously he wanted to throttle the woman but was valiantly trying to restrain himself. If I were a bitch, if I cared nothing for any of them, I'd have encouraged him to kill the traitor. But I knew in my heart Zar wasn't the type of man to intentionally harm a woman. Even if she deserved it. Even if it was his right by law to punish her for grievous crimes. Like treason.

With a sigh, I touched his arm, bringing his fist to my mouth for a kiss. I brushed my lips over his knuckles until he relaxed, then I pried open his fingers to kiss his palm. "I'm covered in blood, Zar. I need help washing the battle away."

With a shudder, he pulled me to him. "You could have been killed," he murmured. "Why would you charge out here like that? And you were naked! Gods!" He scooped me up, shaking Iris loose from his leg before striding to his rooms with long-legged steps and not a single look back or a word of instruction to the other men. I glanced over his shoulder to find Dak and Talon grinning at us. Iris looked stunned, more than a little scared. I should have maybe felt bad for her, but I couldn't. I meant it when I said she had to deal with the consequences of her actions. Bitch nearly got my men killed. For that, I wasn't certain I could ever forgive her.

When Zar and I were alone -- Talon and Dak stayed behind to deal with the aftermath -- he put me in a tub of cool water and washed every inch of my skin and hair until I didn't feel so filthy any longer. I smiled up at his grave face and knew he'd truly been worried, but I thought maybe I saw at least a little respect in his eyes.

He completed his task in silence. When he'd finished, he lifted me out, curling his arms around me to bury his face in my neck. Water sluiced over my body, wetting his clothing, but it was soon not to matter. Zar stripped until he was as naked as I, then carried me to the plush furs in front of the gently crackling fire. Sitting behind me, he ran a brush through my long hair over and over.

"You know," he began, never pausing as he continued with the brush, "I could have lost you."

"Yes, but --"

"Shh," he said gently. "Let me finish." When I gave a small nod, he continued. "You ran out there completely unprotected, with only a sword and a torch, completely naked. No armor. No shoes. Only your cunning and ferocity." He sighed and paused then. "That was the bravest thing I've ever witnessed in my life. That doesn't mean I'm not going to spank your ass for it, but I need to know why you didn't stay put and let us protect you."

I turned to him. He knelt on the floor behind me, sitting back on his heels. The puzzled expression on his face made me smother a smile.

"You really don't understand, do you?" When he shook his head, I rose to my knees and took his face between my palms and brushed my lips with his before meeting his gaze boldly. "I will always fight for what I want. Protect what I hold dear. When Talon approached me with the idea of staying with him, I agreed because I had nowhere to go. But, as I got to know all of you, I realized that you were all honorable men. Better than any man I'd ever met. I knew that not only would I be safe, but I'd be treated well." I grinned. "I just had no desire to be a pet. While wandering the Outlands alone wouldn't be the best alternative, I would have done it if being your pet were the only alternative. When you agreed to my condition? Well. I wasn't going to give any of you up so easily. If that means I have to fight to keep you, know I'll fight to the death. Always."

He sighed before leaning down to kiss me again, this time a bit more thoroughly. When he finally pulled back, we were both breathing hard. "So, what do we do about Iris and her cronies?"

I shrugged. "Give them a choice. Either they go to this Blackheart's territory, however they're welcomed, or they're exiled into the Outlands. You can't let them stay knowing they'll likely do something like this again."

"You don't think I should execute them? I would have bet you'd demand it of me. Most women I know would."

"Haven't you figured out I'm not like most women?" I grinned. "Besides, you don't strike me as the kind of man to want to carry out that kind of sentence on a woman. Since you wouldn't expect others to do what you're unwilling to do, I don't think there is a better alternative."

Zar looked at me as if he were seeing a creature he'd long studied about but had never seen in the flesh before. "How did I get so lucky?" he murmured. I got the feeling he was talking to himself, or whatever deity he believed in, so I just smiled at him. He scooped me up then and carried me to his big bed. "Tonight, I intend to show you that you've been blessed as well."

"Oh?" I managed, if a bit breathlessly. "How's that?"

"Once Talon and Dak return, we're going to spend the rest of the night taking you over and over. My goal will be to make you so delirious from pleasure and lust that you can't even cry out our names. If the three of us make it to the morning without your scratches of passion over our bodies, I'll be quite disappointed. I plan to keep you on the edge of sanity all fucking night. Then, as the first rays of the sun shine on your sweat-dampened skin, we're going to make you come until you pass out in our arms."

I couldn't help the moan that escaped me. "Ah, fuck!"

"Oh yes. Definitely."

I had a feeling I was in for a long night. But oh, what fun it would be.

I never thought being enslaved as a pet would bring such joy. Or pleasure. Perhaps it was because I refused to give in to my mates' every demand. Perhaps it was simply the men themselves. All I knew for certain was, not only had the theft of that spoon bread been worth my troubles, but the prize had never tasted -- or felt -- so good.

The Triad's Pet (The Outcasts 2)
Marteeka Karland

A feisty outcast...
Arryn's life has always been awkward. The daughter of a traitor and his pet, the only reason she is allowed to continue to live in the village is because of her exceptional talents in both healing and engineering. Even still, she knows how to pick her battles and lives a contented life.

A triad pledged to another...
Being taken as a pet is one thing, but to be taken by a trio of men who have pledged to be the promised of another woman is intolerable. Perhaps the impression Arryn made when she saved Storm's life was a strong one, but she certainly didn't sign up to be a pet. Dealing with her budding feelings for the three warriors is hard enough, but knowing she can never have them is enough to break her heart. Not that she'd ever let it show.

A village under siege...
When danger is deliberately brought into their midst, it's up to Arryn to direct her men. But how can a pet convince three stubborn warriors to trust in her unique abilities?

Chapter One

The battle in the distance had everyone in the village on edge. Not a single person here didn't have someone in that fight. Even our kings, the Triad, were in this one because we all knew it was a fight for the city. A fight to the death.

"Arryn! You're needed at the wall! The mechanism on the main catapult is frozen!" That was my best friend, Lassa. She was the fastest runner in the village and, at times like these, she was needed everywhere.

I wanted to protest -- organizing medical supplies and a place to bring the wounded was necessary, too. But Lassa was already off to carry the next message. Besides, Lorgan, our village healer and head of the Council of Elders, had made it clear he didn't want my input. He needed it, though. When the wounded started coming in, assuming we weren't overrun and invaded by the opposing tribes, he was going to have a mess on his hands.

Oh, well. Not my fight.

Yet.

As I hurried off to the wall, I noticed the shift in the breeze. Now it came from the sea rather than inland. Never a good sign. Off in the distance, a black cloud loomed menacingly and lightning flashed, filling me with dread.

As if the fates had heard my fear and misgivings, I heard soldiers gathering near the city gates. In the midst of them was one of our Triad. The other two were already on the battlefield. One always stayed back to see to the city defenses. If the last king was readying to enter the fray on the battlefield, things were bad indeed.

I watched as the tall man on a tall horse directed soldiers with every expectation he would be obeyed without question. His hair was black as night, his skin bronzed and glinting with sweat. Plate armor encased a powerful chest, leather his arms and legs. The powerful steed he rode had guards for the king's legs built onto the saddle that acted as additional armor. Though I'd lived here most of my life, I did my best to stay away from anything to do with the ruling factions. I knew who the kings were, the Triad, but I wasn't sure which was which. I *thought* this one was Asher. They were important people and, because of my shady background, I tended to avoid them.

His sharp gaze scanned the ranks at the wall, calling several soldiers to his side and snapping orders. He'd readied a contingent of cavalrymen to go into battle. Then he looked up... directly at me. Clear blue eyes caught my gaze. Held me captive as easily as if he'd wrapped those brawny arms tightly around me, as if he'd been completely aware of me and where I was no matter what was going on around him.

The hard planes of his face were starkly beautiful, with masculine lines that seemed to have been designed to take a woman's breath. If I'd actually been the type of woman affected by men like him, my heart would be beating faster, my breath catching in my throat. Instead, I'm sure I was just out of breath, my heart pounding from hurrying through the village. Had to be.

Then he nodded once in my direction, actually acknowledging me, before swinging his mount around and charging onto the battlefield with his men.

"Get over here, girl!" one of the guards snapped,

completely shattering the spell King Asher had woven around me. The soldiers were usually courteous, but urgency stripped everyone of niceties. I understood and respected that, not taking offense in the least. "The pin won't release the break!"

As I approached at a run, I could see the problem. "The spring's melted!" I shouted to him over the din of soldiers. "Get the payload off and I'll replace the spring!"

Easier said than done. The payload was a cauldron of flaming oil. Even as I told him what to do, I realized that wouldn't be possible. "Never mind," I muttered, snagging an iron bar next to the hulking catapult. All I had to do was release the break. Which was controlled by the spring. The heat from the payloads they'd been firing had melted the spring. That didn't happen with proper maintenance and care in loading the payload. Either someone got in too big a hurry, or no one had maintained the equipment. During the heat of battle, that was understandable.

I swung the iron bar with all my might. It took three tries before another guard snagged it from me and gave one mighty swing, snapping the spring free. When it finally broke free, the brake handle flipped up, the recoil knocking me on my ass into the mud when I jumped out of the way, but the arm swung, sending the flaming projectile hurling through the air. I didn't notice where it went because I'd had to scramble to my feet and was frantically trying to free the broken bits of the release lever to get at the spring and break.

The soldier in charge of this engine was hurrying to bring me the parts he knew I'd need. Tools were already scattered around where men had been attempting to solve the problem.

I worked as swiftly as I could, repairing what I'd

broken as well as replacing the vital spring that allowed the weapon to launch. I have no idea how long it took -- seemed like forever -- but finally, I was able to give the go ahead. "Test the fucker!" I shouted.

Soldiers cranked the wheel, creating tension. The sling was empty, but we couldn't risk loading it before it was tested in case I'd fucked up.

"Release!" the guard snapped. The arm let go and swung upward in a smooth motion. Without another word, the soldiers began cranking the wheel again, readying the catapult for its payload.

They loaded another cauldron, filled it with oil, then set it ablaze. The guard gave the command to release it and, again, the weapon functioned exactly as it was supposed to. He turned to look at me. Nodded once, then turned his attention back to his duty.

I was the one everyone went to when things broke. The only problem was, I was a nobody. The bastard daughter of a traitor and a pet not his own, most thought me incapable of anything good.

My mother had been a nomad. Captured and sold as a pet, she'd run off with my father, having his child shortly before they'd landed in our village. Years later, my father, having worked his way up as a tradesman, betrayed the Triad by showing an enemy scout how to navigate the maze leading from the village to the Triad compound. He'd been jailed for a trial that had taken months when most times justice was swift and sure. In the meantime, the Council of Elders had given my mother to Lorgan, the head of the Council, in anticipation of my father's execution. Things had gone horribly wrong after that. It was said that my mother "forced" Lorgan into what was considered "deviant behavior." Lorgan had convinced the council to sentence my mother to death. At least, that was the official account. I had no idea what had happened immediately following that horrible incident, but my father, having been found guilty of the charges against him, had been exiled instead of executed.

That left me on my own at eleven years old, so I learned to fend for myself. By the time I was sixteen, I could fix anything. Which is how I'd come to design reinforcements for the city wall four years later. But, I mean, what could anyone expect? Their plan was piss poor and mine wasn't.

While I was at the catapults, I hurried to inspect the area where the wall crossed the river. If there was a weakness in the defenses, it was here. Instead of building with the river on the outside, the elders had wanted it inside, so there was a ready supply of fresh water, which meant the iron gate was the only thing preventing invaders from breaching the city walls. It was fortified with guard towers and all kinds of weapons, but from the looks of things, every man not needed to operate crossbows and catapults was outside on the battlefield. There were a few soldiers on the battlements, but they were mostly boys in their teens. All of them looked terrified. This was why I'd insisted on making sure the design of the wall over the river was strong. I knew the Elders would demand all the defensive strength be focused on the main part of the city. Had the builders followed the original plan designed by some fuck dumber than dirt, we'd have been screwed the second the enemy engaged that section of the wall.

Looking through the grate to the battlefield beyond, it seemed like the fight was still far off. If they broke the lines, however, any enemy who'd studied the layout of the village would know the river was the weakest point and would charge it with everything they had.

I picked up a rock and threw it at one of the boys on the wall. Missed. Tried again. Didn't make it to the wall that time. Fuck. I was definitely not warrior material. "Hey!" I yelled, waving my arms over my head. "Hey, hey!" One of the boys turned around. Cristiano, his name was.

"Arryn? What are you doing over here! The catapult's messed up! They need you at the gate!"

"I fixed it, Cris. How is it looking from your end? Can you hold them if they break the line?"

The young man looked around, fear on his face. "I don't know, Arryn. We've got weapons ready, but if it comes down to it…" He shook his head. "All I know is, I'm scared now and we're not even in the fight."

"Hold them together, Cris," I said, scanning the inner wall for anyone I thought might be able to help. "I'll see what I can do."

"I'd sure love to have Granda here about now," the younger man commented. "He isn't very strong in a fight, but he's a fierce leader."

Which was a great idea. We needed something more at the river than the iron grate, but in this situation the men on the wall needed an experienced leader worse. "Drop the reinforcements!" I called to Cris. "It's the best stationary defense you've got for the river."

"We're not supposed to do that except when it's imminent we're going to be charged," he called back.

"Do you think your men can get the heavy son of a bitch in place if the enemy breaks the lines? Because you'll need to be firing at them with everything you've got."

"I'm on it," he said, as I knew he would.

With one last look at the wall, I sprinted off to the main gate. The largest contingent of guards and soldiers was there. If there was a plan in place to defend the riverside, someone there would know.

"Where have you been, Arryn?"

That angry voice belonged to Lorgan. Head of the Council of Elders and all-around dumbfuck, Lorgan was all about making himself look good. He never wanted me anywhere around unless he was about to fuck something up. Or needed someone to clean up something he'd already fucked up.

Much as I wanted to make sure he wasn't actually killing anyone with his horrible techniques, if the river wall wasn't as fortified as it could be, the entire village could be in jeopardy. "Not now, Lorgan," I said as I sprinted by. He sputtered and swore at me but didn't bother to give chase. Which was my test as to if he was actually about to kill someone with ignorance. If Lorgan was in real trouble, he wouldn't let up. I'd have to deal with him later, but right now, I had more pressing concerns.

"Who's in charge?" I'd reached the main gate, out of breath and panting. Sweat dripped from my forehead into my eyes. My thin, sleeveless dress clung to my damp skin and my wine-red hair stuck to my face and neck uncomfortably. The soldiers were in full leather armor. As hot and miserable as I was, they had to be even worse.

"Arryn!" That was Hadin. Third in command of the city watch and training to be a captain in the Triad's guard, he took his job very seriously. One of the reasons he'd make a good leader.

"The defense at the river. Those boys are good and throwing their heart into it, but really need a strong leader."

"Cristiano is on it. He'll be fine."

"Just one experienced soldier, Hadin. Please. Just one."

Hadin glanced in my direction before turning back to the group of men who'd begun to gather around him. Hadin was one of the few of the villagers in a position of power who actually took me seriously. "I don't *have* one, Arryn. They'll be fine. It's not likely the Blackheart soldiers will break the line in any event. Especially if we keep pounding them with fire bombs."

"Cris is asking for help. He's a good guard but knows he's in over his head."

"No doubt because you asked him if he was overwhelmed," Hadin snapped. "The city is under attack. We all have a job to do. Including you, Arryn. I suggest you get to yours and leave me to mine!" The man normally wasn't so snippy, but I understood and would never hold it against him.

I also knew better than to argue. I'd expressed my opinion and Cristiano's fears. That was all I could do. At least, it was all I could do *here*. My philosophy? Why waste time arguing that could better be spent doing something about the problem?

Whirling, I ran to the inner wall. Our city was formed in a circle. The Council of Elders and their families lived in the center, which was walled off. The theory was, if the city were ever under attack, women and children from all over the village would gather inside the inner wall and be protected from invaders. At least that was the argument the elders had put forth to have it built in the first place.

It was also a last line of defense for everyone. In reality, the elders generally locked themselves in, hunkered down, and expected everyone to protect them and their families. For the most part, any women and children who were not helping the soldiers and healers huddled just outside the inner walls in hopes that, if the outer wall was breached, those behind the inner wall would let them in.

I knew better.

At the festival square, the entrance to the inner wall, I found Cristiano's granda, Malachi. Though the older man was completely white headed and missing a leg below his knee, with his tall, muscular frame, he was still a commanding presence.

"Take the little ones to the underground shelter," he said, his voice booming. The shelter was supposed to be used for food storage, but I could see some of the items not heat sensitive were stacked outside the shelter entrance next to the wall. "Any woman who wants to go with them would be most welcomed and appreciated. My Tessa can only control so many of the little varmints."

He sounded put out, but I knew Malachi wanted every single woman and child in that shelter and would use any means necessary to convince them, even making it seem like Tessa was too frail to care for the children on her own. Not that Tessa needed the help. She was a force of nature.

"Cris needs you, Malachi," I said without preamble. "At the river wall."

Instantly, the old man's gaze seemed to burn through me. "Are they under siege?"

"No, but they need a steady hand to guide them." Malachi met my gaze with a level one of his own. "They're scared. If they come under attack and panic…"

"You make sure everyone who needs to be there gets into the shelter," he said. "Tessa can handle it once they're all inside, but some of them will try to stay outside to help their men."

"Do you need help getting to the wall?"

He gave me a look that said, *If you ask me that one more time…*

"Never mind. Stupid question."

He grunted in satisfaction and snagged his crutches. The man really shouldn't have been able to move around as easily as he did, but he could move as quickly as a man half his age with both legs. Of all the people in the village, I admired Malachi and Tessa the most. Not only were they intelligent and hardworking, but they were fierce in their protection of those they considered family. The gods knew they'd been there for me when I needed them desperately.

Tessa ushered women and children inside the shelter. She looked frail and damned near helpless, but I knew better. So did everyone else, but it still worked. No one she ushered inside refused her.

"You should stay with me," Tessa said decisively. "We could use your calming influence with the children."

I blinked. "Tessa?"

"I mean," she plucked at her apron, "I want you to be in here with us. Where it's safe."

"You know I can't," I said gently. "Is something wrong? Is there something you need you're not telling me?"

The older woman sighed, dabbing at her eyes with her apron. "I'm just getting emotional in my old age." She gave me a watery smile. "I have seven children and twenty-four grandchildren. None of them pull at my heart the way you do, child. I love them all, but I worry over you when I shouldn't."

"I'll be fine, Granma," I said, giving her the title all her grandchildren used. "You know I'm needed in the city."

She pursed her lips. "Just don't you let that Lorgan push you around. Someone needs to pull that man down a peg or two."

I grinned. "I'm sure you're the very one to do it, Granma." I kissed her on the cheek. "I love you, Tessa. Take care of the young ones."

"I love you, too, Arryn. Take care of *yourself*."

I had just given Tessa a hug and closed the door to the underground shelter when I spotted Lassa running toward me. In the distance, it seemed like the sounds of battle were growing louder. As if an army were approaching the city.

Impossible!

"Release!" Haden's shout penetrated through the din of battle closing in around us. Several flaming cauldrons were launched from the eight catapults along the walls. The big crossbows on the top of the walls were loaded with flaming arrows, which also released. A barrage of flaming arrows from archers behind the walls were shot as well. Which meant the city's soldiers were close to the wall, likely in retreat.

Never had the Triad been bested in a direct battle for the city. My heart pounded. Just as I was about to head to the river to make sure the water grate was as fortified as it could be, I saw a group of riders enter the city at a gallop, heading for the healer's tent. The doors were closed once more, indicating they were standing their ground outside.

"Protect the Triad!" a voice called. Which was odd. I'd never heard of the Triad putting their protection over any of the men they led. The trio always led the regiments into battle. One at the front, one with the cavalry, and one with the siege engines...

How could I be so stupid! King Asher had left

the wall. None of the Triad had replaced him with Hadin. Which meant one of the Triad had fallen. That was what Lorgan had been fussing about. The king must not have been at the healer's tent yet when Lorgan called for me. A runner would have been sent ahead to give notice for the healer to prepare; otherwise, had Lorgan needed my help with this particular problem, he'd have run me down immediately. He'd likely thought he could handle it on his own but wanted backup. The man they'd just taken into the healer's tent was one of our kings.

Fuck.

Chapter Two

I sprinted to the healer's tent. Lorgan was leaning over a big man, trying to pull off his armor. Soldiers standing around were helping but seemed afraid to touch the man on the table. Probably because Lorgan was shouting at them to be careful and not injure him further.

As I approached, I could see an arrow protruding from the man's chest. It looked like the armor had stopped much of the arrow's penetration, but it had definitely done damage. When I pushed my way through the crowd of soldiers, I saw another wound high on the king's thigh. Lorgan had an assistant holding a rag over the wound to stem the flow of blood, but it still pooled on the table and dripped to the floor. Lorgan looked up at me, panic in his eyes. "I would very much appreciate your input, Arryn," he said politely.

Well, *fuck*. Lorgan was never nice. Never polite. Hell, the man never acknowledged my skills no matter how many times I helped him out. "I need the big cutters. The ones I brought in a few weeks ago with the long handles."

"We need to get the arrow out first," Lorgan hissed. "There's no way to get the armor off with the shaft protruding."

"We're going to cut the shaft off below the feathers," I said. "Then we're going to cut the armor off with those cutters."

"But the arrow --"

"Has barbs on the head. If we pull it out without seeing how deep it went, we could kill him." I hated having to explain even the simplest things to Lorgan. Though he was being cordial, I was convinced it wasn't in his makeup to simply do what I told him to. He just *had* to argue.

Cutting the armor off would be no easy task. One of the assistants -- a young teen named Kora -- braced her hand on the king's breastplate while wrapping her fist around the arrow shaft to hold it steady. Yanking the arrow out could cause more damage than pushing it out the other side, but this one was precariously close to his lungs and heart, so pushing it through wasn't even an option. Before we cut the armor away, however, I needed to check the thigh wound.

"We need to stop the bleeding before we do anything else. If not, he'll bleed out before we can deal with the chest wound."

Without a word, a young boy -- Lorgan's son, Milo -- laid a tray full of instruments on the table next to the king. He looked at me expectantly. With a sigh, I nodded to the boy. "I need hot water," I said. "Hot water, clean rags, and the pumice soap. Quickly." I glanced at Lorgan. "Until I tell you to stop, work on cutting away his breastplate. Start with the leather ties at the sides and work your way around with the big cutters. Cut close to the shaft, but make sure there is still enough room for Kora to stabilize it. It's very important to keep it immobile while we're cutting away the armor so I can see the actual wound. Also, the second you can put something between the armor and his chest, do it. A brace will prevent the weight of the armor from forcing the arrow deeper."

When Lorgan cut away the leather ties from the breastplate, I snagged one he'd thrown on the floor, using it as a tourniquet. I knew I couldn't leave it on long, but I was hoping it would be enough to stem the flow of blood until I could make sure the artery wasn't severed and sew up the wound. I used a stick -- one of the many discarded arrow shafts on the floor -- to twist the cord, cranking slowly to tighten it just until the blood flow slowed, then I set about cleaning the wound.

Surprisingly, it wasn't too deep. The way he was bleeding, I had suspected the king had cut something vital in his leg -- an artery or vein. Now that I could see the wound better, I was fairly certain he'd only gotten some minor vessels. Or probably just muscle in a bad spot. The gods knew the man had enough that anywhere he took a hit would be on a slab of muscle. Right now, those muscles were tense, though he hadn't made the first sound of pain.

"Mix a potion for pain," I murmured to one of the assistants lining the wall. "He'll need it before we're done." Taking a deep breath, I moved to stand in the king's line of vision. Lines of pain were etched on his face, sweat beading over him that was also streaked with mud and blood. There was so much blood, it ran from his face in brownish-red rivulets to soak into his nut-brown hair. Though he had it braided at the temples and forehead to keep it out of his eyes during battle, the long mass was tangled and stiff with dried blood and mud. There was no question the warriors out there had been in a fierce fight.

"My king," I said softly and with as much respect as I could. "I have to sew the wound on your leg to stem the flow of blood. I've tied it with a tourniquet, but I can't leave it on long or we risk losing your leg." His amber gaze snapped to mine. I knew that fierce look. It said, *Don't you fucking dare take my leg, bitch.*

I nodded to let him know I understood. Resting

one blood-covered hand on his shoulder, I lowered my voice, trying to be as soothing as I could. "I need you to relax as much as you can. I can better close the wound if the muscle isn't so tense. I know it's difficult, but please try. It will help the bleeding to ease as well."

He closed his eyes, as if willing himself to do as I asked.

A girl handed me a tonic for the king to drink. I looked at her, eyebrow raised. "It's poppy-based," she said.

The moment he heard the girl speak, his eyes flashed open. "No," he said. "No drugs." He closed his eyes once more, only to let out a long breath before opening them again, looking straight up at the ceiling. The muscles in his jaw clenched several times, but he was able to relax his leg.

"As you wish," I murmured. "This will hurt. I'll do my best to make it as quick as I can, but the wound is long. Let me know if you need a break or change your mind about the tonic. This will take a while."

"Just do it," he snapped.

"Okay, then."

After cleansing my hands in the hot water and scrubbing them thoroughly with the abrasive soap, I set to work. It took nearly an hour. I removed the tourniquet halfway through, slowly, a little at a time. There was no swelling in his thigh, which suggested the bleeding had stopped completely.

During it all, the king never made one sound. His thigh bunched only once at the very end. The top of the wound was dangerously close to his groin. Any man would have flinched. Instead of reminding him to relax, I let him work through it on his own, pausing until he'd relaxed once more.

With a heavy exhale of relief, I backed away,

setting aside the needle and thread to wipe my brow. Sweat made my clothing cling to my body uncomfortably, but there was nothing I could do about it now. I was only half done.

"That was the easy part," I muttered.

Lorgan was nearly finished with cutting away the breastplate, leaving a good platform for the assistant's fist where she stabilized the arrow, but allowing me to see the entry point of the arrow.

"You were right," Lorgan said, grudgingly. "The arrowhead is barbed. If I'd yanked it out…"

"But you didn't," I said softly. "And you did an excellent job of getting his armor off." The praise was a double-edged sword. On the one hand, it let Lorgan know I appreciated his work and found it more than adequate. On the other, it made it seem like Lorgan deferred to me. Which would grate on the other man's nerves. But really, what was I supposed to do? I had to acknowledge his effort or seem like a bitch. "If you want to do this, I'll defer to you," I said, eyes cast down. "You're the healer. The king is in your care."

Lorgan straightened, looking at me with narrowed eyes. No doubt looking for a trap, though I honestly was only trying to let him save face. "Your work has been good thus far. You've started. I should let you finish, as you have a feel for the injuries."

"Shouldn't the healer be the one to extract that arrow?" a guard asked.

I didn't know the men in the Triad's personal guard, but it was obvious this man was one of them.

"This is a serious injury. The most experienced healer should be the one to remove the arrow. If the king dies…"

"As you observed, I'm the healer," Lorgan said, his tone arrogant. "I wouldn't let the girl near the king if I didn't feel it was in the king's best interest that she be here. Her hands are smaller than mine. She'll be better able to get to the wound under the armor than I."

That was at least plausible. As I'd hoped, Lorgan took the opening I gave him and ran with it. At least maybe he wouldn't hold a grudge that he'd had to enlist my help with the most important patient to come into the healer's tent since I'd been born.

I didn't give anyone time to protest more. Lorgan had cut away most of the metal, but the king's clothing still needed to be removed. Carefully, I snipped around the arrow until all of his shirt was removed but the bit surrounding the arrowhead.

"Part of the arrow made it in, but, thankfully, that's all. I don't know how long the arrow is, so we've still got to be careful."

"What's your plan?" Lorgan asked as if questioning a student to see if she'd get the answer right.

It grated on my nerves, but I only gave him a sidelong glance before answering. "We cut a small space on either side of the arrowhead in the direction of the widest barb. I'd like to know exactly how long the arrowhead is, though. If I don't make the cut deep enough, I could still damage tissue when it comes out."

"I can help there," the same soldier said. "Give me five minutes." He left only to return a few minutes later with an arrow with flights and a shaft identical to the one protruding from the king's chest. The flights were different from the ones littering the floor. Clearly, the arrow in the king's chest was designed for a special purpose. Probably to pierce his armor.

"Good," Lorgan said as he inspected. "My guess is less than an inch and only one barb parallel to the one at the end. Two clean slices should do it. You should be able to slide it right out with no problem."

"I'd be happy to defer to your steady hand, Healer," I said formally, knowing the bastard wouldn't offer to do it. It was one thing to take the opening I'd given him to save face. Quite another to try to make me look like an apprentice. Fucker.

Lorgan's gaze snapped to mine, panic flashing before he raised his chin. "You could use the practice."

"No one is practicing on the king," the soldier growled. "The girl did good with the thigh wound, but she's not doing something she's obviously not done before."

I smirked as Lorgan tried to backpedal. "It's not that she's not done this before, she's just --"

"I don't care what she's *just*! It's obvious you don't think her capable enough to do this. She's not touching the king!"

Sweat beaded on Lorgan's upper lip and he gave me a venomous look. With as innocent a look as I could muster, I handed him a small knife. With a shaking hand, Lorgan made the first cut. The king grunted. It took all I had to bite my lip and stop myself from telling him he needed to make the cut clean and swift. It would sting slightly, but not so much it made the obviously stalwart king show his pain. After the first cut, Lorgan looked at me, pleading in his eyes though he refused to acknowledge it.

"Oh, for fuck's sake," I bit out, snatching the blade from Lorgan. Before the guard could protest, I'd slipped my hand under the remaining fragment of armor and sliced the second slit. As I examined both cuts, pulling the edges apart slightly to better visualize the arrow's barbs, I realized Lorgan's cut was at an odd angle. Again, I simply slipped my hand under the armor and made a third cut. Thankfully, the king didn't make a sound.

"Your majesty," I said as I straightened and stood over him. He met my gaze with those intense amber eyes once again. I reached for a wet rag, unable to keep myself from washing the blood from his face any longer. With the mud, blood, and soot streaks vanishing, I was struck at how handsome our king was. Had this been any other situation, I might have stared into his eyes all day. But he was injured and in pain, his eyes glassy with it. And there were too many people around for me to start acting like a lovesick schoolgirl. "We're ready to extract the arrow. I can't just yank it out because I'll have to stop if the barbs snag on tissue. I'm more worried about your lung than the muscle around your ribcage. I don't think it went that deep, but it found a space between your ribs so there is that possibility." When he nodded slightly, I asked again, "Are you certain you don't want something for the pain? This won't be easy."

"Need my wits," he grated. "Do what you have to to get the fucker out."

I smiled gently at him. "Just so, your majesty."

Taking a deep breath, I looked at the assistant stabilizing the arrow. "We're going to need to swap out," I said. "Let it go slowly."

She did. No problems.

"I need you on the other side, Lorgan," I said, not caring now whether or not I sounded like I was ordering him around. "You'll need to gently part the edges of your side of the wound. I'll do the other. If the barb looks like it's hanging on anything we have to stop. Understood?"

"Just do your job. I'll do mine," he snapped.

The king growled. "When this is over, I want the

two of you to strip. I'll be the judge of who has the biggest dick."

Lorgan's face turned red. I just chuckled. "Good thing you wouldn't let me sedate you, your majesty. Just think of all you'd have missed."

He grunted in response.

Back on track, I bent down again to get a good look at the arrowhead. "Ready?" I asked, not looking at Lorgan.

"Go," he said.

Slowly, careful to make sure nothing was hanging, I lifted the arrow out. A second later, the tip slipped free and I released the wound edge, lifting the armor off the king to toss the whole thing to the floor.

"I've got it from here," Lorgan said, immediately moving around to my side and all but shoving me out of the way.

"Make sure you use something to counteract any poison."

"I know what I'm doing!" Lorgan snapped. "Your assistance is no longer required."

"Fine," I snapped back. "Let me know when you're in over your head again. I'll be more than happy to let you *drown*!"

The king growled and I immediately felt bad. "I'm sorry, sir," I said softly. "Let me know when you're ready for us to strip. Not sure I have the bigger dick, but I'm sure I look better naked than that pompous ass."

A strangled sound came from the King and my alarm spiked. "Your majesty!" A quick glance at his face told me the sound was amusement, not annoyance.

"Get on with you, little girl," he said between chuckles. "I know who saved me this day. You have my thanks." Though he was amused, he still sounded weak. I couldn't stop myself from laying a hand on one brawny shoulder. He met my gaze. And laid his hand on top of mine.

The moment his hand touched mine, an electrical current seemed to zing through my skin. Instead of pulling away, however, I wanted to get closer. My breath caught as I gazed into his eyes. There was something there I couldn't define. Something carnal. Something... exciting. "Go," he said again, his voice gruff. "There are many more in need of your assistance."

I nodded, murmuring my acknowledgement as I walked off. Lorgan had his many assistants tending to the other patients so there was no need for me. I noticed he had many more assistants than he normally did. True, there were many more patients than usual, but there still shouldn't have been this many.

Then it hit me. "Lorgan, you bastard." Swearing under my breath, cursing Lorgan in as many languages as I could, I sprinted to the village clinic. He'd taken his extra help from the clinic. I just knew he had.

Fucker!

* * *

Though the healer's tent was supposed to be for everyone in the village in need of immediate assistance, it was an unspoken rule that only the village elite were allowed inside. With such a vicious battle being fought, *all* the injured should have been brought to the healer's tent.

Instead, from the looks of things, Lorgan had his assistants directing the common foot soldiers to the clinic, where there were fewer resources available for the patients. The only ones being allowed into the main tent were officers and any villager of prominence unlucky enough to have been injured during the ongoing battle, which wasn't many. Bastards were mostly holed up behind their inner wall.

As I entered the clinic, the first thing that hit me was the stench. Death permeated everything around me. Blood, sweat, and excrement mixed to form an unholy fragrance that nearly made me vomit on the spot. There were inexperienced assistants weeping as they tried their best to care for the soldiers. Men were moaning everywhere. Some were screaming in pain. Others had stopped making sounds.

"Who's in charge?" I didn't want to step on anyone's toes, but there needed to be some order here.

"That's the problem," a young man about Cristiano's age said as he approached me. He was wiping blood from his hands on a rag. "No one is. I'm doing the best I can, but I'm no healer." He limped forward and I saw his withered leg. I knew the man now. His name was Brandon. His father was senior captain of the Triad's guard.

Brandon could always be counted on to be where he was needed most. Like now.

"Would I offend you if --"

"I'd welcome your help," he said. He didn't smile, only gave me a level look that said I was getting into a hot mess from the start. "What do you need?"

I looked around. The first priority was clear. "Hot water," I said. "As much as you can find. Open all the doors and windows and put as many people as you can to cleaning the patients, bedding, and floors. In that order. I'll make a round and prioritize the wounded. We'll need three sections. One for the critical patients, one for those who can wait until the others are stabilized, and one for those we can't help."

"Not a problem. You should know, Lorgan took

everything we had by way of medicine and bandages for use in the healer's tent."

"Of course he did," I muttered. "Have someone go house to house and collect clean sheets and clothing items we can use for bandages. Anything will do as long as it's clean. I'll get some supplies and be back."

I didn't wait for him to reply. The need was too great. The only problem was, my herb garden was at the north end of the city, in the great maze that separated the city proper from the Triad's compound, which, in turn, separated the city from the fringe of the Outlands. That was a problem because it was strictly off limits to everyone but the Triad and a very select few of the elite guard. The theory was, if no one knew the way through the maze, no one could get to the city from the fringe without circling around the wall.

I had no idea how the maze worked, but every few days, the walls moved on their own, altering the path to the center and the quickest route to the castle. The ground inside the maze was the most fertile in the village. No one was allowed inside the maze but the Triad and their top captains. Basically, a handful of people and I wasn't one of them.

I'd studied the maze for years so I knew its patterns. I'd put my garden in a perfect spot where the walls moved around it but never over. As a result, I had as many of the best healing herbs and flowers as I could grow. I'd need everything I could harvest now.

It took little time to gather what I needed, get my satchel from my hut, and head back to the clinic. By the time I hurried back inside, Brandon had everyone organized. The place already smelled better and the wards were being set up as I'd directed. More than anything, I was glad to see they were cleaning the place. From the looks of things, everyone was glad to have something to do other than mourn the dead and dying.

I set to work, making sure I saw every single person, especially the most grievously injured. It took time but I wasn't about to let anyone be shuffled aside if there was even the slightest chance they could be saved. Besides, a second set of eyes was always good.

It took hours, but I'd finally eyeballed everyone and done what I could for those who needed immediate help. Now it was time to deal with those who'd waited patiently for their turn.

Brandon and his small group of assistants had done much. All that was left for me was to ration out medication where I could, which wasn't as easy as it might seem. Lorgan had never been very conservative with what we had, and his own garden was never optimum yield or potency. As a result, I used most of what I'd harvested to make fresh pastes and tonics.

The sun was just rising again when I finished with the last patient. Normally, I would have made a morning walkthrough, but I was simply too exhausted. If I was lucky, I might get a couple hours' rest before everyone started waking. I moved behind a curtain I'd set up so I could have a small amount of privacy. I'd just removed my dress when I heard an unfamiliar male voice.

"I'm looking for a girl named Arryn," the deep voice boomed throughout the clinic. I'd been moments away from lying down on a small cot in only a light shift. Maybe if I didn't say anything, the man would go away.

"She's in the back," a woman's voice said. She sounded breathless and subservient, and I got a sinking feeling in the pit of my stomach. Apparently, I wasn't very godsdamned lucky.

With a groan, I pulled on a fresh dress over my shift -- the one I'd been wearing was stiff with blood and mud -- and wrapped a light shawl around my shoulders before I stepped from behind the curtain. "I'm Arryn."

Three men had invaded the peace of my clinic. Two of them looked me up and down. It felt like they found me lacking. I was so tired, my vision was nearly blurred. The third man had the hood of his cape over his head so his features were further obscured in shadow, but there was something familiar about him.

He was taller than the other two -- who weren't short by any means -- encased in leather and bloodstained battle armor, but I got the impression he was a powerful man in both physical and political means. His breastplate was so dented I couldn't make out the crest, but I was certain this was a high-ranking member of the Triad's guard.

"You are the healer here?"

I found the question vaguely insulting and more than a little irritating. It was the slight sneer in his voice he couldn't quite suppress -- probably at the thought of a woman as young as I was being in such an important position. Or maybe it was just me being a woman.

Either way, I didn't appreciate it. "Nah, I'm just wandering around here killing myself with no sleep for a couple of days for the fucking fun of it," I snapped. "Who the fuck wants to know?" The two men flanking him exchanged a look, bowed slightly, and left us. The woman who'd pointed them all in my direction gave me a wide-eyed look of panic, her hand flying up to cover her mouth before she turned to flee from the clinic. "Well?"

With a slow, deliberate movement, the man

pushed back the hood to his cloak. Eyes the color of steel met my gaze. He didn't look at all amused. I had to admit, this wasn't exactly my finest hour. I'd now officially met two members of our Triad. Too bad we hadn't hit it off as well as I had with the other one.

"I'm Hildar. You might not know my name, but you know who I am."

I swallowed, warring between apology and looking like a strong, capable healer/engineer/all-around-smart-chick. Sleep deprivation said *fuck him*. He invaded my space, not the other way around. My brain said, *are you a complete idiot*? "I'm sorry, sir. It's been a long day for everyone, you and the soldiers most especially."

I tried to save face as best I could. Besides, maybe it wasn't so much that the man irritated me with his attitude as it was my lack of rest. I could have imagined his sneer. Maybe. "What can I do for you?" Another thought struck me. "Is the King doing well?"

As he stared at me, I did the same to him, meeting his gaze as boldly as I dared. His eyes were a clear gray, the color of steel, and just as hard. The planes of his face were harsh. More than one scar streaked across his stubbled cheek. One wicked slash ran from his forehead through his eye down his cheek. It was a miracle he'd not lost his eye from that wound.

He wasn't what I'd call handsome, but there was definitely no denying his appeal. In our world, his scars equaled the number of times this man had survived. He was a strong, cunning warrior. One capable of protecting those he cared for.

He was silent for a long moment, his gaze seeming to touch every inch of me. Sizing me up. Finding me lacking in every way. I was uncomfortable with his perusal, but did my best not to fidget.

Finally, he said, "It seems the other village healer, Lorgan, is… struggling. He is in need of your assistance with a patient." He reached out a hand. "If you'll come with me, please."

"Wait," I said, even as he took my arm and pulled me toward the door. "I can't leave this clinic filled with injured for one patient. There's no healer here since Lorgan went to the compound."

"You misunderstand me, girl. I'm not *asking* you."

"At least tell me what I'm dealing with. I need to know what's going on so I know what to bring. I may need fresh herbs and flowers to make medicaments. Is it the king?" When he gave me a level look, I sighed. "Fine. I'll just get what I can together. It's doubtful anything Lorgan has is useful."

"You have three minutes," he said. "Then we're going whether you have what you want or not. You can improvise when we get to the compound."

I started to argue, but the hard, unyielding look on his face said it wasn't a good idea. I gathered needles and thread in case his stitches had broken loose, and herbs I used to make a poultice for both pain and infection. There was no doubt in my mind the king had taken a turn for the worse. But, honestly, how bad could it have gotten in less than twenty-four hours?

I was careful to take only what I thought I might need. There were still two wards full of injured. I didn't want to leave everyone else to fend for themselves. Brandon had his instructions and, really, most everyone just needed rest and supportive care at this point.

Squaring my shoulders, I turned to the hard-faced Hildar. "Let's go."

Without a word, he snagged my arm and led me

outside to his horse. He mounted swiftly, then reached for my hand. I expected he would swing me up behind him. Instead, he pulled me straight up by one arm, hauling me in front of him. I couldn't suppress a little gasp of surprise when I found myself astride his horse, my backside settling firmly against his groin. His swift intake of air -- and the stirring of his cock against my ass -- told me he hadn't been any more prepared than I was.

One brawny arm slid around my middle, his big hand splaying wide over my belly as he pulled me even tighter against him. The woodsy scent of him surrounded me. It was a wild, almost feral scent, one that dared anyone to fuck with him. The strength in his arms was as comforting as it was restraining. Why, I didn't know. But some part of me that ran only on instinct loved this. I knew it was a dangerous attraction, one that was more about lust and a primal drive to claim something intangible, but it stirred something inside me I never knew existed.

I was about to protest the contact with him -- honest -- when he kicked his horse into a full-on gallop. My dress rode up, leaving my legs bare past mid-thigh. If he'd been going at a leisurely pace, I might have protested; instead, I hung on as best I could. I was certainly glad I'd thought to pull on a dress over my shift.

To my surprise, Hildar galloped straight into the maze. The mighty war steed cut through the twists and turns without hesitation. Once inside the maze, the king dropped the reins and held my waist with both hands, holding me tightly as the animal bounded through the maze at breakneck speed.

We passed by my garden and I couldn't help but stiffen. Did the Triad know about my little patch of earth inside their territory? The garden was out of the main path, but his horse had gone straight to it.

He didn't say anything, only urged the animal faster. Once the horse burst free of the maze, he dropped his head and *sprinted*. The king held me tight against him with both arms around my middle. When the horse skidded to a stop, I was glad of it.

Before the dust and gravel had a chance to settle, the king slid off the horse with me in his arms, and hit the ground running. All I could do was hang on for dear life.

Everyone seemed to be expecting him. A servant had the door to the compound open and ready when he reached it. Two more ran ahead of him, clearing the way. He hurried up a grand staircase, taking the steps two at a time even carrying me, and he wasn't even winded.

Minutes later, we entered a large but dimly lit chamber. Heavy drapes covered the windows. There was no breeze and, even as large as the room was, the heat was stifling. Near the center of the room was a large bed. A man lay upon it, a thin sheet draped over him. *The king.* He should have been better. His wounds were still too new for him to be back on the battlefield, but he shouldn't look like this…

I sucked in a breath. He was pale, the dark stubble of his beard standing out starkly against his skin. His eyes seemed to be sunken into his head, dark circles prominent underneath them. When I'd left him in the healer's tent, he hadn't looked so bad as this. Had his leg wound started bleeding again?

Lorgan sat at a long table filled with various items of alchemy, none of which would aid an injured patient. Which told me two things: first, Lorgan was, indeed, in over his head. Second, Lorgan was a shitty healer. I already knew that last part, but it wasn't comforting to have the proof in front of me *now*.

"Here she is," Hildar said, plopping me on my feet. The movement was so sudden, I nearly stumbled to the floor. Had Hildar not managed to snag my upper arm, I probably would have. "Fix him," he demanded.

Lorgan looked up from whatever he'd been doing. The man had sweat pouring down his face and looked terrified beyond imagining. What the hell had gone wrong?

"Poison..." I breathed, the realization hitting me like a boulder to the skull.

Well, fuck.

Chapter Three

"It's n-not that s-simple," Lorgan stammered. "His wounds are very extensive. The b-blade he caught must have been t-tainted with p-poison or s-something."

I'd never seen Lorgan this terrified. Should I be scared, too? "Let me look," I said. "Fill me in on what you've done, Lorgan. I don't want to repeat anything that could cause him harm."

"Nothing," Lorgan hissed. "I've done nothing but re-bandage his wounds." He spoke quietly. I was sure he hoped to have a private conversation with me but knew doing so when the patient was a member of the Triad -- and a second member was standing in the same room -- was impossible. Still, he glanced at Hildar as if awaiting a killing blow from the other man. "I know you can't do anything either, but he was demanding I use every resource available to me. One of the guards asked about you so I had no choice but to bring you here."

"Was not the very last thing I said to you before I left to be careful of poisons?"

"If I knew what kind of poison they got him with I'd know what to do!" Lorgan snapped but was still very quiet, as if he could keep Hildar from hearing. Likely, Lorgan had no idea what to do for poisonings or even what to look for. King Storm could just as easily be bleeding out as poisoned.

Preparing for the city to be stormed was frightening, but this, just like fixing the catapult, was something I could handle. If the patient couldn't be saved, I'd know. If there was a chance, I could give

Hildar realistic hope. Either way, I knew what to do. I could handle this situation.

"Let me examine him," I said again. "Get me hot water, clean rags and towels, clean bedding, bandages, and two servants to clean the room." As I talked, I went to the windows and opened the curtains, pushing open the shutters to let in a cool breeze from the sea. The sky was a deep, brick red, surely a bad omen. Ominous black clouds were now closer on the morning horizon. The storm would hit soon and with fury. I had a feeling it was about to mirror my battle for the king's life.

"I had the windows closed to keep out the flies!" Lorgan snapped. "Do you want him infested with bugs?"

"Once the room is clean and the blood removed, there will be no chance of that." I wanted to tell him he should have done this first thing, but there was no use in starting a fight. "Your majesty Hildar. I need to remove the king's coverings to examine him. I'll leave it to you to decide who stays and who must leave."

Honestly, I didn't care if anyone stayed or not. This gave the king something to do while I did my work. If his Triad brother moaned in pain, he'd be less likely to interfere if he was focused on a goal. I had Lorgan seeing to the other things I needed, getting him out of my way, as well. I wasn't a warrior like these men, but I could manage people when I needed to.

I reached the king's side, noticing his hair was still stiff with blood and mud. Had no one seen to anything other than bandaging his wounds? His breathing was shallow, his features a mask of pain. Every now and then, he'd take a deeper breath only to wince as if it pained him. Sweat dotted his skin and ran down his face in huge drops. Blood stained the sheets but, thankfully, no fresh blood. His thigh had bled, but not recently. The blood on the sheet was dried, the material stiff with it. Beside the bed, a bucket sat, vomit still in the bottom. No blood, only yellow, foul-smelling bile. I immediately moved it aside, instructing a servant to empty and clean it thoroughly with stout disinfectant before returning it.

Not wanting to startle him or subject him to the indignity of being uncovered without at least attempting to get his permission, I laid a hand carefully on his bare shoulder. "My king," I breathed. His eyes fluttered open and he turned his head toward me. His gaze was glassy with pain, his skin cool and clammy. I was right in believing this was going to be a fight for his life.

"You," he rasped weakly. "The girl from the village."

"Indeed," I said, smiling at him. "Do you mind if I examine your wounds?"

"At your leisure." His words were slightly slurred. "Should have insisted on bringing you home with me instead of that one." He tried to wave his hand in Lorgan's direction but didn't quite make it. "Knew he didn't have a bloody clue what he was doing." He chuckled weakly. "Besides, I truly believed you'd look --" he took in a labored breath "-- a sight better naked than he would and I didn't have the time to appreciate it properly."

I chuckled softly, sharing the memory with him. Then I tilted my head, studying the king carefully. It hit me. "You knew the guards would insist the healer return to care for you, but you deliberately let them choose Lorgan? Why would you do that?"

His eyes were still filled with pain but the feverish glaze seemed to lift briefly. It was obvious he struggled to breathe. "Because I'm not the only one injured. There are many --" he gasped "-- who followed me into battle and suffered for it. I would not deprive them --" another gasp "-- of their best chance for survival."

"Bloody hell!" Hildar bit out the curse, scrubbing a hand over his face. "You had no right, Storm," he all but thundered. "You are the head of the Triad. You're needed more than either of us!"

"Not at the expense of the people, Hildar," Storm said gently. "We serve them. Not the other way around."

"Dammit, I know that! But we can't lose *you*!"

"I'm not gone yet, brother. Let the girl work. Perhaps I bought her enough time to save a few before she had to come to my rescue once more."

"No pressure there," I muttered. "Know that I take exception to your recovery being put on my shoulders, my king." I intended it to be a reprimand, but it came out softer. In truth, I admired him for his sacrifice. None of the elders had been willing to make any sacrifices, let alone one that could be life or death for them. "Once you've recovered, we shall have words over this."

"You and me both," Hildar bit out.

Carefully, I peeled back the sheet covering King Storm. As I did, a flash of lightning followed by a loud thunderclap sounded outside from the sea. It was like a portent of things to come. The servants in the room hastily knelt, hands to their foreheads in supplication, probably hoping to appease the gods so they'd spare their king. As I uncovered and examined both wounds, I tried to puzzle out the problem. Both wounds were pink and clean. Neither looked to be poisoned or infected. So what was it?

Most poisons would act quickly. Chemicals, too. It had been nearly twenty-four hours since the king had been injured. What poison would take that long to act?

I leaned in closer…

The faint but unmistakable smell of almonds teased the air.

I snapped up straight, my gaze darting around the room. I spotted a servant cleaning on the other side of the king's bed. "You," I ordered. "Your name."

"Sara," she practically squeaked.

"Good." I looked at Hildar. "We need a bath for the king. His hair needs to be scrubbed thoroughly and his face washed and shaved." I turned to Sara. "Burn any clothing he wore during the battle, as well as his bedding and pillows. Have the stable masters wash down his horse, assuming the beast is still alive. Burn any cloth or blanket used as padding under his saddle and wash all his tack thoroughly with disinfectant before it is used elsewhere as well as anything the tack came in contact with after it was removed from the horse."

I held the girl's gaze. "Sara, you see to this and see it's done well. Wear a wet mask over your mouth and nose as you work and make sure anyone helping you does the same." The girl looked wide-eyed and fearful, but I could see she would do as I said. Already she was enlisting help from others in the room to take care of the king's clothing and bedding.

"What is it?" Lorgan looked interested but was smart enough to realize I thought the poison was on the king's person.

I struggled to help the big man out of the bed, but he pushed me away weakly. "Take your own advice, little girl," he said. "Mask. Hildar as well."

"Fuck," I swore, giving him a quelling look that did nothing but make him smile.

"You'll not intimidate me, girl. Men with bigger balls than you have tried."

"That one's not going away any time soon, is it?"

"Not as long as I live." Which wasn't saying much if I couldn't get him clean.

Hildar handed me a damp cloth to tie around my nose and mouth, then helped me lift Storm to a sitting position. Once the servants had dragged in the tub and filled it with water, we half-carried, half-dragged my naked patient to the water and helped him into the tub.

I did my best to avert my eyes, the gods know I did, but, even in this weakened state, his body wasn't like any other man I'd ever seen. Strong, scarred, hair-roughened... I did my best to suppress a shiver as I tried to ignore his sex. Hard to miss, that. But this wasn't the time or place, and he was definitely not the man to be eyeing hungrily. I had a job to do and his very life depended on me. "I need you to slide down as much as you can and get your hair in the water so I can wash it."

"What do you suspect?"

"I think it's some form of cyanide. Not a gas bomb, but maybe in damp dirt or something similar. Something that would expose your men and stick to them but not be overly obvious or kill them immediately. This was supposed to make anyone exposed sick over time."

He ducked under the water briefly. While he was submerged, I worked through the strands, fluffing them out to allow the mud and blood to be rinsed away.

When he rose, Hildar handed me a bar of soap from his spot on the other side of the tub. I dunked it under the water to wet it before working it with my hands into a lather. I tackled Storm's hair while Hildar soaped the rest of his body. The open windows faced the water, and I could see the tide white-capping with the approaching weather.

"Looks like you're named perfectly for the day, my king," I said with a smile.

"I hear the sea starting to rage." His breath continued to be labored. At his neck, I could see his pulse heightened.

I washed his hair three times to make sure not a spot of mud remained. I had the feeling that was where the toxin had been introduced. Once exposed to the air, it would make a gas. If it was in contaminated soil, dampened into mud, it was possible it would be weak enough to not hit the victim all at once, but rather release more gas as the mud dried.

"We were hit with a cauldron of debris," Storm confirmed. "Not directly, but it rained over us. Damp, like you said, but not a liquid. It hit directly in front of a group of men I was leading. I think I was the only one to get hit with more than a minimal amount. I remember thinking I was lucky it wasn't burning oil or I'd have been severely injured." He gave a bitter laugh. "Guess I wasn't so lucky after all."

I glanced over my shoulder. Sara had taken my instructions to heart. She'd even had the bed removed and a new one brought in. She and other servants were finishing up with it as Hildar and I helped Storm from the tub and dried him.

"Get him in bed," I instructed Hildar. "I need to mix a potion for him."

Lorgan was furious. "What could you possibly have to counteract something this lethal? There's a reason our enemies use it -- it's deadly!"

I could see in his eyes he knew I could probably pull it off and was livid that I could do something to help the king when he couldn't. "It's one of those pesky 'chemistry nonsense' things you told me were useless." I whispered my vehement reply to Lorgan, not wanting to make a scene, but too tired to care what he thought of me. "It's difficult and time consuming to make, not to mention tedious, but in cases like this, it's invaluable as an antidote. I use the same chemicals to cure pork because it prevents bacteria. To use as a treatment for cyanide, however, it has to be mixed differently and given to him through his veins."

"Impossible," Lorgan spat. "You'll kill him with that!"

"Kill him with what?" Hildar asked, approaching us with death in his eyes.

"My king," Lorgan said, bowing his head in difference. "The girl thinks to inject King Storm with a substance we use to preserve meats. Who knows what something like that will do to a person?"

Hildar looked at me, eyebrows raised.

I ground my teeth. "It's in Old Earth texts, if you care to read them, Lorgan. You do know how to read. Right?"

With teeth bared, Lorgan lunged at me. Only Hildar's larger frame moving in front of me prevented him from grabbing me, probably by the throat.

"Witch!" Lorgan hissed the word. "This is nothing short of witchcraft! She said she makes this in one of her laboratories. She scoffs at alchemy when looking for a remedy but doesn't hesitate to employ magicks!"

"Would you shut up!" Hildar snapped at Lorgan, shoving him away. "Guards." He snapped his fingers. "Please escort the *healer* back to the village. There are many patients in the clinic and the healer's tent awaiting his assistance. Pray to the gods he doesn't let any of them die for worrying about King Storm."

That was a threat if ever I'd heard one. Apparently Lorgan thought so, too, because he paled under Hildar's steely gaze.

"You know she will kill the king," Lorgan said as he was led away. "Let it be known that I warned you."

"If you've got a better alternative, speak now," Hildar said, exasperation in his voice. "Because I have no idea what else to do. It's possible he'll recover on his own, but an even better chance the damage is already done. Will you take responsibility if we do nothing and he dies?"

Lorgan raised his hands in capitulation. "It's true I know of nothing else. I just happen to believe what she's proposing will hasten his death."

"So, you believe to do nothing is better?"

"I only wish to see that my daughter's future mates come to her unharmed and as a Triad whole, not a broken unit."

Now, that was a surprising turn of events. The Triad hadn't made an announcement they'd taken a mate. Though it was tradition the ruling triad took a mate from the village, they always did it through a selection process where all the eligible maidens were presented to them. I should have known such a process was merely a formality.

I snorted. "Nobles." The word came out under my breath as I dismissed Lorgan and Hildar from my thoughts. My job was to do everything in my power to save the life of King Storm and that's what I intended to do.

Lorgan and Hildar could go fuck themselves for all I cared.

Fuckers!

* * *

"I know the remedy you spoke with Lorgan about," Hildar said, coming up behind me. He looked over my shoulder as I carefully measured the white, crystalline powder before putting it into an equally carefully measured beaker of water. This was a delicate process when given to someone in this manner. I had to be exact in my mixture or it could cause more harm than good. "Sodium nitrite," he said. "Difficult to make now, but very effective."

I glanced sharply over my shoulder at him. "Are you interested in chemistry, too?"

"Not really. But I knew our enemies used chemicals as weapons and had to find out as much as I could about what they might come up with. Cyanide was a popular chemical weapon during wars of the past before being banned. Though, I confess I never understood how either side could expect the other to keep that pact. Old texts also declare, 'all's fair in love and war.'"

"True," I said, turning back to my work. "I'm not a warrior, but I love science of any kind. Chemistry and medicine seem to go hand in hand, so they interest me in the ways they work together. In my studies, I found ways men have incorporated both into war." I shrugged. "It always seemed sad that people found ways to turn something good into something so destructive. Sometimes, the good was merely an afterthought or a reason to develop a scientific principle when the real purpose was more efficient ways to kill."

Unexpectedly, the king grinned at me. "I've had those same thoughts on more than one occasion." He nodded to my work. "I'll leave you to it. Please let me know if I can be of assistance."

Damn. Now that he wasn't so angry or intense, Hildar was as personable as I was certain Storm would be if he were well. "I'm not a warrior, nor a general well versed in battle tactics," I said. "But you might want to consider the enemy knew their little stink bomb would take a while to act. It almost seems like they were counting on it. If that's so, they will be sending all they have at you when they believe the high king is incapacitated."

"I've thought of that," Hildar replied, sitting in a chair beside King Storm. "Asher will hold them." His tone was matter-of-fact, waving aside any danger. Which told me two things. First, King Hildar had complete confidence in King Asher as a warrior and part of their Triad. Second… he didn't completely trust me. It was obvious he was waiting to see how King Storm responded to my treatment.

"If this doesn't work, are you going to kill me?"

He shrugged. "Depends," he said, not a hint of emotion in his voice or body language. He merely sat there, long, strong legs stretched out in front of him crossed at the ankle, muscular arms crossed over his chest. "If he dies and I believe your effort is genuine, then no. If I believe you deliberately poisoned him…"

I shivered, my hand trembling so much I had to move away from the mixture I was preparing. If I made even one mistake…

Glaring at King Hildar, I retorted, "If I were a coward, like Lorgan, I'd simply back off and tell you the risk wasn't worth it. I'm not going to lie. If I do this wrong, it *will* kill him. On the other hand, if I don't do it, he may recover, but there is a very real chance he will be a shadow of his former self. This stuff will continue to deteriorate his internal organs until it either expends itself or he dies. Given he's still alive and the compound is still working on him, there is reason to believe it's only cyanide-based. There could very well be other things working, or they could have modified the toxin to last longer before it is metabolized."

King Hildar smiled at me, raising his hands in surrender. "I'm not expecting a miracle, girl. Only that you do what you feel is best and gives the High King the best chance of recovery."

"Which is what I'm doing," I snapped. "Go see to the city's defenses before they bring the big guns!"

The king leveled his gaze on me, a look of menace on his face.

Had I been less tired and cross, that look might have cowed me. Instead, I was just sleep deprived enough to flip him off. "Fucker," I muttered.

Storm laughed heartily, choking on the end so that he took a coughing fit before he could stop. He tried to sit up straighter in the bed but seemed to lack the strength. He coughed several times, gasping to catch his breath before waving his hand at Hildar. "She's right," he managed. "If they planned this, Asher will need help."

"Asher can take care of himself," Hildar snapped. "You can't."

"If you really don't trust me enough to administer my treatment to the king without your presence," I said, looking at Hildar with what I hoped was a withering gaze, "Why should do it at all? I've cleaned him up. Your *future mate's* father believes leaving well enough alone is the best option. Why continue?"

All of a sudden, I found the thought of the Triad taking a mate... uncomfortable. As if they were giving away something they shouldn't. Something I wanted to be mine. Which was ridiculous because I knew I wasn't mate material. Not for any man in the village. Certainly not for our kings. Still, that flash of jealousy coursed through me hard.

"Easy, there," Storm rasped out. "No one is questioning your abilities. Hildar is just protective of me."

"Fine," I said. "He can be protective. I've got too much to do in the village. I'll send Lorgan back to watch after you while I work with those I can do more for."

"Stop," Hildar barked. "Your point is taken. I'll find Asher and do what I've been trained to do. You do what you're best at."

With a look at Storm, Hildar nodded at the leader of his Triad. "I'll leave you in the capable hands of this young lady." He still gave me a look that said *I will totally fuck you up if you hurt my brother.*

After Hildar left I looked at Storm. He still had a faint grin on his face though he had lines of pain and stress etched deep. "Do you trust me? Because, I'm telling you right now, I have no guarantee this will work. All I know is that the old texts swear by this for cyanide poisoning, so much so it was mandatory it be kept on hand in any poison kit."

King Storm gave me a lopsided grin that did nothing to dispel the aura of pain that surrounded him. "Honey, anything has got to be better than this." His breaths were ragged, his lips tinged with a bluish cast.

"It may be too late for this to help."

"If it is, we will have a talk before this vile stuff takes me."

"Talk?"

He nodded at the glass bottle in my hand. I'd

poured the solution into a bottle I could attach a rubber tube to. On the end of the tube was a needle capable of delivering the solution straight to his veins. "I'll tell you like I told Hildar: just do what you're best at. Let me worry about everything else."

"I'm not sure this is it," I muttered.

"I am." The king met my gaze. His eyes spoke volumes to me. He was confident in my abilities. Had no doubt I would do what needed to be done. If he could be saved, he had confidence I could do it. In a weak movement, the king lifted his hand to brush his fingertips over my cheek. The touch was light, but struck a blow to my heart. It was a tender gesture, one that should have been bold and determined but, in his weakened state, Storm just couldn't manage any more. Then he let his hand fall atop his chest, never dropping my gaze.

I shivered under that look. What if I was wrong? What if the old texts couldn't help me?

No. This was the only thing I knew that could save the high king. The only other alternative -- the *only* one -- was to do nothing and hope he was strong enough to fight off what he'd already been exposed to, and that was a mighty big gamble.

Resolutely, I slid the needle into the vein at the bend of his arm and strapped it down. "This takes about thirty minutes. Then, it's up to your body. There is another compound that is supposed to follow, but I can't make it. From what I've read, both substances combined provide a greater chance for recovery, but what I'm using is the more important of the two."

He smiled as he closed his eyes. "I have faith in you, little girl. If you say this is the best for me, then do it. You don't have to convince me otherwise."

King Storm slept fitfully over the course of the

day, his body racked with pain, sweat beading over his skin as he shifted restlessly in his sleep. Outside a storm the likes of which I'd never witnessed raged from the sea, seeming to mirror the strength of the battle within the king. Though I was nearing the end of my own endurance and longed for sleep myself, I washed his face and neck with a cool, damp cloth, doing my best to make him more comfortable even though he wasn't fully awake. I urged him to drink fluids when he could but it wasn't as often as I would have liked.

A couple of times he did wake fully, wanting water, which I gladly supplied. Always, he'd smile at me, thanking me for my care. Which I thought odd for a king. Even Lorgan didn't thank me for helping out. It was expected of the villagers of lower class.

After a while I quit thinking about it. Mainly because I was so fucking tired I couldn't. I wasn't sure, but I thought it had been close to three days since I'd slept more than a catnap here and there.

Many times, Sara, the servant girl who'd done such a marvelous job organizing help and cleaning the bedchamber, came to check on us and bring food and fresh water. Always I thanked her, ever aware that she was the same station as I and therefore subject to the same indignities.

"Sara?" I asked when she came in just before dawn. "How old are you and how long have you worked in this compound?"

"Nearly a year, mistress. I'm only fifteen summers. It was an honor for me to be chosen to work here at my age."

I shook my head. "Arryn," I said. "I'm no better than you that you must assign me a title."

The girl only smiled. "If you say so... mistress."

I frowned. "Why would you argue with me over that?"

"I see the way the high king looks at you. You're an equal in his eyes. He even let you order King Hildar to leave in order to aid in the defense of the city. He would not do such a thing if you were a mere servant."

"Sara, I'm not even a servant. I'm an orphaned villager with a questionable background. My only saving grace is that I've fought my way out of poverty and made myself useful." The girl only shrugged. "Anyway, you've worked here a year. How are the servants treated here?"

She smiled. "As family, mistress. The Triad are stern and very protective of their people, but they are good to us. Strict, but fair to all."

"You've worked all this day with me and now well into the night, yet you're of schooling age. Do you not attend?"

"Oh, yes, mistress. But you needed my help. Everything is second to the Triad because they always put us first. It is a small price to pay to miss a lesson or two."

"I'm not certain of your interests, but you'd make a good healer's assistant. You have the compassion for it and a quick mind. Perhaps you could speak to Lorgan."

The girl wrinkled her nose. "Rather that I muck out the stables every day for the rest of my life than work for the likes of him. But I'd gladly work and learn from you, mistress." She said the last with a shy smile as if she craved my approval.

I grinned. "Well, I'd welcome the help, but I work in the clinic where the village peasants seek help. We don't make much. Mostly what each villager can afford by way of food or services."

"After this night, you may find all that changes." She grinned. "Mistress."

"I'm not your mistress."

Sara laughed softly, but merrily. "Yet." She glanced at the king lying peacefully on the bed. Already his color was better, but he still had a long way to go. "With any luck, the Triad will rethink that silly business about Lorgan's daughter, Sunja, being their promised mate. She's not suited to them anyway."

I watched Sara leave, confused by her words. Sunja was a vain, spoiled girl. She was also a year or two too young for marriage. Perhaps that was why they hadn't yet made the arrangement known. I was sure Lorgan had talked the village elders into deciding she'd make a good match. Who had, in turn, probably talked to the Triad about it. Apparently, the Triad thought the elders were correct if they'd already made Sunja their promised, even if it hadn't been announced.

A soft groan from the bed pulled me out of my musings. Storm turned to his side, moving until he was comfortable. The lines of pain on his face had eased considerably. Had he finally turned the corner?

I wet a cloth in cool water and wiped his face tenderly as I sat on the bed next to him. He wasn't handsome in the most conventional sense, but he was every inch the warrior. His face had hard angles and planes, a wide, stubborn chin, and a nose that looked like it had been broken more than once. Sleepy amber eyes opened slightly, looking up at me. His lips curled into a warm smile. "You're still here."

"I am," I said, stroking his hair gently. "King Hildar hasn't managed to get rid of me yet." I smiled teasingly at him. "How are you feeling?"

"Weak," he said, closing his eyes briefly. He

seemed to struggle opening them again, but managed. "Better. No pain. Did you drug me?"

"As tempting as it was, no. You didn't want any so I abided by your wishes."

"There were a few times I wished you would just knock me out."

"Then you should have said something."

There was a bit of silence while he simply looked at me. Then he raised a hand to my face, smoothing a finger over my brow then under my eyes. "How long has it been since you slept?"

I snorted a laugh. "In the immortal words of… someone I can't remember, I can sleep when I'm dead."

His chuckle flowed through me like warm honey. Had this man been anyone other than who he was in the condition he was in, I'd have melted on the spot. He was powerful, kind, handsome, and very intelligent. Catnip to a girl like me. Combine that with a sexy smile, and it was hard to see him as a patient instead of a man sated and sleepy from hours of bed play. That's what that satisfied smirk looked like.

"Lie down," he commanded. "You need to rest if you're to continue to care for me properly."

Truth was, I was so weary I could barely function. "Can't argue with you on that." I stood. Now that my body was still, my brain was getting more and more sluggish by the second. Storm reached out, taking my hand and tugging me back to the bed. "What?" I was confused. Hadn't he just told me to rest?

"I said, lie down," King Storm said, pulling me down to the bed very gently. Somewhere deep in the recesses of my sleep-deprived brain, I knew this was a bad idea, but I couldn't seem to make my body resist. Instead, I lay down beside the king, my back to his front.

Even though I knew he was bruised and battered, Storm wrapped his strong arms around me, holding me close. I had a few seconds to register how good it felt before my brain completely shut down. I closed my eyes, and gave in to the blessed blackness of sleep.

* * *

"What were you thinking?" The unfamiliar voice tried to rouse me from sleep, but my body was having none of it.

"Thinking that, if you wake her, I'll fucking kill you." That voice I recognized. Storm's breath feathered out softly over my ear. Though his words were harsh, his tone was matter-of-fact. The moment I shifted my position, his arms tightened around me, reminding me I was somewhere I really shouldn't be. Try as I might, though, I couldn't rouse myself further. Especially when Storm whispered in my ear, "Shh, little girl. All is well. Rest for me."

And I was out again.

Chapter Four

"Though I still hurt, much better. I think her treatment worked."

I knew I'd caught the middle of the conversation but was relieved all the same. Storm was healing. I couldn't make my eyes open. Storm's warm arms still surrounded me, but I'd moved positions. Now I lay with my head on his wide chest. Worse, I clutched him to me, my fingers digging into his skin as if he were all mine.

That was enough to help me wake, open my eyes, and attempt to sit. "I'm sorry," I said, my heart pounding. I'd slept? *In the king's bed?* "I didn't mean --"

"Didn't mean what?" Storm asked, pulling me back to the bed when I would have stood. "To fall asleep? You'd been awake for nearly three days. No one can keep going like that."

"I should have at least moved to a pallet on the floor."

"And left me alone?" The big man actually managed to look weak and helpless, when I knew he was anything but. Even in the grips of the poison he hadn't looked like anything other than the strong king he was. "What if I'd needed you? You slept soundly for the most part. I doubt you'd have known if something had happened to me."

I was torn between shame and mortification. Until I looked into the king's eyes. They seemed to twinkle in merriment, looking directly into mine. "You're having fun at my expense." I made it a statement since it was obvious. "What if I'd hurt you? You had stitches in your thigh that could have come loose. You could have bled to death!"

"No worries, little girl," he said tenderly, brushing a curl of escaped hair from my forehead. "I didn't die. You got to rest, and I had my own personal healer right beside me. All is well."

I carefully fought my way up and away from Storm's grasp, sitting on the edge of the bed. My body was sore from the previous three days' work and stiff from sleep, making it hard to stand. I managed, glad I did when I looked around me. Not only was Hildar there, but the third member of the Triad, King Asher, stood at the foot of the bed, arms crossed over a massive chest and an angry expression on his face. It was all I could do to suppress a groan. On the plus side, the ferocious storm outside seemed to have abated.

"If you'll excuse me," I said, doing my best to ignore the other two kings, "I need to freshen up, then I'll check your injuries."

Shamelessly, I darted to the other side of the room behind a curtain I'd set up the night before, intending to use it to change clothes. I had to stink. The more I thought about that, the more humiliated I became. Falling asleep in a strange man's bed was one thing. Doing it after sweating all day without washing was quite another.

Undressing quickly, I dropped my dress, shift, and underwear in the corner in a heap. I glanced in a nearby mirror only to see my hair, all wild, red curls reaching my waist, sticking out in all directions. With a groan, I sagged against the wall, dropping my head. I looked like shit.

There was a small basin of water on a nearby table and a clean cloth next to it. I dunked the cloth and wrung it out to wash my face and neck. The rest of my body followed. The cool water felt good on my heated flesh as I trailed the cloth over my skin. As I washed away the sweat and sleep, I contemplated all that had happened.

How was I ever going to look the king in the eyes again? *Any* of the Triad? It wasn't because I'd fallen asleep on the job or that I'd somehow managed to crawl into Storm's bed with him so injured, not to mention that he was a fucking king. It was the fact that it had affected me. Like *really* affected me. For some reason, when I looked at him now, I couldn't see him any other way than how he looked at me when I woke this last time. The feelings were slowly sinking into me, but I instinctively knew they were going to get worse -- not better -- with time.

There was a soft light in his eyes, as if he were looking down at a woman he cherished. For a girl who'd had very little physical affection from anyone in her life, that impression was like a drug. I craved it. Had to have it, even knowing it could never be from Storm.

I finished washing myself before pulling a fresh dress from my bag over my head. Never had I been more glad I always kept a change of clothing in my emergency pack. As I pulled my hair atop my head, securing it in a loose knot, I glanced in the mirror once more. To my utter mortification, Storm's eyes locked with mine. He'd been watching me the whole time while the others talked, informing him of the day's events. Had all three of them seen me?

Fuck!

I couldn't help but scowl. How dare he invade my privacy? My ire at the ready, I stomped from behind the partition, ready to confront him head on. "Have a nice look, your highness?" My tone was icy.

Scornful. "Next time, I'll be sure to let everyone know what time the show will start so you can have time to draw a crowd and charge admission."

Instead of looking sheepish or contrite, or, gods forbid, ashamed, the king just grinned. "How much of a percentage do you plan to take from admission sales? I'd be willing to give you the total portion if you'd let me have a seat up front."

"What the hell are you doing?" Asher hissed, moving to stand beside Storm so he could converse quietly. Like I wouldn't hear. "We've already got a promised and we swore after... after that *last incident* we would never take pets!"

That made me suck in my breath. My own mother had been a pet. I'd seen first-hand how my father had treated her -- and me to a lesser extent -- and wanted no part of it.

"She's a beautiful woman. Why would any man *not* want to look at her? I tell you, brother, after holding her warm little body in my arms for several hours, I'd prefer to be doing more than looking." He said this, not looking at his brother, but at me. The heat in his gaze called forth an answering need in my own body. My belly gave a flutter, and an involuntary gasp left my lips.

"Perhaps this isn't the time," Hildar said, raising his eyebrows and glancing my way several times, as if the entire situation made him uncomfortable.

"Apparently, you're just like almost every other man in this village. You have a woman you're not faithful to. Big fucking deal." My tone said it was most *definitely* a big fucking deal. Great. I sounded like a prude. "King Storm. You're certainly on the mend. I believe you no longer require my services."

"I'll argue that point until I die," he muttered.

Which made me see red. I took two steps toward him, intending to slap his handsome face, but Hildar stepped in front of me.

"Stop, little girl," Hildar said softly. There was no trace of amusement in his voice, but I thought I detected the twitch of his lips. "He meant no offense."

I bared my teeth, angrier than I could remember being in a very long time, and I wasn't even sure why. Part of me thrilled at the hot look in Storm's eyes as he gazed at me. I was woman enough to acknowledge my attraction to him. And Hildar. I didn't know how I felt about Asher, having only just met him -- which I hadn't really done. He'd just been standing there looking all disapproving. But he was the only one pointing out they already had a woman. *A promised!* At least maybe he would be loyal and true to a mate. These other two...

Which was the other problem. I was jealous at the thought of Sunja being their promised, of *any* other woman being their promised. Knowing that if I was their promised, they wouldn't be any more faithful to me than they would be to Sunja infuriated me even more.

"I'll take my leave of you, sirs," I snapped. "I'll be sure to send Lorgan to check on you and see to your needs from here on out. With him being the father of your promised, I'm certain he'd be a more appropriate person to assist you anyway."

* * *

It had been two weeks since I'd last seen any of the kings. Lorgan had been absent for most of that time. When he was in the village, he kept casting me dark looks. Oh, well. If he'd wanted the credit for saving the king, he should have taken the opportunity to learn all he could before the need arose. He'd had the same resources as I did: old texts from before the wars when medicine was nothing short of miraculous. He'd glanced over most of them and dismissed them, believing that none of the medicines and chemicals they talked about could be reproduced in this time.

Whatever.

If there was one thing I firmly believed in, it was that if you could make something once, you could make it again. It might take a tremendous amount of effort or hard-to-come-by resources, but it could be done. I'd picked three or four chemicals I'd thought were the most important, the most beneficial to the most amount of people, and devoted myself to figuring out a way to make them and make them safely.

Anyway, Lorgan knew where to find me if he needed me. I took his continued absence -- and distance -- to mean King Storm was, indeed, on the mend.

I almost wished something would happen for Lorgan to summon me to the kings once again. I regretted leaving, even though I'd been mad as hell. I missed their all-consuming presence. At least, Storm and Hildar. Why, I didn't know. I just felt like, somehow, I was supposed to be with them. All of them. Which was stupid. Apparently, that was Sunja's job. Why would I expect men like that to take on a woman like me for their mate? I was nobody. My sire was a traitor. My dam a pet. The only reason I wasn't sold as a pet myself was because my father hadn't been one. Someone -- and I always thought it had been Malachi and Tessa -- had pointed out that one of my biological parents had been free when I'd been born. That should afford me the right as well.

On the other side, even though Lorgan had made it abundantly clear he expected his daughter to be the

Triad's mate, that announcement still hadn't been made throughout the village. Which was puzzling indeed.

Fuck.

I hated thinking about my past. At least, my parents' pasts. My mother hadn't had many choices, but my father had. I had no idea what had really happened, but I always liked to think there had been a reason he'd betrayed the Triad and the entire village.

Or not. Who knew?

Lorgan. He knew. And there was no way he wasn't taking that secret with him to the grave. He'd taken my mother in, since she was a pet, but I had to wonder at that as well. Why would he have done that when every other person in the village was against the taking of pets? There wasn't a single pet here. Even the Triad never took them, as Asher had voiced. So the question had always stuck in my mind. It was something I'd probably never find out, but I'd made my peace with all of it at an early age. I'd had to or it would have driven me crazy.

For the first time since the battle, I was finally getting to go to my own house. Sleep in my own bed. I'd taken a spot near the river wall for my home. Despite assurances from the council that the wall was perfectly sound during an attack, no one -- the council included -- wanted to live anywhere near the river. Which was fine with me. I had the place all to myself; welcomed solitude after two weeks with little to no privacy.

My home was small, a hut really, like most of the houses in the village. It was basically one big room with a hearth for cooking, a small table, and a bed in the corner separated by a privacy screen. Though things were a little dusty after my absence, I was never so glad to see the place.

I raised the windows to let in the afternoon breeze. Coming off the river, it felt wonderful, cool and cleansing. With a sigh, I shrugged out of my clothing. I had a pile of dresses, tunics, and light breeches I needed to wash, but I was tired. Instead of taking the whole pile, I chose my favorite, most comfortable dress and underwear. I didn't even snag a shift. The rest could wait until tomorrow.

With no one near my hut, I usually bathed in the river. The cool water was blessedly refreshing, and I knew this evening would be no different. I had a well-worn path to a small wooden landing where I could wash and have a clean place to put my linens when I'd finished washing them.

As always, the cool bath felt wonderful. I washed away the sweat I'd only been able to rinse, and my hair… I hadn't washed it thoroughly since before the whole thing started. I felt grimy and knew I smelled awful.

It took me a good thirty minutes before I was satisfied. Though I was now beyond exhausted, I felt a thousand times better. As the sun began its slow slide behind the mountain, I stood in the water next to the tiny pier and combed out my thick tresses, braiding them to work with later.

Gods, the cool water over my naked body felt delicious! I groaned as I sank down to my chin. The water wasn't deep, but it was enough I could sit on a nearby bolder and be in over my chest. It was where I headed now.

Not too far from the shore, I stretched out, leaning back against the rock above the water and stretching my legs out in front of me. My breasts bobbed in the water, peeking out only occasionally as the water flowed past. I soaked up the last rays of sun, turning my face up to the breeze and warmth.

I looked in the direction of the Triad compound. Situated on a slight hill to the north of the city, it was like a beacon to me. Was King Storm all right? Surely King Hildar would have come for me if he wasn't. Thinking about the kings brought on a wave of longing. Not for companionship, either. No. I couldn't help but focus on the lustful way Storm had looked at me in the mirror. Had that been merely because I was an available woman, or had he meant what he'd said? Had he thought me beautiful? I know I had certainly been taken with him.

All three of our kings were striking. Asher was probably the most physically flawless of the three, but they were all prime males. Any woman would be proud to have any of them. To have all of them? Well...

Not for me. They *weren't* for me.

Yet, my traitorous mind wandered into forbidden territory. As did my hand.

What if... what if they *did* find me beautiful? Would they want to touch me? Make my body their own? Men in our village universally left me alone. I'd seen more than one look at me with lust-filled eyes, but I wasn't exactly what one would call a great catch. Naturally, I knew about sex, but had yet to experiment with anything other than self-pleasure -- which I was very good at. But to have a man touch me like that...

One hand cupped my breast while the other rubbed the length of my belly to settle over my mound. My clit was swollen and slick with my own lusts, needing the contact. I gave a lazy stroke, sighing in contentment as an exquisite pleasure rolled through me. What if that were Storm's finger petting me? What if Hildar were cupping and squeezing my breast? The mental image elicited a whimper from me.

I arched my back in offering to imaginary lovers, tweaking one nipple as I did. My fingers continued to stroke my clit under the water, the hot and cold sensations of my skin and the cool water an erotic stimulation.

Seconds later, my body clenched and my breath seized in my lungs. I gave a small cry as my orgasm rushed through me, over me, just like the flow of the water.

The wave had started to settle when I opened my eyes, an uncanny sense directing my gaze south of my little haven. There, on the bank of the river a little way from my hut, stood King Asher. Tall and proud, he stood, legs slightly apart. He rubbed one hand over the front of his breeches as he watched… me.

As if someone had suddenly doused me in aphrodisia, lust hit me hard. A solid punch to the gut. I cried out as another, stronger orgasm overtook me. This one seemed to go on and on, never ending as I watched Asher take out the length of his cock and begin stroking himself.

He. Was. *Magnificent*! Long and thick, his cock jerked before he took it in hand once again and stroked. I watched transfixed, my fingers still busy below the water. I had the mad urge to raise myself more fully onto the rock so he could see all of my body, see what he was stroking off to. Thankfully, I managed to control myself. In the back of my mind, I knew the euphoria of the situation wouldn't last, that I'd come crash-landing back to reality and the impact would destroy me if I embarrassed myself like that. Instead, I continued to watch, not moving but for my fingers still flicking my clit and plunging into my pussy beneath the water.

It wasn't long before Asher's movements became more insistent, frantic even. His lips pulled back from his teeth and I imagined I heard him growl. Then he tensed, threw back his head and groaned to the night. One white rope after another erupted from his cock, semen spilling onto the ground where he stood. I licked my lips, wanting to taste what he offered. Wanting to suck his cock into my mouth and clean him, readying him for another round, this time with me participating.

As I watched, he relaxed, his gaze finding mine. The heat I saw there pushed me over the edge once more, my pussy contracting around my fingers as the heel of my hand pressed and rubbed on my clit. I cried out, my gaze still locked with his. I couldn't seem to break away, even to preserve myself. I felt vulnerable. Stripped bare by his heated looks. I couldn't seem to look away, though. Couldn't disengage myself. Probably because I wanted to be with him, to feel what it would be like to have a man like him take me and teach me the pleasure to be found in his arms.

Asher tucked himself back into his pants and hesitated. For a moment, I thought he might approach me, but he didn't. Instead, he sketched me a small salute and turned to leave. Back to the compound with the rest of the Triad. I'd never been so emotionally and physically battered in my life. This display had been just the last in a long line of mentally and physically taxing events of the last two weeks.

I needed to think about this. Figure out the best course of action, because I had the feeling it wasn't the last I'd hear of it. Right now, however, I just wanted to get back to my home and fall into bed.

Which I did, falling facedown atop the quilt, not

even taking the time to dress and dry my hair. God, it felt wonderful! With a groan, I drew up one leg and promptly fell asleep.

* * *

I awoke in a rush, an orgasm the likes of which I'd never known existed crashing over me in wave after wave of searing ecstasy. I was still on my belly, my legs still parted where I'd bent my knee for comfort. Between my legs a tongue stroked my slit with sensual flicks, every so often dipping further down to catch my clit. Strong hands held my legs in place while fingers spread my lips to open me up for his sensual assault.

When the sensations ebbed somewhat, I looked back over my shoulder to find the wildly handsome King Asher. His eyes blazed with intent as he lazily licked my slit, licking up drops of my cum while holding my gaze, which was, I had to admit, sexy *as fuck*. I still wasn't letting him think he could get away with invading my privacy and sexually assaulting me.

"Touch me again without my permission, and I will poison you at the earliest opportunity," I said, doing my best to keep my expression blank. "I'm pretty sure you know I can do it, too."

The damned man simply gave me a sexy smirk and dipped his head back to my cunt -- never breaking eye contact -- and took another long, slow lick. I nearly groaned at the erotic sight of my juice glistening on his lips. To cover my reaction, I turned over and scooted up the bed, sitting on my ass and covering myself with my pillow.

"You need to leave."

He shrugged. "I only wished to thank you for the lovely view earlier. You gave me pleasure. I returned the favor."

"That should never have happened. Besides, you were the one trespassing. I'm the only one who lives out here. Everyone else is afraid of an attack at the river wall."

"Which begs the question, why do you live out here alone? You should reside closer to the village. A woman alone needs protection from sexual predators."

"Like the Triad? Tell me any one person in this entire region who would stop you or any other member of the Triad from doing anything he wanted to anyone he wanted?"

"Wasn't necessarily talking about me," was his mild reply. "But there are others who would take advantage if they so desired. If they did, could you fight them off?"

"I think you know the answer to that question." I was proud of my abilities and the knowledge I'd worked so hard to hone and procure, but I was embarrassed that I was piss poor in a fight. Our society worshiped strength because strength kept the Outlands from encroaching on the villages. We weren't as big as the great, walled and fortified cities, but we still had wealth and resources other villages or bandits would gladly kill to acquire. As evidenced by the recent attack.

"You need to move inward," he said, shifting his weight off the bed to stand before me, massive arms crossed. This was the king giving an order to a peasant.

"I'll get right on that," I snapped, my temper getting the better of me. "I'll send you a notice once my things are transferred to the great compound so you can assault me there."

He nodded once. "Good. See that you do." Then he walked out.

What the hell just happened?

Chapter Five

"All citizens, young and old, male and female, must assemble in the festival square one hour before sundown! No exceptions!"

The town criers were all over town. Which included Lassa. She was all excited, telling me the Triad was making an announcement. Passing judgment on one of our citizens.

"Passing judgment?" For some reason, that phrase sent a chill down my spine.

"I know! I wonder what happened?" For some reason her question brought to mind the conversation I'd had with King Asher the night before. Seemingly, one had nothing to do with the other. So why did I feel like I'd just walked under a cloud of doom?

Naturally, everyone in the village converged on the meeting place long before the specified time. The moment I walked through the city's inner gate, I knew whatever was happening revolved around me. Lorgan stood with his inner circle of elders and moneymen all around him. As one, their gazes shifted to focus on me. Lorgan gave me a sneer. I flipped him off.

Precisely at the allotted time, the Triad's party rode through the inner-city wall to the festival square. The three looked resplendent in their formal armor, a sign that whatever was about to happen was serious. King Storm still looked pale, but, somehow, he managed to sit his steed as if he were in the best of health. The slight beading of sweat on his upper lip told another story and made me want to go to his side to make sure he was well enough to be out. My gaze snapped to Hildar's. The damned man shouldn't have let Storm out like this. He was still sick and needed care.

Everyone hushed, turning to the kings expectantly. Looking around, I could tell there were some who were eager to see someone punished. I wasn't worried until I saw Tessa. The older woman looked on the verge of tears as I met her gaze. Malachi looked ready to do murder but seemed undecided if he wanted to go after the Triad or Lorgan. Seeming to make up his mind, he started in Lorgan's direction, but Tessa stayed him, nodding in my direction and speaking to him frantically, if quietly. Before I had time to go to the other woman, however, King Storm spoke. Despite his obvious weakness, his voice was clear and strong, as if his appearance were all an illusion.

"As you know, we have rules governing travel to and from the Great Compound." In life, everyone has an "oh shit" moment. This was mine. I knew what was coming. "Arryn, ward of Lorgan, *apprentice* to the healer, please step forward."

The "apprentice" part made me want to scratch Lorgan's beady little eyes out. The fucker should be *my* apprentice, not the other way around. No. Scratch that. I would never have him as an apprentice because he was dumber than fuck.

I hesitated a moment, then started forward. Malachi intercepted me, his face a mask of grim determination. Again, I was amazed at the ease and speed with which the older man moved with only one leg. Tessa held tightly to his hand, and the couple planted themselves firmly in front of me.

"I will not let you harm this girl, Highness," he said with a complex combination of deference and defiance. Malachi spoke to the king as an equal, but giving respect all the same. "She saved your life.

Anything she's done, she did for the good of the people."

"Be at ease," Asher said softly, kindly, to Malachi. There was no malice in his voice or visage, but I could tell none of the kings would be moved from whatever was about to happen.

Reluctantly, Malachi let me move in front of him and his wife. Tessa gripped my arm hard, her touch firm and reassuring. In that moment, I was struck at exactly how much Tessa and Malachi had to lose. If the kings truly had ill intentions -- or thought I did -- the older couple could be severely reprimanded. More, there was every possibility that, by defying the Triad as they were, they could be made to share my punishment. They knew this and still came to my defense.

"Arryn, ward of Lorgan --"

"My mother may have been given to Lorgan after my father's death," I interrupted King Storm, "but he has never taken responsibility for me, nor has he been the mentor he should have been for me to be considered his ward."

"You ungrateful little brat," Lorgan spat. "If not for me, you'd have been burned alive with your mother!"

"Silence!"

That was Hildar. The king actually moved forward on his steed, a purely menacing gesture directed at Lorgan. Lorgan backed up three steps before stopping and standing his ground. Likely, he only grew a pair because he bumped into one of the members of the Council of Elders -- the council he was supposed to be head of. Showing weakness of any kind would get him demoted or kicked off the council entirely.

"She has no respect for anyone, my king. You can see I could have no influence over her when even such respected members of our society as Malachi and his wife cannot sway her."

"If memory serves," Hildar countered, "you were the one to insist on taking in both Arryn and her mother. It would seem that you've been the one to not follow through with your obligations. Which we will get to later." It was a threat. Pure and simple. Lorgan knew it, as did every member of the village, including the council.

"Arryn," Storm continued as if he'd never been interrupted. "It is my understanding that you regularly enter the maze. Is this inaccurate?"

I thought briefly about denying it. After all, it worked for Lorgan and the rest of the council when needed. Their M.O. had always been, "deny, deny, deny," until proven otherwise. Then pretend you hadn't denied and that everything was someone else's fault. But I'd always hated that about our elders. Despite my time in Lorgan's house, even as an outsider, he'd made that impression on me. Rather than emulating him, I'd decided early on I would be the exact opposite. I would own up to my actions. Accept any consequences. I might not like them, but at least I would know I was doing the right thing, no matter what. My conscience would be clear.

"It is not, your majesty. I purposely planted my herb and flower gardens inside the maze because the soil is much richer than any in the village."

Storm raised an eyebrow. "Think carefully about this. If you can't deny your accused actions, we will have no choice but to render punishment now instead of having a trial." He sounded like he expected me to deny it. Maybe even wanted me to deny it.

"I am many things, King Storm, but I am not a liar. I will say that anything I have done in the maze, I did to aid the people of this village. And you as well."

Hildar raised an eyebrow. The corner of Asher's mouth lifted slightly. Storm, however, looked impassive. The only reaction I could discern from him was how he leaned forward expectantly in his saddle.

"So, there is a free admission of guilt," Storm continued.

"No!" Malachi interjected. "You will not pass judgment on her! I will fight you to the death!"

Several villagers stirred uneasily. Tessa openly sobbed, clinging to me as she tried to put herself between me and the Triad, throwing them fierce looks even through her tears.

King Asher dismounted and strode forward, his steady gait taking him to Malachi instead of me or Tessa. "It will be all right," he murmured to Malachi, laying a comforting hand on the older man's shoulder. "Trust us to look out for her best interests."

"I can't," the older man whispered. "She is the daughter of my heart."

"You have watched us grow from boys to men, Mali." The nickname Asher gave the older man seemed to startle Malachi. His face took on a look of realization, like he'd just remembered he *had* watched the kings grow from boys into the men they'd become. "You were with us when we made the transition to the Triad, and once called us all sons of your heart. Put aside what you fear and trust us to be the men you taught us to be."

"The penalty for entering the maze without express permission from the Triad..." Storm paused, shaking his head slightly as if even voicing the penalty was abhorrent to him. "Is death." The silence in the village was deafening. No one spoke. Not the children. Not the elders. Lorgan gave me a triumphant smirk but said nothing. Tessa clung to me, her arms around me in a fiercely protective gesture.

"I won't let you," she hissed. "I won't!"

"Death has always been the penalty for treason," Lorgan chimed in with a strong, loud voice. "Without exception."

"She saved your life!" Sara cried, addressing King Storm as she shouted and shoved her way through the crowd to stand with her shoulders back alongside me and Tessa. I shook my head, but she plowed on, Lassa at her side. "I was there!"

"Saved the king's life," Lorgan scoffed. "She used the king as a test subject, using questionable methods. She could just as easily have killed him." Lorgan pointed at Asher accusingly. "You have to follow through with our laws, laws *you* enacted!"

Storm pinned the other man with a gaze so deadly it gave me chills. "Protest in protection of a loved one is one thing. Outright disrespect quite another."

"She deserves to die! Being in the maze without permission is treason!"

"Am I to punish her in that way when those same actions saved my life?" Storm's voice was deceptively quiet. Lorgan should have heard the menace but either didn't or didn't care. "Death for life?"

"If not death, what will her punishment be? What could possibly be fitting enough for her crimes other than death?"

Storm sat straighter in his saddle, looking at me once before back at Lorgan. "She will be taken by the Triad as a pet."

The elders let out a collective gasp at the same time Lorgan erupted into a tirade. Personally, I felt like I'd been punched in the gut. I couldn't breathe, could barely register what Lorgan was saying, or Storm's response. All I knew was the argument went on for long moments before Lorgan brought up what, as far as I knew, few people in the village were privy to.

"You're promised to *my daughter*!" Lorgan shouted. Was he too stupid to realize even a single king, much less the entire Triad, wouldn't stand for such blatant disrespect? "I will not allow you to take a pet! It would be the greatest insult to Sunja! If Arryn is to be a pet, then you will sell her to the markets to the north. Let someone else deal with her. My Sunja will *not* be humiliated by one such as her in her own home! *I will not permit this disrespect*!"

Hildar dismounted and strode to Lorgan, menace in every footfall. His superior height towered over the other man. With an expression as scary as I'd ever seen, Hildar got right in Lorgan's face and hissed. "Like *you* didn't disrespect your own wife when you insisted on taking in Arryn and her mother, Lila?" There was a tense silence all around, no one daring to say a word or make a sound. "I was *there* when the previous Triad debated what to do with the young woman -- a pet -- and her daughter when Famar was imprisoned waiting his trial. You lied about having your Gretta's support. I know you did because I was the one to deliver both of them to your home. Your wife was cut to the bone. You, her beloved husband, bringing home a *pet*."

I winced. Hildar uttered the word like it was the vilest of terms to be applied to anyone. Hadn't Storm just designated me the same?

"I also happen to know not all of what you

accused Lila of was true. I happen to know *you* were the aggressor in the situation, and that you had much the same planned for Arryn."

Lorgan paled, and my breath caught.

Hildar knew something I didn't. More, Lorgan had reacted viscerally to the accusation. Whatever had happened, it hadn't been my mother's fault. At least, not entirely. Certainly not enough to warrant being burned alive.

"Nonsense," Lorgan spat. "I tried to help both of them --"

Whatever he'd been about to say was cut off when Hildar backhanded him hard enough to spin him around and land him facedown in the mud. Hildar stood over Lorgan, his lips pulled back to bare his teeth, just waiting for the other man to get up. Hildar's fists were clenched at his sides as if he just prevented himself from pounding the other man into the ground. Instead, he waited for Lorgan to get to his feet. It was telling that none of the elders aided Lorgan.

When he stood before Hildar, the other man raised his hand and snapped his fingers. From the group of soldiers surrounding the Triad, a man emerged carrying a black whip. We all recognized it, though few had actually seen it. Stinger. It was a whip specially modified to feel as if one's skin was being split open when in reality it only left a painful welt with every lash.

"Fifty lashes for Elder Lorgan," Hildar said. "For insubordination and attempting to undermine the authority of the Triad."

No one spoke. The silence continued to blanket the village. Where Malachi, Tessa, Sara, and Lassa had come to my defense, no one spoke up for Lorgan. Not even his wife. The woman looked almost smug, as if the punishment didn't bother her in the least.

"Come," Storm said to me, reaching a hand out to me. "It's time to go."

"No," I whispered. "Please." I hated to beg, but I was terrified. While our village had allowed my father to bring in my mother, after that incident they'd refused to allow pets into their midst. This very Triad had supported and enforced the unwritten law themselves. Lorgan had terrified the village into believing pets were sexual predators concerned only with their own pleasure. I'd always figured the Triad held much the same beliefs, but apparently, the Triad had their own reasons for not wanting pets in their territory. Honestly, I had no idea what pets were normally like. I only knew my mother hadn't been like Lorgan said. She was a good woman, a good mother who hadn't deserved what had happened to her.

"It will be all right," Malachi whispered to me. "Tessa, let her go."

"No," the other woman sobbed. "Please, Mali. Don't let them do this."

"Trust in the men we raised, wife. Trust them to be decent."

She looked over her shoulder at Storm. I had no idea what passed between the two, but Tessa sagged, seeming defeated. Then she released me. Malachi guided me to Storm's steed. He urged me to reach for the king. Once his big hand circled my forearm, he hauled me up in front of him, much as Hildar had done all those days ago.

Again, I was filled with apprehension, only this time I had reason. What would they do to me? It was obvious that all three had at least some level of attraction to me. What exactly would they expect of me? I had no idea, but I was terrified.

As they turned around to head back to the compound, my gaze found the soldier, Hadin, who had led the men at the city gate and the catapults during the battle. I knew he respected my abilities, no matter that I was a woman and wasn't worth a damn in a fight. He gave a slow shake of his head as if he knew I was debating bolting at the first opportunity. If I did, there was a high probability Hadin would be the man tasked with bringing me back to the Triad. Once he saw me sag against Storm, he nodded as if to tell me to just go with them. To give them a chance. He didn't leer or look disgusted or any number of other things I expected from the villagers, just quietly encouraged me. It steadied me.

I could do this.

Maybe.

In the distance, the sound of Stinger cutting through the air was punctuated by the sound of leather lashing flesh. Lorgan's cry was followed by a deep voice booming "one," as it counted down Lorgan's punishment. I suppose I should have felt bad for the little weasel, but I didn't. *Have fun with that, Lorgan.*

With a resigned sigh, I settled myself, centered my thoughts. Storm grunted, his arms tight around me, one palm resting on my belly as he urged the horse onward. It wasn't long before I felt his breath whisper over my ear. "I'm proud you didn't make a scene."

"Why are you doing this? You have a woman willing to be your mate. Why make me into a pet? Is it to have an acceptable means of seeking pleasure so you don't have to rely on one woman to service three men?"

He sighed, not answering. Instead, he simply nuzzled my ear before sitting up straighter. The arm around my waist tightened, as did the palm on my belly. "Resign yourself, little girl. You're ours to do with as we please."

Now, why did that statement thrill me instead of repel me?

* * *

On the ride back to the compound, no one said a word. Asher and Hildar flanked Storm the entire way. I was strung so tight I feared I would snap. The soldiers kept a respectable distance behind. When I could take no more of the maddening silence, I asked again, "Why are you doing this?"

"Well," Storm said, "it's either this or we put you to death. You'd rather the second option?"

"Depends," I snapped

"Relax." That was from Asher. "No one is going to hurt you."

"Relax? *Relax?*" Hyper aware of the guards several feet behind us, I tried to calm myself. "How can I possibly relax?"

Hildar shrugged. "You could trust us. Then you'd be relaxed."

I wanted to hit him over the head. He must have read my expression because he grinned. "Must remember to get you riled often. That expression you get when you're thinking about doing murder is more than a little sexy."

I was definitely in over my head. None of the men in the village had ever paid much attention to me. I tried a different approach. "Look, let's be reasonable. Everyone in the village knows I'm… weak." I tried my best not to trip over the word, but it left a bad taste in my mouth nonetheless. "I'm less than useless in a fight and my head is filled with math and science, and all kinds of things no one wants to know about. I'm not good mate material and, therefore, I'm not sexually experienced in any way. I wouldn't make a good pet for anyone. Especially not for *three* kings."

There. I'd said it. My face felt like it was blistering, but I'd gotten it out.

Silence followed.

"Fucking *say something*!" I thought I might be going mad.

"There's really nothing to say," Storm said. Was that amusement in his voice? I looked back over my shoulder. Sure enough, a smile played at his lips.

I noted sweat dotted his brow and upper lip. "Are you even going to make it back to the compound?" I asked, alarm spiking through me.

"I'm weak, little girl, but strong enough to ride a horse a short distance. I'm probably even strong enough to hunt wayward little pets through the woods should they attempt to flee us on foot."

"Not-so-subtle hint there, big guy?" I wasn't respectful, but then, what did I really have to lose? Strangely, my sassy tone seemed to amuse him.

"Just so. Though, once I'm better, I'd welcome the challenge."

"The fun of the hunt," Asher added, a wicked gleam in his eye, "isn't the chase. It's delivering the punishment afterward."

I wasn't touching that. Especially since my intimate interlude with Asher was playing on a loop in my mind at the moment. My dress had crept up my thighs, baring skin that was now kissed by the night air. Given the erotic images in my head, it also made me wonder what it would feel like to ride in this position naked. Would Storm enjoy it? Would I? Despite the warmth of the night, a fine shiver swept through me I couldn't suppress.

"That's not a shiver of cold," Storm murmured

right at my ear. "Nor one of fear. What is playing through that tricky mind of yours? Hmm?"

When I refused to answer, Storm simply made his own suppositions. "Asher told me about your encounter. I'm betting you're wondering what that same incident would be like played out with each of us. How different would each of us be during sex? Which of us would be the most aggressive? Which the most passionate? Which the most... dominant?"

I could actually hear the lust in his voice. Not only that, but his cock, which was right at my butt, was swelling. And the size simply to the gods *couldn't* be right. For emphasis, he pulled me even closer so that he was mashed hard against my ass. He actually pulsed against me as he rocked his hips.

A tiny whimper escaped me before I could suppress it. In that instant, I knew I'd made a grievous mistake. Asher and Hildar closed in so that all three rode side by side, so close they could touch me if they chose.

"To be clear," Storm began. "We will never do anything you don't want."

Before I could open my mouth to tell them I didn't want them to do anything at all, he qualified, "But you have to say it with your mouth *and* your body. Once we prove to you we can make any kind of sex with us pleasurable, I think we can ease your fears about your permanent place with us."

Until he'd actually said the words, I hadn't realized how much the prospect of them selling me terrified me. The relief was so overwhelming I actually sagged in his arms. Still, I had to ask. I wanted at least that much clear. "You're not going to take me north? To be sold?"

Storm halted his horse. I gave a little squeal as,

with little effort, he lifted me, turning me so that I faced him, my legs hooked over his own as I straddled him as well as the saddle. The plain dress I'd worn slid up my thighs even farther. I tried to keep my distance, but Storm looped his arms around me, forcing me tight against him. His erection pressed against me intimately, separated only by his breeches and my underwear. As if he'd given a spoken command, Hildar and Asher fell back, blocking any view of us from behind.

That gesture, more than anything, eased my fear somewhat. I might not be with them under ideal circumstances, but they wouldn't be needlessly cruel to me. Keeping any sexual activity out of sight from those around us wasn't something the kings needed to do with me. I was a pet, after all. But they *chose* to. Without me asking.

With gentle hands, Storm cupped my face, moving me so that I had to look straight into his mesmerizing amber-colored eyes. "Understand me, girl. We will never sell you. Either you're ours, or you go free. No matter what."

That shocked me. "You'll let me go?"

"I didn't say that," Storm said with a chuckle. The dark rumble vibrated sensually through me. "At least, we won't let you go until you've at least given us a chance to prove we will be good for you. We already know you're good for us."

"You're confusing me," I said, shaking my head. "I'm a *pet*. Why do you care if you're good for me or I'm good for you in the first place? One has nothing to do with the other."

"Just put it all out of your mind. Forget all this pet and mate stuff. You're with us. We're with you."

"What of Sunja?"

He waved my question off. "She is enamored with the power we would bring to a mating. She doesn't care about us or our needs. A pet shouldn't bother her in the least, no matter what Lorgan says."

That irked me. It might not matter to Sunja, but damn it, it mattered to *me*! "Men," I muttered under my breath. Though I'd clutched his shoulders in reflex when he'd turned me around, now I crossed my arms over my chest, looking away from him and pouting a bit. I couldn't help it! Storm was talking like I might mean more to him and his Triad than a pet, but he was planning on taking an actual mate in the process!

Fucker.

Again, Storm's warm chuckle vibrated through me. Had I spoken that last thought out loud?

"Just rest easy, little girl. I promise to keep your mind from Lorgan and Sunja and everyone else but me, Asher, and Hildar for many nights to come." With that, he gently turned my face to him and brought his lips down on mine.

He was right. The instant his lips touched mine, my world narrowed to him. His mouth. His cock pulsing against my sex. Those big hands of his wrapped around my body, one covering my back, the other palming the back of my head to hold me right where he wanted me. Storm wasn't dominating or fearsome in his kiss. He was gentle. Coaxing. A would-be lover trying to soothe his chosen female. There was no way to suppress my whimper. Had he swooped in and took what he wanted, I might have been able to resist. Maybe. But not this gentle persuasion.

As if he that one little whimper signaled my surrender, Storm growled deep in his throat and pulled me even closer so that I sat fully on him. One of his big hands slid down to my ass, holding me to him while he thrust slightly, a small reminder of his need of me. I wanted to push him away, to claim this was too much, but something inside me clawed and fought to get out and claim this man before he had a chance to take another woman for his mate.

Surrender wasn't a word in my vocabulary. No matter how physically weak I was, my tactic in any situation -- physical or mental -- where I didn't have the upper hand was to back off and go at the problem at a different angle. This time, my instinct screamed for me to meet Storm head on. Also, there was this aggression inside screaming for me to claim what I wanted before they could take Sunja as their mate. The combination of emotions I'd never experienced before nearly made me lose my mind.

Before I actually realized what I'd done, my hands were fisted in his hair and *I* was taking *him*. I thrust my tongue between his lips to taste him fully, tangling myself with him as I gripped his hair tightly to keep him from escaping me. His taste was *addicting*! Masculine, wild, and powerful. His fingers dug into my ass and moved me on him as if we were actually fucking.

"That's it," he praised between licks at my mouth. "You need us as much as we need you, don't you?"

I didn't know how to respond to that. *Need* was a strong word. Want? Sure. I wanted them with a lust like I'd never before experienced. I wasn't sure I *needed* them. I didn't *need* anybody. I'd been alone and dependent on myself most of my life. To suddenly have this fierce passion to keep someone, to be jealous they might take another, left me reeling. I didn't know what to do with it, or Storm.

Through the lust haze, I suddenly perceived

Storm's body tilting at an odd angle. Then Asher was at our side, steadying his king with a firm hand.

"Turn back around, Arryn," he said softly. I pulled back to assess Storm's face. He was breathing rapidly, his face dotted with perspiration. At first I thought it was merely the heat of the moment, then I noticed his lips and the skin around his eyes was pale, the dark circles standing out starkly now.

Embarrassment scalded me. "Godsdamn it," I swore softly. I tore a strip of cloth from the hem of my dress to dab at his forehead, placing the back of my hand to the skin there. He wasn't with fever that I could tell, but he was certainly reaching the end of his endurance. "He shouldn't be out of bed." Carefully I turned around. Storm's brawny arm still snaked around my waist to balance me as I did.

"Once we get to the compound," he said at my ear, "I'll gladly stay in bed if you stay with me."

"Stop it," I hissed. "You need rest and medicine. I can do that."

"Rest easy, little girl," Asher said as he moved so he could converse with me more easily. Hildar hung back but was well within conversation range. "We all intend for Storm to get better. Besides, I think you were the aggressor in that little display." His wink took the sting out of his words, but not my embarrassment.

I sat staring straight ahead. Though Storm's arm was snug around me, I still clung to the saddle horn, mainly because I was afraid I'd clutch that big arm if I didn't. "Just get us to the compound so I can see to his needs." When Hildar coughed behind us -- a sound suspiciously like a laugh -- I clarified, "His *medical* needs."

"At this point," Storm said with a small chuckle, "I'd classify this --" he thrust his erection against me again --"as a medical need."

"Fuck off," I muttered. I had fallen right into his trap, revealing the tension inside me Asher had started. He'd known he was too weak to do anything else. I'd bet my life the damned man had initiated that kiss simply to prove to me I wanted to be with them. But to what purpose? They had me! No one in the whole of the Outlands would question this Triad's right to take me as a pet. The civilized lands wouldn't even care. *They had me!* Why this show?

Confused, now near tears, I sat in silence while the horses made the last hill to the compound. Once inside, I'd take care of Storm, then retreat to lick my wounds and take stock of the situation free of distractions. Then, when I'd cleared my mind, I'd face them again.

Chapter Six

Storm barely made it into the compound on his own. The second the door to the Triad's chamber was closed, he sagged against the wall. It looked as if he would have fallen to his knees had Hildar and Asher not been at his side to prop him up until he was steady once more. Everything inside me screamed for me to go to his side, but after the ride up here, I forced myself to retreat behind the curtain I'd erected when I was there before. Strange it hadn't been moved.

There was talk in low murmurs as they helped Storm out of his armor and tried to get him into the bed. "I'm fine," Storm insisted, though, clearly, he wasn't fine. "Just a little weak. The ride was long."

"The bloody ride was long because you couldn't steady yourself on the fucking horse going any faster than a slow fucking walk," Asher snapped. "Even the horse knew, by the way his ears were laid back and his eyes rolled. Get in the fucking bed!"

"I'm still the leader of this Triad," Storm snapped, though he sounded too weak to back up that statement. "I'll do whatever the fuck I want."

"Fine," Hildar said. "Fall on your ass in front of the servants. See how that works for you."

"And seeing me lying in bed is better?" Storm sounded as irritated as the other two. I could almost see his stubborn chin jutting as he stood up to the other men. "Just don't let them in. They won't be expecting to be needed tonight anyway."

Because the kings had brought home a new *pet*. Embarrassment flooded me again. I couldn't believe I was in this situation. I'd saved Storm's life, damn it!

They should be grateful to me. Not… this. I stepped from behind the curtain to find Storm swaying on his feet in nothing but thin breeches, sweat soaking his body.

"Oh, for heaven's sake! Get in bed, you big oaf!" I stomped toward him, pushing him back when he refused to sit on the bed behind him. Unexpectedly, he lost his balance, tumbling backward with a groan.

"Fuck," he gasped.

"Not in this condition," I muttered. "Get him fully on the bed. He needs fluids and rest," I said, trying to sound no-nonsense. "Bring me some warm water and a couple of cloths. I need to wash him."

Surprisingly, both Asher and Hildar followed my instructions without hesitation. I crossed my arms and met those amber eyes with my own. They were glazed slightly, almost feverish, though he was cool to the touch.

"If you take a setback because of this stunt, I swear, Storm, I'll let you die." I didn't really mean it, but I needed to look put out when, in reality, I was becoming alarmed.

The infuriating man only grinned at me. "Not to worry, my little girl. I'm only playing to your sympathies. Trying to get you to sleep in my arms once more. I rather enjoyed having my own personal healer in bed with me last time."

"Forget it," I said even as I sat on the edge of the bed next to him. "You're not in any shape to make me, either."

"I just need a little rest," he said, finally acknowledging his weakness. "This was the first time I'd done more than walk around the room since you left me." He managed to look hurt, as if the separation had been all my fault and he'd been the one to suffer for it.

"At least this time I can honestly say you aren't being unfaithful to your *promised*. Taking liberties with a pet hardly qualifies." I knew I sounded sulky. Really, I was acting like a child.

"What bothers you more?" Storm asked, his eyes suddenly clear as if my answer were the most important thing in the world to him. "The fact that we've declared you our pet, or that another is promised to us?"

I was saved from answering when Hildar returned with the requested wash water. Asher wasn't far behind with a meal of stew and a large pitcher of drinking water.

Instead of answering directly, I simply said, "A man should be faithful to his mate." Then I paced to the window, leaving Asher and Hildar to wash Storm.

I stood with my back to them, trying to get my emotions under control. I wanted to take my meal in the relative privacy behind my curtain, but a big set of hands on my shoulders stopped me.

"You can't hide from us, little girl." That was Asher. After the previous night, I'd recognize his voice anywhere. "The sooner you get accustomed to us, the easier all this will be."

"I don't want to get used to you," I said quietly, not looking at him.

"You might find you like us."

I did turn to him then. "And what good would that do me? You've got a woman waiting for you to claim her."

"This bothers you." He didn't make it a question.

Frustrated beyond belief, I honestly didn't know how to respond. "If it does?"

"Then perhaps we need to figure out why."

Without thinking, I picked up a glass of water and threw it in his face. "Stop it! Just... stop!"

Instead of getting angry with me, Asher simply wiped his face with his sleeve and grinned at me. "You're jealous," he stated baldly.

"I'd have to have a reason to be jealous," I spat. "All I know about the three of you is that you're not true to your promised."

"And do you think that fits with our character?" Hildar asked. "Don't you even wonder why?"

"Why is any man unfaithful to his woman?"

"Perhaps because she isn't his woman to begin with," Storm said softly, sitting up on the edge of the bed instead of in it. "Did you ever wonder why we'd agree to mate a woman like Sunja in the first place?"

"I assume it has something to do with letting yourselves be bullied by Lorgan. To take a mate from outside would make it seem like you didn't find anyone in the village good enough for you. Then, of course, he presented his daughter as the perfect solution. A woman from the village, daughter of the leader of the Council of Elders. She'd be accepted readily by the people."

Storm grinned at the other two. "Told you she was intelligent."

"You let us worry about Sunja and Lorgan," Hildar said to me. "You worry about accustoming yourself to life with us."

When I snagged another flagon of water, Hildar raised a hand, giving me a "don't even think about it" expression. Naturally, I did. Which prompted Hildar to snag the pitcher of water and fling it over me. Not in my face, but over my chest.

Typical male.

"Can't say that was a bad idea," Storm said, grin

firmly in place.

"Which brings me to my first command to you as a pet, girl." King or not, Asher was starting to get on my last nerve. "Take off your dress and join us for supper."

"I will not…"

"Or," Asher interrupted, "*we* could take off your dress and have *you* for supper."

A punch of lust hit me so hard, I sat down abruptly in the chair behind me. If it hadn't been there, I'd have collapsed to the floor.

"And I guess that's that," Hildar said, reaching for me. There was no fight in me when he helped me stand and whipped the dress over my head. I hadn't worn anything under it but short panties, which meant my breasts were bare.

Not waiting for permission from me, Hildar wrapped one muscled arm around me and took one puckered nipple between his lips suckling gently before letting it go with a little *pop*. Then he lifted me in his arms, carrying me to the bed and Storm.

"What are you going to do to me?" I couldn't keep the trepidation out of my voice, but there was anticipation and excitement there, as well. Wouldn't you know it, the devil heard it all.

"Anything we want," Storm said with a wicked grin.

The moment Hildar placed me in the bed, Storm reached for me, settling in to lie beside me, pulling me close to him so that he cradled my head on one muscled arm and placed the other hand on my belly. To restrain me? If so, he used very little pressure. It was more that he took in as much skin as he could with that big hand, fingers splayed wide.

Hildar sat next to us, his eyes seeming to devour

me. I wanted to cross my hands over my chest or something, but Storm merely pressed lightly with that one hand and shook his head as if reading my thoughts.

With gentle fingers, Hildar brushed back a lock of my hair that had fallen over my forehead, then pushed back several locks concealing one nipple, the feel of his touch whispering over the peak making me shiver.

"I believe I'm the only member of this Triad who hasn't had the sincere pleasure of sampling your little body or your drugging kisses," Hildar said, his voice low and rumbling. "You can't think to deny me a taste, can you?"

Before I could answer, Hildar lowered his head to my chest, flicking his tongue out against the same nipple. I couldn't suppress the cry that burst from my lips. The sensation was electric! Both nipples hardened in a flash, tight peaks insisting on more from his tongue and mouth. I arched to him, encouraging him to take that nipple into his mouth. There hadn't been a conscious decision on my part; my body had simply expressed what it wanted. I was torn between mortification and a desire to take what I needed…

And there was the problem. That all-consuming need, when I refused to allow myself to need anything. Yet there it was. A force I couldn't deny. It went beyond companionship or physical attraction, or even sex. What I felt was a… a connection. A physical and emotional bond I had never known existed that I was beginning to realize I couldn't live without.

Need… With a cry, I surrendered to it, knowing it was futile to resist. I wrapped my arms around Hildar's head and held him to me, thrusting my chest at him. The king maneuvered himself over me, his body between my spread thighs. His arms circled my torso to hold me to him as tightly as I held him. Growls and slurps came from my chest where he feasted on my tits. Stubble from his jaw abraded my tender skin deliciously so I knew he'd leave his mark on me. It was primitive. Raw. A primal need neither of us attempted to deny.

For a long, long time, my cries and Hildar's growls were the only thing I heard, the vast chamber of the High King's bedroom echoing with those sounds of passion and lust. Hildar's mouth moved from one peak to the other in increasingly rougher movements. His arms tightened and loosened around me reflexively, as if he were trying to rein his own lust the way I was. And failing, just as I was.

I tilted my hips, grinding my clit over his belly for friction. Before I realized what I'd done, I'd wound my legs around him, squeezing him to me for even more friction. "Oh, gods above," I whimpered, my breath coming in little gasps. "What's happening to me?"

"Just let it happen," Storm whispered next to my ear.

I turned my head to look straight into these mesmerizing amber eyes. Words escaped before I could censor them. "I'm afraid."

"I know," Storm soothed, petting my hair and nuzzling my forehead. "I know. Trust me. Trust *us*. We'll not hurt you. Ever."

I wanted to disagree, but when I shook my head slightly, he cupped my face and brought his lips to mine in a gentle kiss. The tenderness and carefulness with which he kissed me was at odds with the way Hildar ravished my breasts. There was no way I could deny there were two completely different men at work here. Two men.

But then, I was a pet. A living doll meant to satisfy the needs of three men, if that was what they wanted. Even that thought couldn't get my traitorous body under control. I still wanted the pleasure they effortlessly stoked inside me. Still wanted these men to teach me about sex with a man. It was humiliating as much as it was titillating. My body gave in to the latter, ignoring the former.

Storm continued to kiss me, giving me wicked flicks of his tongue when I opened my mouth to him. I wrapped my legs around Hildar even tighter, rubbing my pussy against him, needing to come. Hildar's growls sounded primitive, a caveman taking what he wanted from his woman. He moved his body with mine, giving me what I needed.

"That's it." Asher's voice was at my other ear. I jumped, probably would have turned my head away from Storm to look at the other king. Asher's strong hand stayed me, keeping me still for Storm's kiss. "Let them have you, beautiful girl. Surrender to them. To us…"

I did.

One arm around Hildar's head, the other around Storm's, I took what they willingly gave. My body was on fire, thrumming with a need so strong I nearly sobbed when I felt my orgasm beginning.

Pleasure crashed over me with the force of a detonation, cataclysmic in its intensity. I screamed so hard my throat was raw and ragged, my ears as well as the chamber ringing with it. Hildar quickly lifted himself off me to free his cock. Asher slipped his hand between my thighs to find my clit where Hildar had abandoned it. With the new touch, another explosion rocked through me. I pushed through it even as I registered Hildar kneeling over me, pumping a massive cock in his fist. Hildar gave his own roar of completion, and his cock exploded in a geyser of cum. Hot seed splashed over my tits and belly in lash after scalding, creamy lash until he was spent. Then Hildar collapsed over me, his sweaty, heaving body heavy on top of me.

I couldn't say anything. Couldn't express my feelings of outrage -- I didn't know what was actually foremost in my mind. Hildar and Storm nuzzled me and murmured words of praise. I was too stunned and lust-stupid to do anything other than try to catch my breath, my thoughts a chaotic mess.

Asher moved in the background. I heard water tinkling as he squeezed out a cloth. When Hildar gave me one last soft, lingering kiss and moved off me, Asher sat beside me, using the cloth to clean the semen from my chest and belly. He took his time, making sure I was completely clean before tossing the cloth to Hildar.

"Now," Asher said, extending a hand to me. "Time to eat."

I was laid bare, raw with emotion, and he wanted to *eat*? What's more, I found myself reaching for the hand he offered, letting him help me from the bed. He walked me to the table where everything was ready, four places with bowls, saucers, and silverware. A large pot in the center held some kind of savory stew while two loaves of bread with accompanying slabs of butter sat next to it.

I couldn't stop trembling. Hyper aware of all three of them, I kept looking around to find them, needing to know where each of them was. The feeling was how I imagined a wild animal would react, sensing predators all around. Only these predators had already pounced. They'd conquered me, and I wasn't sure how I felt about that.

Naked as the day I was born, I sat in the chair Asher held for me. I was self-conscious, but figured it was expected of me to eat naked with them. As a pet, would they expect me to forgo clothing all the time?

The next thing I knew, Hildar was behind me. "Arms up," he said softly. When I obediently followed his direction, he slipped a soft tunic over me, covering me adequately. "That should do until we can retrieve your own clothing and buy you new garments." Hildar patted my shoulder before brushing a kiss over the top of my head, then taking his own seat. Quickly, I tucked the long garment under me and pulled it as low over my thighs as it would go. It came almost to my knees even sitting.

Bread was passed around the table as we began to eat. I was still in shock, but the stew smelled too good to ignore. It would be easy to digest as well, allowing for Storm's recent sickness. High in protein and carbohydrates, it should stand him well.

The men talked amongst themselves for a time, sharing a breakdown of the recent attack on the village. They obviously hadn't discussed it before, probably because of Storm's condition. Seconds on the stew were dished out and the last piece of bread fought over, but I barely paid attention. I was sure the stew must have tasted as good as it smelled, but I simply had no appetite for it beyond a bite or two. It was rich and filling for Storm, but in my present condition, too much for me.

"They knew where to hit us," Asher said. "Or thought they did. Thanks to the reinforcements on the riverside, our walls weren't as easily penetrated as they'd expected."

"We have you to thank for that, Arryn," Storm said, including me. "I had my doubts about including the river inside the city wall, but the Council insisted it was necessary in case of a siege."

"The Council doesn't know anything about siege warfare," I muttered, still feeling vulnerable and out of sorts.

"I think we can all agree on that," Hildar acknowledged. "But I'm curious as to why you'd think so."

Why was he deliberately drawing me into the conversation? Actually asking my opinion? I cleared my throat. "Well, they wanted the river enclosed so there was always a source of fresh water, giving us unlimited resources as long as the wall remained intact."

"That was the excuse they gave me," Storm said, resting an elbow on the table as he spoke to me.

I looked at him like he'd lost his mind. "Do you not realize that river is the exact wrong place to rely on drinking water during an all-out siege?"

"Of course I do," Storm said, not batting an eyelash. "I'm just curious as to why *you* believe so. You were the one who designed the wall in that area. If you thought it was a bad idea, why would you agree to do it?"

"I agreed to do it because they were building it anyway, whether or not I helped. It's a bad idea, but there's no point on wasting resources and energy and manpower on something that serves absolutely no purpose. At least, built the way I instructed, the structure is sound. It just won't work for the intended purpose."

"To provide water for drinking and crops."

"Exactly," I said. "The river runs through the

mountain, but that doesn't mean there is no access on the other side of the mountain. Further, that river fills the groundwater for miles downstream. Likely, all our wells on the other side of the village, as well as wells to other villages deeper into the Outlands, are supported by that river. Does anyone know where the mouth is or who controls it?"

"The Triad of a Jesuit village controls the river on the other side of the mountain, where it begins its flow underground. The village is pretty much filled with monks of that order, living a life of poverty, obedience, and chastity. They were placed there by the leader of the New Catholic Church just after the Great Wars in an effort to control this region of the Outlands." Storm imparted this with seeming indifference, his gaze lazy as he lifted a piece of bread to dunk in the stew before taking a bite.

I snorted. "And we all know how the new church sees things. They're even more corrupt than they were in the dark ages."

"Not the Triad," Asher said with conviction. "They follow the letter of their vows, working to better the lives of the people around them. Which is why the river has been clean and free of pollutants from the Outlands all these years."

"If they take their orders from the church, wouldn't they contaminate the river if their leaders instructed it?"

"In the past, I'd have said a solid yes," Storm admitted. "This Triad, however… They think for themselves. Their vows are more to their god than to the church or the priests."

"Then it would seem the elders were correct," I said, not following where they were going and unable to truly concentrate on the conversation given all that had happened to me mere minutes ago. "The Jesuit Triad will protect the river from their end."

"Unless that Triad were overthrown," Hildar said quietly.

All three men looked at me as if they expected me to follow the hidden meaning of their conversation. I shook my head once, intending to tell them I didn't understand, then I stilled. "How likely is that to happen?" I asked, suddenly needing to know the answer. "How easy is it to trek through or around the mountain to their village?"

"There is no pass into the mountains from this side of the Outlands that anyone has ever found," Storm said. "And the river through the mountain has nothing but sheer rock facing and rapid-moving water. We've not explored outside our territory so it's likely any way up the mountain is deep within the Outlands and outside our sphere of influence."

"Seems like it's impractical to reach," I said, shrugging. Though I was beginning to get the feeling I didn't want to know more.

"Which would negate running messages from upstream to our village," Asher supplied. I got the feeling he was stating the obvious conclusion, something I'd heard more than once but discounted because I was so focused on why it was a really bad idea to enclose the border wall on the outside of the river bank.

"Unless someone had access to trained birds," I murmured. I stood, needing to pace, the tension inside me coiling tightly all of a sudden. "But why?" I was talking more to myself than anything else. Presented with a puzzle -- any kind of puzzle -- I had to work it out. "What purpose would it serve to capture this village? For that matter, why did Blackheart send an army to attempt to take our village this time?"

"That's easily enough answered," Storm said. "Between this village and the Jesuits, deep below the water table, is the biggest salt mine known to exist outside the Wastes."

"Whoever controls that mine has an almost infinite supply of revenue," Asher added. "When the wars ended, there weren't many unaffected areas where existing mines could be accessed safely. While there are other salt mines, none of them have the yield of this one."

"Do we profit from this mine?" I asked.

"No. It's always been an agreement between our Triad and the Jesuits that they controlled it because they have vowed not to be motivated by profit."

"And if they didn't?" I countered. "Would they feel the need to take over our village to ensure there would be no resistance on our end?"

There was silence for a long while. No one moved, but all three men looked at me so hard I felt like a bug under a microscope. It was all I could do not to fidget.

Storm set down his cup carefully, placing both hands on the table. "What you're suggesting would mean the Jesuit Triad had either been overthrown or no longer followed the principles they were founded upon."

"Either would be equally bad," Hildar mused.

"Also," I said, "consider if either of those situations is true and they managed to figure out how to navigate the river through the mountain…"

"They'd come in through the river inside our walls and catch us unawares."

"I need to know something," I said, a sudden thought catching me. I might be wishful thinking and grasping, but I needed to know. "Were you around when my father was found guilty of treason?"

All three stiffened. Storm pushed up slowly from the table and paced to the window. He moved slowly and like he was still stiff, but seemed to need the separation. Hildar glanced at Asher, and for a while I wasn't sure any of them would answer me.

Finally, Storm said softly, "I was a young man. One month before, we assumed responsibilities from our predecessors. It was our first act as Triad. Their last act, the one that prompted us to take control..."

"Why banish him? As you pointed out with me, the penalty for treason is death."

Storm turned around, meeting my gaze directly. The look on his face gave me chills, and I knew my world was about to be tilted. "Because they didn't believe he was guilty. Neither did we."

My breath caught, my lungs seizing. "And my mother?"

"Her death was the reason we assumed control when the reigning Triad was still in their prime."

If I hadn't been sitting, I'd have passed out. The room seemed to spin, and my vision narrowed. "You didn't believe she was guilty either," I said. Not a question.

"Neither did the previous Triad," Storm confirmed.

"Then why?" Tears pricked my eyes. As laid bare as I'd been, sitting there at their table in nothing but one of their big tunics, I had reached my limit.

"Why do you think?" Asher said, harshly, obviously angry. "The Triad gave in to the village council. Not all at once, and not with this incident initially. Slowly. Over time." Asher looked at Storm and sighed. "Your mother's death was merely the last in a long line of failures. I can't prove it, but I'm certain any inappropriate behavior was all Lorgan's doing. He just happened to get caught and needed a scapegoat."

"It's a failure we risk repeating if we continue down this path," Storm muttered, turning back to the window, the musing more for himself and his Triad than for me.

"I don't understand," I said. This whole day had me reeling, but this last exchange had turned my world upside down. I was light headed, probably hyperventilating, and my stomach rolled. The soup that had smelled so appetizing before now made me nauseous.

"The previous Triad allowed Lorgan to push through the execution of your mother. Because of the lack of evidence on your father, we banished him instead of hanging him," Hildar supplied, "but I suspect Lorgan set your father up in order to eliminate him so he could have your mother. Then he wanted your father executed so he wouldn't retaliate for the death of your mother."

"The previous Triad knew there was something off with the council's accusations," Storm said softly. "Since your mother was a pet, she wasn't afforded the same courtesies and proof of guilt your father was."

I wanted to cry hysterically but managed to hold it together. Just. "What happens to me if Lorgan decides he wants rid of me to make sure his daughter's position isn't threatened?"

Instantly, Asher and Hildar were at my side. Asher's hands rested heavily on my shoulders while Hildar knelt before me.

"No one will ever lay a hand on you, Arryn," Hildar assured. "Not even if we perish. You will always be protected." The fact that he called me by my name and not the pet name of "little girl" they'd taken to calling me said volumes. They truly meant what they were saying.

"You can't know that!" I shook my head, tears burning behind my eyes. I hated feeling so out of control and emotional. "Gods! This is intolerable!" In a burst of desperate temper, I swatted my water cup off the table, the contents spilling all over the place.

"I know," Hildar continued, taking my hand and brushing his lips over my knuckles. Despite my anger, confusion, and, I was willing to admit, fear, I clung tightly to his hand, not wanting to let him go. "But just trust us to take care of you."

"Can I?" I wasn't normally so belligerent -- okay, so, sometimes I was -- but with the lack of sleep and the bombshell they'd dropped I thought I was a little entitled.

"You, above all others, can trust us," Storm said, his voice soft. "Just stay close to one of us at all times and don't worry about anything else." He sounded more like a king now, the leader of the Triad. "Your one job is to make sure you stick to one of us like our godsdamned shadow. All the time. If that means you defy an elder, then you do it. Anything else is optional. This one order… is not."

To my surprise, Storm stalked back to the table, looking much steadier on his feet, and crossed to me. Taking my other hand in his, he indicated the massive bed we'd shared two weeks before with an inclination of his head. He didn't ask or order me there, just made a suggestion. An invitation.

"What do you expect of me?" I lifted my chin, meeting his gaze and refusing to be cowed. If he demanded I… service him, I'd do so. I wouldn't be happy about it, but I'd do it.

Okay, so maybe I might be happy about it…

No. Definitely not. I wouldn't!

He grinned. "Nothing too terrible," he answered. "I'm still ill. I might need a healer, so I expect you to lie with me like you did before."

"Right." I narrowed my eyes in suspicion. "You know I'm not going to believe that."

Storm shrugged, sitting heavily on the bed, somehow managing to look weak and tired, not at all the strong king I knew him to be. "Come," he beckoned. "I swear I won't do anything you don't want."

"That sounds like you're setting me up for something."

"Consider this your second order," Asher said, amusement tingeing his deep voice. "Storm wants your company in bed. It's your duty to obey."

I still had on the big tunic, and they didn't instruct me to remove it, so I climbed in next to Storm still wearing the shirt. With a satisfied grunt, he wrapped his arms around me and nuzzled my neck until he stilled with his lips next to my pulse.

"That's it, my beautiful girl. Just relax with me."

With his big body wrapped protectively around me, there was no way to *not* relax. Even through the tunic, his body heat soaked into me, taking away my anxiety. It was then I realized exactly how much the worry and fear had zapped my energy. My eyelids drooped.

"I don't want to be a pet," I whimpered softly, hating that I sounded so weak and scared.

"Trust us," Storm said, his breath tickling my neck. "Just let us take care of you and this situation. I swear you won't be sorry."

Something inside me… gave way. I relaxed

completely, my mind shutting down from pain and worry and heartache. I was in the arms of one of the three most powerful men in the region. All of them had been nothing but gentle with me. Good to me. They'd given me what I needed sexually even when I didn't know I needed it. I truly had no choice but to be here and the men hadn't done anything to really warrant my *not* trusting them. True, Asher had touched me without permission, but it hadn't been with malicious intent or for his own pleasure. Did I trust them? *Could* I trust them? If they'd meant to harm me, they could have killed me or humiliated me in front of the whole village or their soldiers. They hadn't.

So, did I trust them? Not yet. But I knew I could, given enough time.

Exhausted and heartsick, I decided the best course of action was inaction. I'd wait. Watch. Really pay attention to the men. I'd start with this.

Taking one shaky breath, I closed my eyes and let sleep overtake me.

Chapter Seven

"Time to wake, my beautiful girl." Storm's voice was rough, his hands exploring my body. At some point, I'd lost the tunic, and my body was bare to him. I was probably supposed to be outraged, but pleasure swirled around my brain as he petted me, though he never ventured into forbidden territory. Those big, rough palms slid over my belly and waist and arms in a rough caress I loved.

I couldn't keep the contented purr from escaping as he continued to roam over my skin. Before I realized what I'd done, I turned over, wrapping my arm around his neck and bringing him to me for a kiss.

The groan coming from Storm was music to my ears. Surprisingly, he let me lead, matching my own exploration but not doing anything I hadn't initiated. When I leaned my head back, exposing my neck, he trailed kisses and licks down the long column to the top of my breasts but never going lower. I knew he wanted to, could tell by the way his fingers flexed and dug into my waist.

"What do you need?" I whispered. "Tell me." I had no idea what possessed me to question him, but once uttered, I realized I wanted to know. Wanted to give him what he needed. Like a mate would. Which made no sense since I'd never be his mate. The thought filled me with an unexpected sadness. Did I truly want to be a mate to the Triad? If so, why? Not for the position. I detested the Elders Council and all it stood for. They wanted nothing more than to live off the backs of those not as wealthy or privileged, thinking themselves entitled to the best of everything. No. I didn't want to be the mate of the Triad for their position. I realized in that moment, I wanted to be their mate because they were good men. All of them.

"I need you to give yourself to me," he responded in a low, husky voice. "All of yourself. Your body and your heart."

"I don't know that I can give you my heart," I answered. I started to leave it at that but frowned. For some reason, I felt the need to be completely open and honest with him. He had, after all, not treated me as I imagined a pet might be treated, even wanting to hear my opinions and assessments. I didn't imagine most men treated pets thusly. "I'm not saying I could never give you my heart. You've been good to me so far and, I admit, I didn't expect that."

"Then give me your body and some time before you decide about your heart. I'll do my best to win it from you."

I laid my hand on his shadowed jaw. "I can do that, my king."

He growled as he turned us over so that he lay on his back with me sprawled on top of him. "Straddle my hips and sit up. Let me see your beautiful body."

I did, sitting up slowly, my hands trailing over his chest and abdomen as I did. His cock prodded my buttocks as I sat settled in front of it.

Storm's gaze roamed over my body from head to the thatch of short, dark auburn hair over my mound. His hands rested on my thighs, rubbing lazily up and down as he seemed to try and memorize every inch of me. Those big hands were rough and calloused, gently abrading my tender skin like an erotic caress. Just the hungry look in his eyes was its own aphrodisiac. Where before I'd resisted the idea of sex with any of these men simply because it would make me more like the pet they'd made me, now I couldn't imagine not having sex with them.

"There will be so much pleasure exploring your body, Arryn," he said, his voice a husky growl. "Pleasure for both of us." He gradually let his hands wander up my hips to my waist and back, still not touching anywhere I might object to if I were so inclined. I wasn't inclined to object.

Keeping my gaze firmly fixed with his, I gripped his wrist with shaking hands and dragged them up my body. Up my waist, to my ribcage, until, with a shuddering breath, I brought his hands to my breasts. The second he cupped their weight, a ragged groan escaped him and his eyes slid shut, a look of something like supreme satisfaction on his face.

His thumbs feathered over my nipples, stroking them to taut peaks. I arched into his palms, urging him to continue. The sensations overtaking me were foreign but welcomed, and I wasn't sure what was natural and what was something wicked inside me clamoring to get free. Lorgan had said my mother was prone to deviant behavior. Was he right in his assessment? Did I have the same inclinations?

The thought was enough to sober me, nearly quelling the desire Storm seemed to effortlessly stoke. I captured his wrists once more.

"Stop," I whispered, fear beginning to overtake me. Would he burn me alive as the previous Triad had allowed my mother to be burned?

"Don't fear this between us, beautiful girl," he whispered. "Let yourself go."

"Can I? It was said my mother was indecent and look where it got her."

He slid his hands up to cup my face and pulled me down to him. "If you believe nothing else, believe

- 236 -

this. As long any in my Triad live, no one will ever lay a hand on you. You are perfectly safe with any of us."

Before I could comment, he took my mouth again, kissing me with a fierce possession that left me trembling. Much as I wanted to question exactly what he meant, to nail down how he planned on protecting me, when he kissed me, I lost my train of thought.

Storm was a big man. Even weak as he was, he was still imposing in size and strength. As he kissed me, his arms snaked around my body, coiling tightly until he gave a slow, lazy roll, taking me to my back. His hands stroked and tangled in my hair as his tongue thrust between my lips to lap at the inside.

The taste of him was addictive. I loved every second of the erotic play between us, needing more but half afraid of losing myself. His weight on top of me was as delicious as his kiss. That big, hair-roughened, muscled body of his was wicked and sinful. A temptation I didn't even want to try resisting.

Though I was naked, he still had his breeches on. As he settled between my legs, rocking his hips back and forth leisurely, I felt his cock rub insistently over my mound, a temptation I wanted to accept as freely as I accepted his kiss.

"This time is for us, little girl," Storm told me between kisses. "Later, the others will want the pleasure of enjoying you, but I'm greedy to have your full attention for a time." He didn't stop kissing me but spoke between laps at my mouth. Even though I had reservations about giving in to the pleasure he so readily offered, I found myself falling deeper and deeper under his spell. I suppose having kissed a man only a few times in my life made me hyper aware of every sensation he stirred within me, but I suspected most of it was all Storm.

His body pressed me deeper into the bed as he lay fully atop me. He took some of his weight on one forearm beside my head, but I was surprised to find how much I reveled in knowing I was essentially helpless beneath his towering frame.

A throaty moan escaped me as I thrust my tongue into his mouth to tangle with his, something that seemed to please him. He started a slow rocking motion with his hips, as if he were already fucking me. In that moment, I found I *wanted* him to be.

"Storm," I breathed, my nails scoring down his back as I lifted myself up to meet his thrusts. "Gods, that feels so good!"

"It certainly does," he agreed, his voice husky. Rough. Sexy. He trailed his lips down my neck to the swell of my breasts. "I'll never get enough of you, my beautiful girl."

When he enclosed one taut nipple between his lips, I cried out, pleasure coursing through me. I could actually feel my pussy wetting, readying itself for him. How had I gone from hesitating to needing with everything in my being? I was out of control, my body aching with an emptiness I'd never known before. Though I'd long ago learned to pleasure myself, nothing could compare to the sensations I'd been shown with all three of the Triad.

Now, with Storm demanding his due from me in such a carnal way, I was glad he chose to do this with us alone. I wasn't sure I'd be able to survive much more. And with the other two, I was certain there would be more.

Storm continued his exploration down my body, his lips, teeth, tongue, and hands learning every quivering inch of me. The pleasure was what I could only describe as... carnivorous. He was eating me alive, and I couldn't be happier. Especially when he settled his upper body between my legs.

Wrapping his arms around my thighs he held me open for his perusal. The way he stared at me, the hunger and lust in his eyes should have given me pause. Instead, it gave me courage. This man, this warrior, this... *king*, who could have any woman he wanted, wanted... me.

"Do it, Storm," I whispered, holding his gaze with mine, willing him to do as I commanded.

"You want my mouth on you?"

"In this moment, I want that more than anything in the world." My answer came without hesitation. Yes, I wanted him to fuck me, but, gods, this carnal delight was rapidly becoming a favorite of mine!

Eyes firmly locked with mine, Storm lowered his head to my weeping pussy and took a long, slow lick. A groan burst from him as he tickled my clit. "Sweet as honey," he murmured. "Never get enough of this."

Gods, I hoped not! The silky glide of his tongue on me was erotic in the extreme. My belly clenched, my sex pulsing under him. Moisture leaked from my body, which he drank with every swipe of his tongue. Over and over he lapped at me, stroking me expertly.

I tried to keep my responses measured, not wanting to draw attention to my lack of experience, but it was a losing battle. Before long, Storm had me writhing beneath every swipe of his tongue, every nip of his teeth. When he speared me with two thick fingers, I cried out, arching my back and thrusting my pelvis in invitation.

Soon, my gasps and cries echoed in the vast bedchamber to mingle perfectly with his grunts and growls at my pussy. He still held me open, his big, brawny arms clamped around my thighs as though he expected me to close my legs and bar him from my body. Nothing could be further from the truth. As I lay there trying to process the sensations he created effortlessly within me, I knew I'd never deny him no matter how much I might want to. It should have been a sobering thought, but I couldn't seem to get beyond the moment. Self-preservation nowhere to be found, I surrendered everything to him on a whimper, letting my body go limp beneath him. Arms over my head, legs spread wide, I simply let go. I was going to fall -- there was no question of it. I'd simply have to trust him to catch me. If he failed, I'd die from the impact because I was definitely too committed to the jump to save myself.

As if he sensed the complete surrender of my body and my heart, Storm focused on my clit, his eyes locking onto my face. With several strokes of his strong tongue, Storm pushed me over the edge into madness.

I thrashed beneath him, screaming as I came apart in his arms. My body seemed to float, my vision growing fuzzy around the edges and my ears roaring as my heart pounded. Sweat slickened my skin, making it difficult for Storm to retain his vise-like grip on my thighs as I slipped through his arms. Instinctively seeking what I needed, I ground my cunt against his mouth, rubbing my clit even harder over his chin. The slight stubble there abraded me deliciously, making the tremors even stronger.

When I finally floated back to reality, I was breathing hard, my body feeling wrung out, but not at all sated. Never had I experienced anything like this, especially without at least a feeling of completion. Instead, I felt like I was just getting started but was terribly afraid he'd expect that to satisfy me.

I frowned, looking up at Storm with what was

surely a bewildered look on my face. He said nothing so I raised my chin. "Is that it?"

He burst out laughing. "Ah, my beautiful girl." I was growing to love it when he called me that. Why, I had no idea. It was slightly demeaning, as if I weren't enough to be called a woman. "We're only getting started."

I tried my best to look haughty. "Well, good then. Because I need something more."

"I thought you might." Storm inched his way up my body, trailing little kisses over my skin as he went. "Rest assured, I'll give you all you need. You'll never leave my bed -- *our* bed -- without being completely satisfied."

With each brush of his lips, each nip of his teeth, my body came to life. I burned for him, a flaming pyre as he effortlessly kept me on the edge of sanity. My body didn't feel like my own.

But then, it belonged to *him*. It was in this moment I realized Storm was taking possession of my body, and there was absolutely nothing I could do to prevent it. Hell, I wasn't even sure I wanted to prevent it. At least, I didn't in this moment. Later I'd probably regret it, but right now this felt too good to regret anything.

With his face nuzzling my neck, his lips sucking at the tender skin he found there, Storm nudged my entrance with his cock. I couldn't stop myself from thrusting my hips up to receive him. The second he entered me, my body clenched all around him. It burned, but the pleasure as he grazed my clit with his body was unimaginable. There was nothing in my life that had ever compared to this. I'd long ago penetrated myself, ridding myself of that pesky virgin's barrier, but he was big. Long and thick. My lack of experience with men made this experience even more earth shattering for me.

I felt full, stretched. It should have been uncomfortable and probably would have been if not for Storm having me so worked up. I was wound so tight, nothing could dampen my lust for this man.

"So tight," he bit out, shuddering above me. He acted like he was in nearly as bad a shape as I was. "So fucking good!"

"Storm!" My cry was sharp, my nails digging into his back as I tried to pull him to me. I slid my hands down to his ass, gripping the muscled flesh there.

He flexed, his body surging forward into me. Again, a shriek was pulled from me as he slid home, fully seated inside me. "How can this feel so good," I whimpered before I could censor myself.

"Because you were made for me," he whispered, his voice grating with his own need. "For *us*."

I couldn't process the "us" part right now. I was simply trying to contend with Storm. He was mastering me with no fight on my part. I was simply letting him have what he wanted because he was giving me so much in return.

His muscled arms slid around me in a tight embrace, his heavier weight pinning me to the bed in a most delicious fashion. One hand found my ass, gripping nearly as tightly as I gripped him. I could tell he was trying to hold me still, to pin me against him for his use, but I couldn't stay still even if I'd wanted to. I braced my feet on his calves and surged upward to meet him thrust for thrust. Anything I could do to get closer to him, to force him to go harder. Faster.

"So demanding," he bit out next to my ear. "Tell me what you want, beautiful girl."

How to answer that? "I just…" I couldn't form the words. Probably because I didn't know how to voice what I wanted. It was intangible, yet so physical it hurt. I needed to come, no question of it. But there was more. "Just fuck me hard and fast," I gasped. "I… I want it…"

"Fuck," he growled. Until that moment, it seemed like he'd been holding back on my account, ever conscious of my untried state. Now, he gave me what I asked for, his body slamming into mine with abandon. The sensations were indescribable. Pleasure. Pain. Fullness. *Carnivorous pleasure*! I wanted to eat him up.

Before I realized what I'd done, I bit him sharply on the shoulder, my teeth sinking into flesh when I didn't think he was giving me all he had.

"Bloody hell!"

It was all the warning I got. Storm pounded inside me, taking me with a force that bordered on violent. I wrapped my legs securely around his waist, hooking my ankles so he couldn't get away. Every move he made, I made one to meet him. The sound of flesh slapping against flesh was loud. The only thing competing with that sharp staccato was our combined moans, cries, growls and whimpers.

Finally, Storm caught my chin in one big hand. "Look at me, beautiful." When I managed to focus my gaze on his blazing amber eyes, he bared his teeth and thrust savagely. "Come for me," he commanded. "Now!"

I was helpless to do anything other than what he demanded of me. With a shrill cry, I convulsed in his arms, my orgasm hitting with unimaginable force. There was no way to control my body as I thrashed beneath him, bucking my hips to him. I clung to him, digging my nails into his back and ass where I pulled him to me in my abandon.

Just as I began to float back to reality, I felt Storm ejaculate inside me. His cock throbbed and pulsed with each scorching jet of seed. I had a thought that perhaps he oughtn't have done that but couldn't figure out why. At the same time, I tilted my hips up, digging my heels into the mattress in order to keep him inside me as long as possible.

Gods, I was confused! Such a mix of emotions warring with instincts I didn't realize I possessed swirled within me, all of them demanding I do something. But I had no idea what. In a way, by taking me as a pet, the Triad had taken those choices away from me. By demanding I let go of every worry I had about the situation and concentrate on finding my way in their lives, they'd forced me into thinking of us as a unit. It was oddly freeing not to have to consider the consequences, though I knew it wasn't the most intelligent thing I'd ever done. Though I had many pressing questions for myself -- not the least of which was why I reveled in the fact that Storm had just come inside me without any kind of protection -- my mind seemed to dismiss them no matter how I tried to focus on them. I kept coming back to the same promise they'd made to me to take care of everything else if I'd only make my way in this new life.

Storm collapsed on top of me, his weight heavy but extremely satisfying. I continued to cling to him, though I did let go of his ass. My hands stroked his strong back, one hand curling in the hair at the nape of his neck. I found myself kissing his shoulder where I'd bitten him as if praising him for giving me exactly what I'd wanted. *Was* I praising him? I didn't know. My mind refused to look too deeply at my own behavior, only that I'd gotten what I needed.

Need.

There was that word again. I'd never before had anyone or anything I couldn't live without. So, did I need the man or the pleasure he gave me?

Yet another puzzle I had no energy for.

With a sigh, Storm rolled off me, taking me with him so that I lay with my head on his chest.

"Don't pull away from me, Arryn," he said softly. Seriously. "Your body stiffens with tension when you think about your situation too much."

"How can I not think about it?" My voice was soft. I didn't want to move from the comforting position but didn't feel like I could stay tangled so intimately with Storm. With a sigh, I raised myself up on one elbow to look into his eyes. "I need your help with something. Just you and me."

"Anything," Storm said without hesitation. It was that lack of thought on his part that gave me the courage to continue. Had he mulled it over or declared he couldn't promise anything without talking to his brothers first, I might have chickened out.

Sighing, I spoke my mind. "I'm not used to being in this position," I started. "I was terrified of being a pet, of all it entailed. Then all of you insisted I forget about all that and simply figure out my place in your lives, and suddenly that's all my mind can focus on." I sounded as frustrated as I felt, my face scrunching up in distaste. "I'm not like that. At all. I have a problem, I work it from all angles until I find the solution. Now, I can't reconcile my feelings with my new station in life."

He frowned. "I don't understand."

I gave an exasperated huff. "I mean, I shouldn't blindly take what you dish out, no matter how much I love it or even simply *because* I love it. There are consequences I need to consider, and I can't seem to muster the effort."

His lips quirked, and I was certain he was going to grin at me. If he did, I might smother him next time he slept. Instead, he coughed into his fist once before continuing. "What consequences have you fretting, love?"

"This, for example," I said, waving from him to me and back. "You..." I looked around us, lowering my voice as if I suspected someone might be listening to our conversation. "You came inside me, Storm. What if I get pregnant? I don't want any child of mine to be in that limbo I've lived in because no one knew what to do with me. The babe might be a child of a king, but it would also be the child of a pet. *Illegitimate*. While I could give two shits about my child being an heir or anything, I don't want others to look down on him or think they can treat him as less than a man simply because his mother was a pet and he's a bastard."

Storm did grin at me then, but not unkindly. I was about to punch him when he said, "You must truly be letting yourself be consumed by us if you're even giving this much thought to having our babe." He cupped my face gently, brushing his thumb over my lower lip. "This is a *good* thing, my beautiful little Arryn. Your instinct trusts us. Just turn off that brilliant, logical mind of yours for a little while longer. Trust us to take care of you, then you can take care of us as you see fit."

"Gods!" I said, shoving away from him and getting to my feet. I knew I should have looked for my tunic or something to cover myself but was too upset to care. Storm's seed trickled down my leg, something

I was acutely aware of as I stalked across the room to the water-filled basin at the window. "You confuse me so much!"

He stretched, all that muscle flexing as he did so. Even though I was upset, I couldn't help but admire his magnificent body. The way he moved was nothing short of awe inspiring. "What is confusing you, sweet? Let me help you."

"You're going to take a mate! Gods, Storm! What do you think that will do to me?" I cleaned myself with angry swipes of the cloth before ducking behind my partition and snagging my last clean shift. I could feel tears burning behind my eyes and, in that moment, hated him for making me feel so much confusion. The shift wasn't much of a cover, but it was better than facing this conversation with Storm while I was naked.

When I stomped out of my refuge, Storm was sitting on the side of the bed. Despite my anger with him, I found myself looking him over with a clinical eye, making sure he didn't look weakened or hurt from the rigorous sex we'd just shared while he was still recovering. The gods knew after what we'd done, he had every right to be weak. Instead, he looked invigorated. Ten times stronger than he had the previous evening. Gods help me, I wasn't unaffected by his incredible, masculine beauty.

"I told you to let us worry about that." His tone wasn't angry or even irritated. If anything, he looked satisfied. Like my unwarranted jealousy was welcomed.

"And I need more than that," I snapped angrily. "I wasn't cut out to be used for sex, no matter how much I enjoyed it with any of you." I closed my eyes, taking a much-needed calming breath.

I was about to go into how having their attention

was heady for me, how I had never had sex with a man before and had craved that closeness I felt with his Triad with everything in me, when Asher and Hildar entered the bed chamber. I wanted to both grind my teeth in frustration and sag with relief all at the same time. Telling Storm how lonely I had been would be the worst mistake I'd ever made. It would give him ammunition to use against me. He'd be able to keep me a willing captive, even after they'd taken their mate. It helped that Storm look just as exasperated as I felt at the entrance of the other men.

"Congratulations on your bad timing award," he muttered as Hildar approached him.

The other man merely raised an eyebrow. "This is our home, too," he said mildly. "Is Arryn not ours as well as yours?"

"We know you claimed her," Asher said matter-of-factly. "I'm not sure but what the entire compound doesn't know."

My face heated in embarrassment and I groaned, covering my face with my hands. "Fucking hell," I said, the sound slightly muffled.

"What?" Asher said, as if he truly didn't see a problem with this. "The whole household is abuzz with the news. They seem quite happy about the whole situation."

"I swear, if any of you live through the night it will only be because one of you insisted on staying awake and standing guard," I bit out. "Are you trying to embarrass me?"

"Me?" Storm said, blinking rapidly as if I'd slapped him or something. "You were just as loud as I was."

I stomped toward him, intending on pouncing and maybe pounding his face. Instead, Hildar snagged me around the waist, pulling me against him with a chuckle. Not only didn't Storm flinch, he grinned.

"Easy there, little girl," Hildar said, his mirth grating on my already frayed nerves. "Much as I'd love to see you go toe-to-toe with Storm, I have much more pleasurable pursuits in mind for the foreseeable future."

"Look," I said, twisting around to look at Hildar. I knew it was a mistake the second my gaze clashed with his. I swallowed. "I... I need to talk with Storm."

Hildar merely shrugged. "So talk. I don't mind." He lowered his head to my neck, kissing and licking the sensitive skin there. I shivered but managed to push him away slightly. "Alone."

He blinked at me. Then looked at Asher, who had an identical look of bewilderment on his face, as if the very idea was absurd.

"I don't understand," Hildar said, looking for all the world as if he truly had no idea why I'd want to exclude him from the conversation.

Asher looked from Storm to me and back. Then a look of realization crossed his face. "I see," he said. As if he *could* see my frustrations. Could he see the vulnerability inside me I tried so hard to refuse to acknowledge?

I had been about to admit it to Storm, though. At least part of how I felt. Now, the more seconds ticked by, the less inclined I was to say anything.

"You know what?" I said, crossing my arms over my chest and hunching into myself. "Never mind. It's not important."

"It's always important when something is troubling you, Arryn," Asher said, approaching me slowly. He looked like a predator on the hunt, determined to get out of me whatever he thought he should know.

Stubbornly, I lifted my chin. "I said never mind."

"Fine," Asher said. "Then I'll speculate. Either way, we're getting through this now."

For some reason, I glanced at Storm, too late realizing what I'd done. I'd looked at him to make Asher back off. All three of them grinned.

"Fuck," I muttered, turning around with every intention of retreating to my little corner. Hildar's big hand landed on my shoulder gently.

"Consider this your third order, Arryn," Asher said.

I ground my teeth, wanting to throw something at him. "You don't need to know my feelings," I snapped. "You only need the use of my body."

"Why would you think that?" Hildar said as he urged me back to the bed. Instead of trying to get me to crawl into it or simply tossing me in as I expected, he had me sit on the edge next to Storm. Asher sat on the other side. Hildar pulled up a chair and sat in front of me, forearms resting on those strong thighs.

"What else would I think?" I bit out. "I remember how my mother was treated by both my father and the rest of the village. The village tried hard to simply ignore her. My father didn't give her a choice in anything. He made the decisions for all of us without her input in any way." I raised my chin. "That's not me. When I go to the village to work or treat those in the clinic, I don't want people sneering at me. At least the way things were I had a modicum of grudging respect. Now…"

"Is that what's really bothering you?" Surprisingly, it wasn't Storm who asked the question. At least, with all I'd told him so far, he could figure out what was really bothering me. Scalding, seething jealousy. At least, I hoped that was what he'd deduced. It was certainly part of it. Instead, it was Asher.

"Of course it is! What else?"

"Indeed," Storm muttered. I caught him just before he smothered his grin.

"Oaf!" Throwing an elbow, I caught him in the stomach. He winced, but simply chuckled and pulled me into his lap. I struggled, but to no avail. He maneuvered me to straddle him, his arms going around me to hold me firmly to him.

"We told you to let us worry about everyone around you," he said.

"Let me tell you what I think," Asher began. "Of the three of us, you've had the fewest interactions with me, but, I assure you, I've had more time to study you than you're aware of." I looked at him, dread filling me. In that moment, I knew, without a doubt, that this man could see straight through me to my very soul.

"You were the one who reminded the others you had a promised," I said. "Surely you can see how wrong this is. No matter that pets are accepted in the Outlands, for a mated man to take one is the height of disrespect to his woman."

"I was," he acknowledged. "And I meant it."

"Then why --"

"We're not talking about us right now," he interrupted. "We're talking about you. You enjoy being with us. You enjoy how you feel when we make love with you."

"Make love," I scoffed, trying to pull away from Storm, but the big man was having none of it. "We fuck," I snapped, my anger swelling from a deep pool, anger and frustration I'd felt all my life swinging fists and elbows to be let free. "That's the only thing pets are worthy of!"

"Where in the world would you get that idea?" Storm looked genuinely puzzled. "Did it feel like all you and I did was fuck?" Was that... was that hurt on his face? In his eyes? "Because that wasn't what I was doing. At least," he added, glancing away as if I'd hurt him and he didn't want me to see how it affected him, "that's not what I meant it to feel like."

"I was barely a teenager when my family as I knew it fell apart," I began, not sure why I was even trying to explain what everyone already knew about pets. "But I saw how everyone treated my mother. Even my father. When we were alone in our hut, it wasn't any different than what was presented to the rest of the village. She was subservient to him in all things. Even things she didn't want to do, she did because he told her to. I have no idea about their sex life, but I can't imagine it was any different. My father likely took what he wanted from her whether she wanted the same thing or not. It was the same when Lorgan took us in after my father was held for trial."

"But your mother fought Lorgan," Hildar said. It wasn't a question. When the Triad had claimed me for their pet in front of the village, Hildar had told Lorgan he knew what had really happened. "She didn't fight your father, did she?"

I thought back. There had been times she'd looked or acted like she might defy my father, but never had. She'd always done willingly what he'd ordered of her. Had it been that way in their bedroom? I didn't know. "I never remember her fighting him," I finally said.

"Perhaps it was simply the way they lived," Hildar reasoned. I was beginning to realize that Hildar was the more methodical thinker of the three. "I was young and still learning my future role, but I don't remember Lila as being miserable or browbeaten. In fact, I remember Famar being very protective of Lila and her giving him loving looks every time he stood up for her. I'm not sure how they lived their everyday lives, but I know she loved him, Arryn." He stroked my cheek gently before brushing my bottom lip with his thumb. The tender gesture did funny things to my insides. It felt like... caring. Like he saw me as someone important in his life. "Perhaps being subservient to him was her way of showing him respect?"

"A woman can do that without turning over her life in every aspect to a man," I muttered.

"Agreed," Hildar said easily, "but I don't think this is what's really bothering you."

I swallowed. It was apparent the men knew me better than I knew them. Any thought I had they'd taken me from my home to their sensual den on a whim vanished.

"It's obvious you know more about me than I do you," I grumbled. "Why don't you tell me what you think my problem is?" I was still clinging to the hope they'd think I was shallow enough to want to be their queen. The reality was just too humiliating.

"Fine. You're jealous." Hildar made the statement without flair or embellishment, though I could tell by the look in his eyes he had more to say. When I didn't rise to his bait, he continued. "Most women I know would be resentful or angry they were giving the use of their body over to us without the benefit of being our mate and queen." It's no doubt what the rest of the village would think. I could just see how Lorgan was spinning this with the council, urging them to make the Triad get rid of me before I could guilt the men into taking me as their mate. It was all I could do not to round my shoulders and hunch into myself, a self-protective instinct.

Instead, I gave them a breezy shrug, quipping, "I guess you have me figured out." It still stung to think they saw me like that.

"I'm not finished," he said gently. "I happen to think you're jealous Sunja is supposed to be our promised, not for her future position, but because you think of us already as yours. I don't think you care if we're kings or farmers. In fact," his lips quirked in a grin, "I suspect you'd prefer us to be farmers."

I couldn't deny it. Shaming though it was. I'd only been with them hours. Had known them weeks, and most of that I'd spent avoiding them. It was the first time in my life the philosophy of "deny, deny, deny," appealed to me. Try as I might, I simply couldn't make myself.

The silence stretched on for several moments. Where I'd once met Storm's gaze boldly, now I turned away from all of them. Struggling to get off of Storm's lap, I felt tears burning, threatening to break free.

"Nothing to say?" Hildar persisted when Storm refused to let me go.

Mutely, I shook my head. I was normally so confident in myself, in my place in life. Now, I felt like I was being turned upside down.

"Then let me make this perfectly clear." I wanted to cringe, to crawl into a corner and just disappear. For a strong, capable woman, I was acting like a baby. "*Trust. Us.* Just a little while longer. Work on finding your place with us. We've said it repeatedly, so I know you understand what we're asking of you." Hildar knelt beside the bed, grasping my chin gently to turn my head to him. "Mali and Tessa would have fought us for you if they didn't trust us to take care of you. If you can't find it in yourself to believe me when I tell you we'll protect you to the death, then trust them. No matter the odds against them, neither of them would have allowed us to take you without a fight if they didn't believe we would take care of your body, soul, and heart. You know that's the truth."

I did trust the older couple. With my life.

With a sigh, I straightened my shoulders. "Fine. What do you want of me?"

Asher grinned. "Right now? Hildar and I want our turn to pleasure you."

"But only if you're brave enough to take on both of us." Hildar's qualifier made me roll my eyes.

"As if the two of you could ever intimidate me that much."

Storm chuckled, clutching me to him in a big bear hug. "There's the woman we thought we were getting." He nuzzled my neck, scraping the tender skin there with his teeth. "I wonder how long she'll stay out in the open?"

Chapter Eight

Hildar plucked me from Storm's lap and tossed me on the bed. I had a moment to be shocked, but it was soon replaced by anticipation. A lustful gleam in Hildar's eyes mirrored my own feelings when he whipped off his shirt to reveal his sinfully muscle-packed chest and abdomen. His arms and shoulders were corded with an abundance of muscle as well, and I wanted to simply eat him up. I was distracted enough that it startled me when Asher urged me to sit up so he could remove my shift.

With a sigh, I surrendered. I'd found nothing but pleasure in these men's arms. Until they proved unworthy of my trust with regard to my body, I'd continue to let them do as they wanted. Which put my heart in a precarious position.

Hildar covered me with his larger frame, mashing my body deliciously with his. I loved the sensation of his hair-roughened skin on mine. Loved the way his lips found mine with little effort and immediately stoked a fire within my belly. I clung to him, raking my nails down his back when he nipped my bottom lip.

"Yeah," he breathed. "There's the little hellcat."

Irrationally, his comment filled me with pleasure, spurring me on. He still had on his breeches, but his cock pulsed against my sex as he continued kissing me. My fingers found their way to his nape, tangling in his hair. The strands felt like silk beneath my fingers, urging me to stroke him like I might a cat. And, really, he was very much like a cat. Intelligent, cunning, predatory, yet playful. They all were.

I'd seen how their responsibilities weighed on them from time to time, but they still found time to coax me to them instead of simply decreeing this was my place and going on about their business. They wanted me to find my own way, but I got the sense they were testing me. To see how far I was willing to go in tangling my life with theirs.

He rolled over in a slow, lazy movement, his arms wrapped around me possessively. Rough, calloused hands slid over my skin in an erotic abrasion making me shiver. A low, rumbling growl vibrated through him, almost like satisfaction. The thought that he was that happy about having me in his arms was an aphrodisiac in itself, but when Asher's arms slipped around me from behind to urge me to sit upright, I knew what lust was.

Asher cupped my breasts, rolling and tugging at my nipples, just hard enough to make me moan. My head fell back to rest on his shoulder while both men worked my body with gentle touches and the occasional kisses.

"There's my beautiful little girl," Storm said from his seat on the edge of the bed. "So responsive to us. You're a little wanton, aren't you?"

I wanted to reply that I really wasn't, but my breath was coming in little gasps and my mind couldn't process all he was saying. All I could do was feel. Hildar's hands rubbed up and down my thighs while Asher stroked and petted my upper body from my waist to my chest. My arms had circled his neck from behind as I arched into his touch and rocked my hips over Hildar. Asher thrust against my lower back, his cock hard and long. I had a moment to realize I'd soon feel him inside me but still couldn't think beyond the moment. Not that my state of mind really mattered.

I wanted him. I wanted Hildar.

"Are you ready for me, beautiful?" Asher whispered the question in my ear just before he nipped the lobe. I yelped, but the pain was as stimulating as their gentle touches. His big hand slid between my legs to cup my sex, two fingers slipping in with little effort. "I think you are."

"Yes," I gasped. "Gods, yes!"

He pushed me down, his palm covering my upper back. When he did, my mouth found Hildar's, and he kissed me with wicked flicks of his tongue. I rocked back when I felt Asher prodding me, his cock seeking entrance. Then he surged forward, burying himself inside me.

"Asher! Ah, gods!" It was bliss, the full feeling an exquisite torment. Hildar clamped my thighs as he rose up to rub much-needed friction over my clit, all the while kissing me and kissing me. Asher's fingers gripped my hips with nearly bruising force, but I love every blessed second of it.

Hildar kissed my chin, my cheek, my eyes. All the while Asher surged inside me. The sensations were too much. Holding back wasn't possible as I gave myself up to the pleasure and simply let them have me.

At once, an orgasm crashed over me, my sex milking Asher with pulsing spasms. His hands tightened on my hips, and his breaths were harsh on the back of my neck.

"My beautiful girl is trying to make me come before I'm ready," he bit out on a ragged breath. His arms slid from my hips around my waist, his body continuing to surge inside me. With a hoarse shout, Asher shuddered above me, his seed spilling hotly inside me.

All I could do was lie there, my limbs too heavy

to lift. I felt like I'd run a race. My lungs were heavy with exertion, my muscles satisfyingly sore from the tension that continually wound tightly inside me. As I lay on top of Hildar, sandwiched between him and Asher, I could actually feel that tension draining away. Why? Fuck if I knew. Probably because I'd decided not to fight them. I was theirs. Until they told me otherwise, I was treating them as mine.

With a satisfied groan, Asher rolled off me. He bent to press a tender kiss to the small of my back, then to what was likely slight bruising at my ass and hips where he'd gripped me so tightly. I didn't care about any bruises. The pleasure they'd given me was worth any slight discomfort they'd caused. Especially given the pain had been because of their own pleasure. The thought that I'd been a part of something that had made two of these three incredible males lose control was heady. The thrill was unlike anything I'd ever experienced.

Hildar brought me back to the present when he shimmied underneath me, freeing his cock. Though it was trapped between us, I could feel it pulse and throb, seeming to strain for my body with every second.

"It's my turn, beautiful," he murmured. I thought he'd flip us again, take me in a dominant position. Instead, he gently searched for my entrance with me on top of him. Once he sank easily into me, my breath caught. Though I was relaxed and stretched from the other two men, Hildar still made me burn deliciously.

He urged me to sit up. This time, as I straddled him, his cock slipped in and out of me in a sensual glide. His hands traced a path from my knees up my thighs to my waist and breasts. Over and over he did this as if gentling me. I could have told him there was no need. I was putty in his hands. I thought I should probably fear they could make me a slave for their use, make sexual pleasure the only thing I lived for, but I couldn't muster the outrage I should have. Or the fear. I was simply rolling with it. It felt too good not to.

I soon found a rhythm we both liked. Slow and sensual, I experimented with my movements, learning what we both liked. When I figured out how to whip my hips forward at the end of my downward slide, Hildar's breath hitched. I knew I had him then. I did this over and over, rolling my hips as I watched his face. Sweat broke out over his upper lip and brow. His lips pulled back from his teeth, and he growled at me. Those big, strong hands gripped my thighs as he seemed to be barely preventing himself from forcing me to go faster.

On a whim, I snagged his thick wrists. My hands couldn't circle them all the way, but that gave me an even bigger thrill as I lay forward on top of him, bringing his hands above his head.

"The three of you have had your turn with me. Now it's my turn." Three deep, masculine groans filled the chamber. "Keep your hands there," I said, not really expecting him to obey me, but loving the glimmer in his eye. He was going to play along.

I sat up again, running my hands over my body, cupping my breasts as I rode him. Storm scooted closer to us, his gaze focused on my nipples as he did. Without hesitation, I reached for him with one arm. Wrapping my hand around his head, I guided him to me until he took my straining nipple between his lips and sucked.

My head fell back. I continued to ride Hildar, the pleasure and anticipation building within me to a fever pitch. Asher must have left briefly to clean himself, because he sat on the other side of the bed to join us after a short absence. He clearly thought I would pull him to my other breast, but I shoved him away when he leaned in to me. Instead, I found his big hand and brought it to my clit. Without any more encouragement, Asher circled my clit. My moisture combined with the seed inside me made his skin glide over my sensitive bud.

With a harsh cry, I tried to hold off my orgasm, to no avail. Though Hildar kept his arms where I'd put them, he planted his feet and surged up into me. The added stimulation hurtled me over the edge into bliss. The pleasure was just shy of madness. I couldn't contain the scream torn from me. Didn't want to. If the whole of the compound heard me, so be it. These were *my* men, godsdammit! If I wanted to fuck them into oblivion, it was no one's business but ours.

Hildar gave a shout as loud as my scream. Louder even. His hips surged up against me, lifting me from my knees. The tendons and veins stood out in his neck and shoulders in his strain, and I thought there could be no more awing a sight than a man this strong and powerful in the grips of such intense pleasure.

When I finally went limp, Storm pulled me off Hildar. I was boneless, like a kitten peeled off a warm lap. Weakly, I wrapped my arms around his neck as he carried me over to the table where a basin of water sat. He cleansed me gently before carrying me back to bed.

"You've made me exceedingly proud this day," Storm said, kissing my temple. "Exceedingly proud."

"Mine," I thought, sleep fogging my brain. Had I said that out loud or in my mind? I didn't know. All I knew for sure was I meant it. These men were mine. I didn't care if they were kings or farmers. I'd thought it before, but in this moment, I knew the truth of it. No matter what they were, what their station was in life, I wanted them with every fiber of my being.

It might have been wishful thinking, but I dared Lorgan or anyone else to take these men from me. That was my last thought before I succumbed to a pleasantly exhausted sleep.

* * *

A week passed with little for me to worry about other than eating, sleeping, and learning all about sex with my Triad. I just didn't know how to rectify that situation, so I ignored it as much as I could.

The entire time, the men had kept me busy with getting to know them individually and as a unit. I'd learned that they needed a woman to accept both sides of them. And they were distinctly different apart than they were together.

When together, they seemed to feed off each other's aggression, each seeming to need to prove his dominance. I realized very soon that Storm had held himself back before, whether because he was still weak or because he didn't want to frighten me off, I had no idea. I had to admit, though I loved every single wicked thing he led them to do to my body, it gave me pause. Until I surrendered fully and just let them have me. There was never a time they didn't ensure my pleasure above their own. When he was alone with me, however, he was unfailingly tender, worshiping my body with loving touches and gentle kisses rather than ravishing me. I found that, though I loved the intense need and fierce lovemaking they showed at times, I needed the caring as well. Maybe even more than I needed the lust.

Hildar was methodical when we were alone. He seemed fascinated with my body's response to him and took every opportunity to experiment. One time he'd pet me to orgasm until I begged him to take me hard and fast, another he'd simply take what he wanted. Other times, he'd actually play with me, tickling me until I shrieked with laughter. Then we'd tangle in a heap on the floor in front of the fire or on the bed and make love until he'd worn me out.

By contrast, Asher got more aggressive when he was alone with me. It surprised me because he didn't seem like the type, but more than once I found myself tied to the bed or suspended from the ceiling while he did anything and everything he wanted to me.

I also learned what my body could do. That, sometimes, a little pain was a serious turn-on. Though they pushed me beyond my comfort zone, they never took me too far and always, without fail, pleasured me so much I couldn't contain the screams.

During what I'd come to think of as the "honeymoon phase" of my new life, I hadn't ventured out of the bedchamber much. When I did, one of my men was always with me. Most usually it was Asher, and he was every bit as intense out of the bedroom as he was inside it. No one approached me or even looked my way most of the time. It was both discomfiting and welcome. Much as I hated being treated differently, I didn't welcome the awkward non-interaction. Everyone seemed to be going out of their way not to acknowledge my presence. At least, that's what it felt like to me. Thankfully, the Triad didn't expect me to go out much. To be honest, I had too much to deal with trying to figure out the three of them.

That wasn't to say we didn't venture out, though. In fact, because of our earlier conversations about how someone might use the river to their advantage and enter the village from the mountains, we'd set about building a grate, much like the one where the river flowed under and through the wall. The temporary one was already erect, with a stronger one in process behind the temporary grate. It wouldn't stop anyone trying to enter the village for long, but it might be enough time for us to mount a defense before they breached it entirely.

I'd awakened a short while ago to find that, for the first time since my pleasurable incarceration, I was alone in bed. No warm male surrounding me with his big body. No one in the bedchamber with me either. There was, however, an assortment of fresh fruits, cheeses, and breads as well as chilled wine and water. I reached for my robe as I climbed out of bed. I still didn't have much in the way of "real" clothing, but I hadn't really needed it.

I snagged a piece of cheese, closing my eyes in bliss at the sharp bite. A dark grape followed, cold and crisp. The meal was simple, but absolutely delicious. I shouldn't have been surprised at how hungry I was. One or more of my men had awakened me several times the night before. Just before dawn, I'd awakened them all. I grinned at the memory but blushed just the same.

Once I'd started with them, Storm had managed to coax me into trying something new. Though they'd all pleasured me together, I'd never actually been penetrated by more than one of them at a time. Not counting, of course, oral sex. I often suckled on the two who weren't fucking me while being pounded by the third and loved every blissful second of it. This time, however, once Hildar had me on top of him and kissing me as he lazily rocked in and out of my pussy, Storm stroked my opening around Hildar's shaft.

"What are you doing?" I'd croaked, unsure

exactly what I was feeling.

"Just relax," he murmured, his voice husky and sexy as fuck. "Let Hildar kiss you.

Everything they'd done to me -- individually or together -- had given me pleasure without fail. I made the decision in that moment to always give them the benefit of the doubt. If they betrayed my trust, I'd reevaluate.

He'd stroked and stroked, circling my pussy with his clever fingers. Hildar never altered his pace or stopped his insistent kisses. One of his hands cupped the back of my head while the other stroked my back up and down in a mesmerizing caress.

Then Storm's finger breached me... beside Hildar's cock. One finger, then two, until I could tell that he scissored his fingers around Hildar. Thrusting in and out with his own rhythm, Storm continued to move inside me. The sensation hinted at more, but I couldn't wrap my mind around it. I didn't have time to worry over it though. Hildar kept me occupied with his drugging kisses and caresses, not to mention his slow, steady fucking. Every now and then, he'd buck his hips at just the right angle and hit my clit with the root of his cock.

The next thing I knew, Storm was mounting me from behind, sliding his cock in my pussy beside Hildar. He went slow, easing the head inside with care. Both men groaned but weren't as loud as my sharp cry. Surprisingly, there was no pain. It burned, but not uncomfortably so. Just a feeling of fullness that rode that fine edge.

It didn't take long for him to coax my body into relaxing and stretching for him, and he soon rode me freely. Hildar had praised me. Storm rewarded me. The teeth-clattering ride I'd enjoyed had forever changed my perception of sex. Asher had joined as well, offering me his cock to suck, which I did greedily. I was amazed at how much pleasure there was to be found with these men. Was it like that with all men or did the Triad know more about women than most men because they experienced sex as a unit rather than as individuals only? I didn't know. Didn't want to know. At last, not first-hand. While I loved every second with them, I couldn't imagine giving any other man this much power over my body. Hell, I'd only given it to them because I'd had no choice. I was glad I had, though. As I'd drifted back to sleep after we were all spent, I realized I wouldn't have traded these experiences for anything in the world.

As I buttered a slice of bread, I heard raised voices outside in the courtyard. One of them, I recognized as Lorgan's. Surprise. He sounded angry. I smirked. I guess he was feeling better after his flogging. I should have been horrified at his punishment, but I couldn't manage. The man was a toad. More than that, he'd had my mother killed. The little bastard deserved everything he got and then some.

Nibbling the bread, I walked to the window to peer down...

And fury blossomed over me.

With Lorgan was perfect Sunja. She'd just dismounted her horse with all the grace of a princess and run into Storm's arms, her glad cry carrying over the courtyard and up to me. Her arms twined around his neck as she pressed her lips to his, a familiar gesture that suggested she'd missed him and was happy to see him. I couldn't seem to get enough air, feeling like something punched me in the gut. I barely registered that Storm caught her by the waist. He didn't, however, circle her slim body with those strong arms I'd found so much pleasure in. It was the only thing that kept me from losing my mind.

Instead of completely freaking out, I watched for several more moments. Storm was gentle with her but didn't appear to welcome the interaction. The moment she pulled back from him, Storm set her away. He seemed to be resisting the urge to swipe his sleeve across his mouth. I looked at the other two. They looked on in stony silence.

"I insist you honor your pledge to me," Lorgan demanded, his anger making his voice carry. Where before I could just make out his words, now I could hear every single one distinctly. "You will marry Sunja this evening."

"You know that's not possible," Storm said. His voice was so soft I had to strain to hear, but his anger was evident. Lorgan didn't seem to be as intimidated as he had been before. Of course, having his daughter marry the kings and setting himself up as the father-in-law to the Triad would be more than reason enough to throw caution to the wind.

"Is the word of the Triad no longer sacred? If so, perhaps the village should look for new direction."

"Be careful of your words, Lorgan," Asher offered. "They could cost you."

After his recent punishment, I'd have thought Lorgan would have backed off. Instead, he took a step forward. No doubt the council had given him an ultimatum or something. Secure the Triad or they'd kick him off.

I frowned. No. Even that wouldn't have spurred Lorgan. He'd have needed more than that to openly oppose the Triad. He was too much of a coward. I'd witnessed it first-hand when he thought Storm would die.

"I want to be queen," Sunja pouted prettily. "I *should* be queen. Everyone says so."

"And why would you think it should be you, love?" Hildar asked, not unkindly, but I could tell there was an edge to his voice.

Sunja blinked. "Well, it certainly shouldn't be that *pet*, Arryn. She's nothing but trouble. I hear she's as deviant as her mother. Even if she's not now, I'm sure she will be eventually."

"Have you met her, then?" Hildar continued.

"Of course! Everyone in the village has, though most of us try to stay away from her. She needs to learn her place. Why, she's nothing but a peasant! She thinks that because she can read she's better than everyone. If I were queen, I'd forbid any but the noble families learning how to read. All the peasants need to know is how to work."

"I see." Hildar's expression hadn't changed, but I knew him well enough to know he wasn't happy. Or amused.

"Everyone knows she's a whore," Sunja continued, as if she knew Hildar didn't believe her that Arryn wouldn't make a good queen and was trying to convince him of it. "Why else would she live off by herself? It's so no one can see men coming and going. She's probably slept with half your soldiers. It's why they all give her deference and turn to her when something breaks. It's an excuse to get her close to them. Surely you can see that!"

I'd had enough. Turning away from the window, I stomped to the door, opening it to bellow, "Sara!" I had never called for anyone since I'd been here. Wasn't even sure how to go about it, hence the bellow.

"Sara's not here this morn, mistress." Julia, a

woman about Tessa's age, rounded the corner. She didn't look put out I'd called but, strangely, curious. "Is there something I can help you with?"

"Yes," I said, grateful she'd offered. "And thank you. I need clothing," I said. "Not a dress, but leather breeches and a top of some kind. Boots." I raised my chin, trying for regal, but wasn't sure I pulled it off in my robe. "I want to go outside to the courtyard and greet the Triad's guests."

Julia's face lit up. "About time," she said, beaming with pride. She looked at the guards outside my door smugly. "I told you, didn't I." It wasn't a question. "Come with me, Miss," she said, taking my arm. "There's a wardrobe all set for you. No one's had time to bring it to your chamber since you moved in, as you've kept the kings busy." When she winked, I realized she was teasing me and welcomed it. The woman had accepted me. Glancing at the guards, I caught their smiles as well before they masked their expressions. Had everyone just been waiting? On me to grow a pair?

"What's going on?" I said, trying to stop the older woman, but she was having none of it.

"Just never you mind, Miss." She shoved me inside another bedchamber before closing the door on my guards. "You need to dress. The guards will escort you to the courtyard when you're ready. Be quick about it now! Do you need help?"

"Dressing?" At her curt nod, I actually backed up a step. "Are you kidding? I've been dressing myself since I was a girl. I think I can manage." Again, she gave me a look of pride, closing the double doors as she left.

Inside, I found two wardrobes filled with clothing, shoes, and undergarments. One seemed to be for formal wear while the other had everything else. I found tight breeches of the softest leather I'd ever touched. A matching vest hung next to them, and I raised my brows. The tight armholes suggested it wasn't to be worn over a tunic, but by itself. The front laced up, showing a generous amount of cleavage, even though my breasts were on the small side. The tight material held me up and together even without a binding. Which was good because I hated bindings anyway. Finding tall boots that came over my knee, I tried them on. Perfect fit.

Examining myself in the mirror, I was a little stunned at my reflection. Having just gotten out of bed -- after hours of play the previous night -- my hair was a wild, curly mass of red and gold. The doeskin leather hugged my body, accenting my rounded ass, tucked-in waist, and making my breasts look a size bigger than usual. The vest hit the top of my pants perfectly, so with every movement, I flashed midriff and back as well as cleavage. I wasn't sure exactly what I looked like, but the one thing I didn't look like? A fucking *pet*.

Ignoring the guards, I marched down the corridor and stairs to the great room, then out into the courtyard. I could hear the guards walking steadily behind me. At the thought that I had at least some kind of backup, my shoulders shot back, and I donned what I hoped was an expression of utter confidence. This was it. One way or another. If the Triad didn't see me as an equal, then this would certainly tell the tale. Perhaps they'd let me go if I'd read the situation wrong and they still intended to marry Sunja.

"Storm!" I wasted no time with niceties. Best to go ahead and stake my claim. His head whipped around, his gaze colliding with mine. Did he actually look... relieved?

"Arryn," he breathed, then straightened. "I believe you know --"

"Sunja and Lorgan. Yes. I know them. Do you want to explain exactly how well *you* know Sunja?"

At first, he jerked his head back as if either he couldn't believe I'd just asked him something in that particular tone of voice. Then he grinned. "All depends, I guess."

"It's not a 'depends' kind of question. You were kissing her as if you know her *very* well."

"True," he conceded, "but in my defense, she kissed me. Not the other way around."

"Either way, your lips still touched hers. I hope you don't expect to be touching mine with yours any time soon." At that, his grin faltered.

"I just said I didn't kiss her back." Storm looked anxious now. I'd never seen him like this. He was always supremely confident and in control. He looked -- and acted -- like my not allowing him to kiss me after kissing Sunja was an actual possibility. Like he wouldn't go against my wishes even if I was a pet.

"I just said that was semantics. The end result was the same."

"Take it easy," Hildar said, putting an arm around my shoulder. I shrugged him off.

"Don't tell me to take it easy. One of my men was letting another woman kiss him. I don't take that lightly." My fingers curled into fists at my sides. I had to go all the way with this, let everyone know my displeasure. Even the Triad. Though, the gods knew, I was happier than I could express knowing it mattered to them that I was uncomfortable with the situation, to put it mildly.

"Are you going to stand here and let this… this… pet talk to you like that?" Sunja looked mortified.

Lorgan looked livid.

"I told you that one should have been executed!" Lorgan took a step toward me, and I noticed something I couldn't have seen from our room above the courtyard. He was sweating. Though the day was warm, it wasn't so hot or humid he should be perspiring so much. Great drops ran down his forehead to his face so that he had to wipe his sleeve across his eyes several times.

At his comment, Asher and Storm both took a menacing step toward him. Unlike in the village, Lorgan didn't move.

"I thought you'd learned your lesson before," Asher growled. "Disrespect to any of us will not be tolerated."

"One would have thought you'd have more respect for the village than to take a pet, let alone to allow one such liberties." Lorgan raised his chin, seeming to ignore Asher's not-so-subtle threat. "I demand you get rid of it and honor your promise to my daughter. If you don't, the elders will see you deposed."

He sounded sure of himself, confident the Council of Elders would, indeed, back him in this. Something seemed... off.

I glanced at Sunja while Lorgan and Asher continued to trade words. Her gaze darted around the courtyard nervously. She shifted from one foot to the other, unable to keep still. When she raised her hand to her mouth to nibble on a fingernail, I interrupted the argument that had broken out between Storm and Lorgan.

"Storm. Look at me." I didn't raise my voice, only spoke loud enough for him to hear me over Lorgan's din. When Storm focused fully on me, I held his gaze. "You need to get soldiers to the village wall. River side. Now."

For long moments, he said nothing, only stared at me, his expression serious. Then he shouted, "Draden! Muster the men! Half to the main gate! Half to the river!"

The captain nodded crisply, "At once, sir!"

Within minutes of the muster being sounded, the first regiment thundered toward the city, some on horses, others on foot. All of them pressed at top speed.

"This is madness!" Lorgan spat, though he started trembling. "The soldiers need rest after the battle mere weeks ago!"

Asher advanced on Lorgan, this time not stopping until he reached out and snagged the other man by the throat. "You presume to tell us how to utilize our soldiers? The better response would be for us to ask what you know that we don't. If it's that there is an impending invasion from the mountain through the river, don't waste your time telling us about it because we already know."

Lorgan clutched at Asher's hand slowly squeezing the life out of him. Everyone's attention was so focused on Lorgan that none of us realized Sunja had sprinted off.

"Fucking bitch," I muttered before sprinting after her. What I was going to do, I had no idea. I couldn't fight, but if I caught up to her, maybe I could take her to the ground and hold her there until someone else took over.

Storm snagged my arm as I passed him, hauling me against his larger frame. "Settle down, little girl. Hildar's already on it."

"But he's standing right here! She's getting away and I'm certain she's as much a part of whatever is going on as Lorgan is!"

At that moment, two soldiers stepped in front of Sunja before she could dart into the maze. She fought them, but the pair hauled her back to Storm, dropping her unceremoniously do the ground.

"I'll have you both flogged for this!" she cried, as if she were truly going to be queen. "Storm! Asher! See to it those idiots are flogged and exiled! I won't have a common soldier putting his filthy hands on me!"

"You're acting as if you're not about to be punished yourself," I snapped. "Shut the fuck up!" I'd reached my limit. "Storm," I turned to him. "We have to get to the village. The soldiers will need direction, and there may be people in need of a healer."

A stable boy jogged toward them, three war horses' reins in his grip. "Triad!" he called. "I got em here as soon as I could. My brother took off with the soldiers."

"You did good, lad," Hildar praised as he took the reins from the boy. He looked no more than ten, his eyes wide. The poor kid was out of breath but beamed under the praise.

Storm and Asher mounted swiftly. Hildar snagged me by the waist and tossed me up to Asher, who settled me in front of him on the horse. I just managed to stifle a girly squeal. After that, there was no time for anything except hanging on for dear life. Asher's arm was like an iron band around my waist as his horse sped through the maze from memory, just like Hildar's had before. Just like before, the horse exited the maze and sprinted to the main gate.

Asher slid from the horse before helping me down. "Go," he said to Storm. "I've got her." With a nod, Storm and Asher kicked their steeds to a gallop and sped off to the river.

"You can't stay with me," I pleaded. "They might need help!"

"Hush, Arryn," he said, bending his head to brush my lips with his. "This is the way we fight. One at the front, one in the rear, one at the wall. I command troops manning the ranged weapons. This is where I belong, and you belong with me."

"But the clinic --"

"Will send for you if needed. If that happens, I'll send two trusted guards with you. Clear?"

I sighed. "Then I might as well help here."

It wasn't long before the familiar sounds of battle filled the air. Malachi approached Asher, though he looked me up and down once before focusing fully on the younger man. "I trust you've been good to her?"

"You know I have, Mali. She is most treasured."

"Good. She's a fine woman. She'll stand with you."

Asher quirked an eyebrow at me. "That she will."

"I'm not going to be a pet," I blurted. "I'm done with that role."

"You haven't been treating her like a pet, have you?" Malachi was incensed. He actually took a threatening step toward Asher. The king raised his hands in surrender and retreated a step in deference.

"We might have at first, but only to force her to accept her place in our life. If you ask her, I think you'll see she's quite happy."

"Are you?" Malachi asked, reaching out one aged hand to cup my cheek tenderly. "Because, if you're not, I'll teach these boys a lesson."

I couldn't keep from smiling. "I am. As long as everyone understands I'm an equal and not a pet, I'll be fine. Because they have made me happy. I love the life they've given me."

"We've not even begun to spoil her yet, Mali," Asher said with a grin. "Just wait until we do."

The older man waved that away. "She's never been interested in material things or power. Only in life. She's like my Tessa -- a rare treasure."

"Riders approaching from the east gate!" a soldier atop the wall shouted as he pointed over the field leading from the city into the Outlands. "They carry the Jesuit standard!"

"How many?" Asher queried.

"Three, sir!"

"The bloody Triad," Asher growled. "Dammit!"

"Could be a trap," Malachi offered. "You ride out to meet them. Their forces ambush you while another group fights to get through the mountain. If a member of our Triad is in danger, the soldiers will fall back to protect you."

Asher laid a hand on Malachi's shoulder. "No worries. I'm not going out there. They can come to us. If they need asylum or assistance, I'll gladly give both, but I'll find out what's going on."

Just as the Jesuit Triad rode through the gate, the first of the wounded started coming in. Surprisingly, Lorgan was at the healer's tent, ushering them inside.

"Why is he here?" I demanded of Asher.

"Where else should he be?"

"You don't think he's an innocent bystander in all of this, do you? His visit to all of you and this battle can't be a coincidence. He had to have known what was happening! It wouldn't surprise me if he had a hand in planning it."

"I don't doubt you're right, but we don't have proof. Though, I suspect the Jesuit Triad may be able to shed some light on the subject. Assuming, of course, they aren't part of the problem."

"You said before you thought them above reproach. Have you changed your mind?"

"No. I think they were probably overthrown. Likely by someone in the New Church."

I nodded. Though I knew very little about the Jesuits, I know the New Church was corrupt to its very core. If there was money involved in the salt mine the Jesuit Triad controlled, there was every possibility the church would use nefarious means to obtain it.

"Go," Asher urged. "Hadin and Garth will go with you. Don't leave the tent unless Malachi or one of our Triad comes for you." The order was given gently, but I knew he meant it as one of those hard-and-fast orders to be obeyed no matter what.

I gave him a mock salute, unable to stop my grin. "Yes, sir."

"Smart ass," he muttered before turning his attention to the approaching Jesuits.

Chapter Nine

Once wounded started coming in, they did so in a steady stream. No matter what Asher had said earlier, I didn't trust Lorgan as far as I could throw him. Which was why I had Brandon sticking to him like glue. The boy knew what he was about, and if Lorgan did anything to harm any of our soldiers, Brandon would know.

Over the next few hours, I forgot about everything. It was hell all over again. So many maimed and injured in various ways. Some wouldn't leave the tent whole. Others wouldn't leave it alive. If I found out Lorgan had anything to do with this, I might kill him myself and damn the consequences.

I had just finished bandaging a soldier's arm when Asher and Storm entered the tent. My stomach rolled when I didn't see Hildar anywhere.

"Finish tending him for me," I hissed at Sara. The girl had been with me the entire time, learning a great deal. She had a quick and willing mind, absorbing everything she could.

"Where's Hildar?" I questioned Storm anxiously.

"Relax, beautiful," Storm said, pulling me into him for a soft kiss. "All is well."

"But --"

"He'll be along shortly, love. Have a little faith in us. We have done this a few times all on our own."

"Are you trying to manage me?"

"Only if it takes that worried look off your face," Asher said, taking his own kiss.

"What's going on?"

"The river is secure." Asher made his voice

louder. I wondered what he was doing until I realized Lorgan was just across the room. "We caught several men helping our enemies cut through the temporary barricade from our side. Once we finish interrogating them, we'll know who the traitors are."

I raised an eyebrow. Asher winked at me. Storm had his hawk-like gaze locked on Lorgan. He glanced up but didn't stop his work. It wasn't difficult to notice he'd started shaking again.

"Brandon, I need more sutures and some antiseptic."

"Sara," Brandon called, taking my order to him not to leave Lorgan's side seriously. "Supplies, please."

"That girl won't know what I need," Lorgan snapped impatiently. Again, he glanced up. Probably to see if we were watching him. "Get them personally. It's already been too long a delay in closing this wound."

"Lorgan," Brandon said, crossing his arms over his chest. "You've been trying to get rid of me all day. You haven't done it yet, so what makes you think this time will be any different?"

"Boy," he bit out. "I said *now*!"

"Problem?" Storm said, crossing the room to face Lorgan, the patient in between them. "Because I'm willing to help if you're in need."

Lorgan's face paled. "Uh, no, my king. I was just asking young Brandon here to get supplies for me. My hands are clean, and I can't risk contaminating them else I'll have to scald them again."

Storm kept his gaze locked on Lorgan. Asher and I had followed, as had several of the king's personal guard. All of them pinned Lorgan with hard stares. "Go, Brandon. I'll stay to aid the healer if he needs it." With a soft whistle, Brandon left to retrieve the requested supplies.

"Funny thing, mercenaries," Storm began. "It's difficult to pay one enough to keep his mouth shut when faced with certain death otherwise."

Without warning, Lorgan snagged a scalpel and sliced a deep laceration over the throat of his patient and then ran from the tent. The man gave a short, shocked yell. Storm instinctively clamped a hand over the man's bleeding neck nearly at the same time the patient brought his own hand to the wound. Brandon shoved Storm out of the way, taking his place. The patient trembled, and blood flowed faster as his heart pounded in alarm.

"Go! Get that bastard. I'll take care of this!" I hissed as I took stock of the situation.

Asher and Storm sprinted after Lorgan. Though I was torn with the need to follow my men and see Lorgan punished, I knew I'd be worse than useless if it came to a fight. My place was here, trying to repair the damage Lorgan had done.

Blood oozed from between Brandon's fingers and around his hand. The bastard had cut deep enough to cut the man's external jugular. With Brandon and Sara's help, I held pressure with thick dressings. Blood flowed freely, but I managed to stem the flood somewhat.

"P-please, d-don't let me d-die," the young man managed.

"I'm going to have to tie off the vein," I said. "Otherwise, he'll bleed out." Ignoring the man's pleas was one of the hardest things I'd ever done, but emotion would only hinder me at this point. I had to be steady else risk a mistake. A mistake in this operation would cost the man his life.

Instead of arguing with me, Sara snagged a bowl

and filled it with hot water, knowing I'd want to clean my hands before starting this. As I scrubbed, my heart thundered. If I couldn't do this, the soldier would die. If Asher and Storm didn't kill Lorgan for this, I promised myself I would.

"Give him enough painkillers to make him sleep," I said. "Make sure he doesn't quit breathing."

"You have it all measured out," Brandon said. "One vial should do at his weight, right?"

I smiled. "You're a very intelligent man, Brandon. Yes. Get him to drink while I'm preparing. Once he's out, I'll have to do it quickly, otherwise he'll wake before I'm done."

This wasn't something I'd ever wanted to do. The risk of infection was so bad I didn't want to think about it. I had some medicine I could give him, but even if I stopped the bleeding and he survived the wound, infection could very well still kill him.

Once he was unconscious, I tied off the vein above and below the cut. Thankfully, there was another vein behind that one to serve the purpose of moving used blood away from his brain, and it didn't look like his carotid artery was cut. The man groaned in pain though I was as gentle as I could be. When I finally finished, there was blood everywhere. My patient was pale from blood loss, his skin clammy and cool.

"You have to lie still and drink as much fluid as you can stand," I said as I placed a hand on the man's brow. "I'll cover you and keep you warm, but you have to promise me you won't try to get up for anything."

When he nodded weakly and closed his eyes, I slumped into a nearby chair Sara had had the foresight to place.

"Where are the Triad?" I looked up at my grim-faced guards.

"Questioning Lorgan and the mercenaries who claim he hired them."

"What of Sunja?"

"She's also in lock-up, still trying to pretend she's the queen," one stony-faced soldier said. "If I didn't know better, I'd swear she was mad. Probably trying to make us all believe she is. Wouldn't put it past her."

"She's not mad," Brandon said. "Just spoiled and stubborn. Thinks everyone should bend to her will." He shrugged. "If she had anything to do with this, she finally went too far."

I stood, going around to the other side of my patient. Before I went to my men, I needed to make sure there were no other wounds that needed tending. I'd just finished cleaning the blood from the other side of his neck when a huge arm yanked me back, snaking around my throat.

"What the hell are you doing?" Brandon's eyes were wide as he looked over my shoulder. One of the soldiers guarding me now had me prisoner and was rapidly cutting off my airway. My heart pounded. I struggled but to no avail. It shouldn't have surprised me when I wasn't able to budge his hold considering what a piss poor fighter I was. Still, I struggled until he squeezed enough to completely cut off my air. He didn't let up until I stilled in his grasp, and then only just enough for me to not suffocate. I'd never been more afraid in my life. The only thought I had was that I hoped I could hold out until my men could get to me.

"Getting out of here any way I can," he growled. The other soldier was nowhere to be found. Had they worked together? How many more did Lorgan have in his employ?

"Just let her go," Sara pleaded, her hands raised. "We need her, or many people here won't survive the night."

"Not my problem," he said. I was beginning to panic. It was harder to breathe with each passing second. I dug my nails into his arm, trying to pry him loose.

"She can't breathe," Brandon said, his voice increasing in volume. "Do you want her to suffocate? What do you think the Triad will do if you harm their mate?"

"Mate?" The soldier's body went tense. I couldn't see his face, but this seemed like it was news to him. Unwelcome news.

"Yes!" Sara cried. "She's their queen! Just… let her go and run. You'll have a head start on them."

The other soldier burst back inside the tent. "They've got Milo and Gerald. We have to get out of here now. It's only a matter of time before they give us up, if they haven't already."

"They have." Storm's calm voice filled me with such relief, I would have sobbed if I hadn't had to concentrate so hard on simply breathing. "Let her go, and we will consider exile instead of execution." I could read Storm well enough to tell there was no way in hell he was going to do anything other than kill the shit out of this guy. I'm pretty sure the soldier knew it too because he began to tremble. Sweat dampened his skin, and he tightened his hold on me. I could almost scent his fear as he came face to face with his executioner.

"How do I know you'll keep your promise?"

I knew there was nothing Storm wouldn't say or do in order to see me safe. It wasn't a stretch to figure the soldier knew that too. Which meant he wasn't going to let me go. Might even do something like what Lorgan had done -- injure me badly enough to give himself a head start before anyone came after him. My heart beat madly, threatening to burst from my chest. I was going to die right here. Like he was my lifeline, I refused to take my gaze from Storm, needing to see his resolve. I knew nothing could stop him if he wanted something badly enough. Now, I prayed he wanted me enough to find a way to help me.

When the guard took a step back, dragging me with him, my thigh bumped a table, rattling instruments with a loud clatter. Groping blindly, I found a pair of scissors and stabbed him in the thigh. The soldier gave a howl of pain, relaxing his hold just enough for me to squeeze through his arm and drop to the floor. Storm leapt on him, tackling the soldier to the floor.

Storm forced the scissors imbedded in his leg as deep as they could go. The guy bellowed in pain, but still fought Storm for all he was worth. Brandon limped around the fight until he was above Storm and the soldier. Bracing himself on the table, he kicked out with his good leg, connecting solidly with the guy's head. The guy was dazed, but not out of the fight. So Brandon did it again, harder this time. The soldier didn't move. Storm sat back, his hand shaking as he scrubbed it over his face. When his gaze met mine, I could see the fear lingering. Fear for me?

Asher trotted in from the back, Hildar right behind him. When they saw Storm on the floor, both of them hurried to his side. Well, Hildar went to Storm's aid. Asher was on me like stink on shit.

"I will bloody flay every single one of these mother fuckers!" Storm was angrier than I'd ever seen him. His eyes fairly blazed with it. "Are you hurt?" he demanded, looking at me like this was all my fault.

"I'm fine," I managed, though I was shaken beyond belief. Had started to tremble, even. "I'm fine." I think I said it again more for myself than for Storm's benefit. Then, to my utter mortification, I burst into tears.

Asher scooped me up in his arms. "Can the two of you handle it here?" I figured he meant Brandon and Sara since it was Brandon who answered.

"If I need help, I'll send for her," the younger man reassured. "I promise I won't unless it's life or death."

Asher nodded once then strode outside with me cradled securely in his arms.

Somehow, we made it back to the compound. I honestly don't know how because I was sobbing into Asher's chest. Once in our bedroom, my men stripped me bare, inspecting every inch of me. Storm winced at the bruising around my neck, dipping his head to cover every dark smudge with his lips and tongue.

"He w-was going to ch-choke the life out of m-me," I managed in a tremulous voice. "If it hadn't been for y-you and Brandon, I'd have *died*."

"Shh, there, beautiful," Storm crooned, pulling me closer to him. They'd put me on the bed while they examined me, only pulling up the coverlet once they were satisfied they'd seen every single mark on my body. "We've got you. No one will ever hurt you again."

I'd stopped crying. Occasionally, a tear would spill, but it had mostly passed. "What did you learn from Lorgan and the men you captured?"

"The whole Council of Elders was involved, apparently," Asher said, wearily. "Though none of them expected Lorgan to actually put their plan into action, they all had a part in it."

"Why?" I was stunned. I'd known there were some really shitty people in our village and that most of them were on the Council, but I'd never dreamed they'd actually try to usurp the Triad. "What was the purpose?"

"To put another Triad in our place," Hildar supplied. "They wanted a Triad more like the old one. One they could bend to their will."

"What are you going to do?"

Storm gently urged me into Asher's arms then got to his feet. Like the others, he was naked. As in shock as I was, as grave a situation as we were in, I still couldn't help but admire his backside. Sculpted muscle made sharp hollows in the sides of his ass. I used all my willpower to stifle a sigh.

"I don't know."

That surprised me. "I figured you'd have them all put to death."

He turned to me. "Is that what you would do?"

The question surprised me, so I thought about it. Really thought about it. "I suppose we need to figure out just how involved each person was. It sounds like Lorgan was the main culprit. As were any soldiers in your employ who participated."

"Indeed," Hildar said. "There is no question of that."

"What was Sunja's part in the whole thing?"

"There was more to her than I'd have thought possible. She seems like a bit of an airhead, but she's actually quite cunning. Turns out, none of Lorgan's plan was actually Lorgan's plan. She did most of it. Might have worked, too, except she underestimated your genius."

"Did she really want to be your mate or was that

all a ploy?" I tried to keep my voice neutral and not sound like the jealous lover, but knew I'd failed epically when Asher raised an eyebrow.

"It was all about the power. We knew that from the beginning. We just didn't know how deep her narcissism went."

"They deserve to die," I said. "All of them."

"I'm hearing a 'but' in there," Storm said.

I sighed. "But, I don't think you should execute them. I don't think they should get to stay in the village, though. The Council of Elders, Lorgan, Sunja… all of them. They have to leave."

"Agreed," Hildar said. "Any sight of them in our territory will be met with lethal removal."

"There is something I want you to do," I said, looking at Storm and holding his gaze. "I want you to agree to exile Lorgan instead of a death sentence only if he agrees to lay out what really happened with my mother and father."

Storm raised an eyebrow. "Continue."

"We know part of it, have pieced together more of it. But there are things I'm convinced he knows that he has refused to say. In exchange for his life, I want to know what happened. I deserve to know."

Storm didn't hesitate. "Done. If we're careful with how we question him, I'm confident we can get the truth out of him."

"What about the rest?" Hildar asked. "Do you think the Council's families were involved?"

Asher shook his head. "Not going there. Their families can stay if they want. If they choose to leave with them, none of them may return."

"That should go for the mercenaries, too," I said. "They were doing a job they were paid for. While it's despicable, I can't hold them more accountable for something a citizen of our own village hired them to do."

"Very judicial," Storm commented. "I think we chose wisely with you."

"Which leads me to another topic," I said, sitting up and crossing my hands over my breasts. "You *all* lied to me."

Chapter Ten

"How do you figure that?" Hildar demanded. His gray eyes held a hint of mischief though.

"You said I was a pet. Clearly that's what you wanted me to think even though you knew how it distressed me."

"Did we ever treat you as a pet?" This from Asher, his voice low and rumbly. He knew full well how that particular voice he used made my toes curl.

"That's not my complaint." I wasn't getting distracted. I wasn't really mad -- *now* -- but I wanted them to think I was so I could make some demands. "You said I was a pet. In front of the entire village. That's what you said." When Storm opened his mouth to say something, I cut him off. "Now, the whole village sees me as nothing but a plaything for the Triad. How long do you think it will be before someone gets the idea he can touch me or refuse to pay me in the clinic?"

"I can answer that one without reservation or hesitation," Storm said, all traces of teasing gone in an instant. "Never. The next time we leave this compound, we're introducing you as our mate and queen. I'll shout it from the bloody ramparts if I have to."

"That's all well and good, but you still lied to me."

Storm put his chin up, challenging me. I knew he'd always challenge me, especially when he knew I was right. I suspect sparring with me turned him on.

"Would you have fallen in love with us so quickly if we had done things differently?" The certainty with which Hildar asked the question made me want to throw something at him. The bastard had trapped me. If I lied and said I didn't love them, I couldn't take them to task for lying to me. If I admitted I *did* love them… well, they were already too arrogant and insufferable.

But I did love them. With all my heart. I wasn't sure how it started or when it happened, but the moment he uttered the question, I knew it had.

Shrugging, I said, "That's not the point."

"So you *do* love us," Hildar said, a big grin breaking out on his face.

"Look. Don't let it go to your head. I'm still not happy with any of you."

"We simply gave you no choice but to find your way with us," Storm explained. "If we'd given you a choice, would you have stuck with us as a Triad? Taken three men willingly into your bed? And into your body?"

"If I said yes would you believe me?"

"No. Because you're a sane woman. Arryn." Storm looked uncomfortable. "Dealing with one man is hard enough. You're signing on for three. I wouldn't expect any woman worth having to take that on willingly. The only ones who would wouldn't be doing it for the right reasons."

"I have no idea what the right reasons are, but I can honestly say I'm doing it because I fell in love with all of you individually. I want you to be happy and cared for. You seem to take care of everyone else, and I happen to believe you deserve to be happy and have a home to relax in when you're not solving the problems of the entire village."

"Then stop whining," Asher said as he reached for me, "and tell us how to make you happy tonight."

Well, when he put it that way.

"All I want is to still be able to help. I worked hard to make myself useful. Obviously, with Lorgan gone, we'll need a village healer."

"You've pretty much got that job locked up," Hildar said. "Everyone already looked to you. Lorgan was only there to make himself feel better."

"True, but, just because I'm your mate doesn't mean I want any of that to change. I fix things. Including people. I don't want my role to change other than to have the authority to make some changes."

"Make any changes you want, beautiful," Storm declared. "If we worry over your safety, we'll make it so we don't worry. In other words, expect one of us or our most trusted guards to be with you at all times. I only hope that, if the danger is too great, you'll respect us enough to be flexible."

Finally, I shrugged. Storm pulled me across the bed so he could roll on top of me. "Fine. It's not like I was really mad anyway."

He grinned. "I thought not. I think this was your way of asking for something to do with sex."

I wrapped my arms around his neck, bringing him down for a searing kiss. "Maybe. What are you willing to do for me in order to make up for this little indiscretion?"

"Anything," he answered without hesitation. "Name it."

"I want more of what you did to me last night." I met his gaze boldly, knowing that if I was skittish about asking, he'd never do it again this quickly.

"I see," he said, gruffly. His cock twitched where he'd nestled it between my legs. "What if I wanted to show you something... a little different, but close."

Wicked man. He knew before I answered I'd

agree to anything. This "different" intrigued me.

"Tell me what you had in mind."

"Why don't we show you instead?"

Storm lowered his head to mine again, kissing me hungrily. I could tell the idea of whatever he and his brothers were about to do to me excited him greatly. Without preamble, he guided himself to my slick entrance and slid inside me. I arched to him, my moan muffled by his mouth.

For long moments, he simply slid in and out of me, kissing and caressing me as he did. He expertly worked my body with his, pushing me to the very edge only to let me float back down without actually peaking.

He did this over and over until I was in such a frenzy I was clawing at him, even looking to Hildar and Asher for help.

With a deep, warm chuckle, Storm slowly rolled us so that I lay sprawled on top of him, his cock still working in and out of my slick pussy.

"Just relax, beautiful," he said at my ear. It sounded almost like a growl. His cock pulsed inside me, as if he were anticipating what came next as much as I. "Concentrate on me. Kissing me. Fucking me."

He gripped the back of my neck, holding me to him as he kissed me with wicked flicks of his tongue. I was nearly lightheaded with need, my breaths coming in little pants. Sweat dotted my skin, and I trembled when he slid his arms tightly around my body. I was so much smaller than him. All of them. Any one of them could force me to his will at any time, and there was nothing I could do about it. Much as I hated to admit it, that loss of control, any blatant show of their strength turned me on something fierce. Did I like the idea of being at the mercy of all of them?

Fuck.

In some intelligent part of my mind, I knew I should be worried about what they were going to do to me. I knew I was incredibly vulnerable, open to all of them in this position. The other part of me, the one that had accepted them utterly, knew that, whatever they decided to do to me, they'd make sure I enjoyed it. Thoroughly.

Storm kept sliding in and out of me at a leisurely pace as if he had all the time in the world and was savoring it as much as I was. My mind went back to the night before when Storm and Hildar had both been inside my pussy. I had never felt so connected to anyone as I did all three of them in that moment. Perhaps it was the new sensations. The wicked byplay. All I knew for sure was that I wanted more.

There was a trickle of something warm and slick over my backside between my cheeks. I jumped and cried out at the sensation but arched to the drops sliding down my skin. The soothing scent of jasmine and lavender filled the air. It was my own special blend of aromatic oils used primarily for baths and gentle cleansing. No doubt Asher had noticed some in my home and swiped some that first night he'd come to me.

"Gods, she's so responsive." The gruff murmur was from Asher. He was beside me, his hand roaming over my back down to the curve of my buttocks and back, over and over in a rhythmic enchantment.

"Because she was meant for us," Hildar responded. He was the one drizzling something between my cheeks, stroking me where I'd never thought to be touched. His touch, though wicked, was gentle and coaxing instead of the usual demands he made. It made me eager for what I knew would happen soon.

"She certainly was," Storm agreed against my lips. "All for us. Only for us."

"Mmmmm…" I moaned helplessly into Storm's mouth, unable to disagree if I'd wanted to. He was right. There was no other man who could ever compare to any of my Triad. Put them all together, and they owned me as if I truly was their pet.

Then it struck me. Maybe, for some people, being a pet wasn't about buying another person and ruling over them. Maybe it was about earning the right to make another surrender willingly. My mother certainly hadn't seemed to mind. In fact, I knew she'd loved my father and he her. Had they shared such pleasures? Had she felt like she might die without him? Because, though I'd never admit it to a soul, I was beginning to believe I'd never be whole without my Triad.

Hildar worked one thick finger inside my ass, circling the rim several times before penetrating me. I thought it would hurt, but it didn't. I just felt… full. stretched.

Full…

When he added a second finger, I arched my back to meet him. Storm chuckled at my anticipation, thrusting up so that my attention returned to him. There was so much stimulation I didn't know where to focus. Then Asher added his kiss to my shoulder. The center of my back. Trailing his lips up my spine, he brushed my hair aside to find the nape of my neck and nip it gently.

"I'm eager to have you, my beautiful girl," he whispered, keeping me on the very edge of sanity. "I think you want this as much as we want you?"

"I do," I breathed. "I never knew…"

"I know, sweet. I didn't either," he said. I could

hear the honesty in his voice. This was new and exciting to him as well. "I've never wanted to share a woman with the Triad before you."

"Then why?" I turned my head to look back at him, truly confused. "Because this feels… right to me. Like this is the way it's supposed to be."

"I feel the same way," Asher breathed against my neck before catching my lips for a kiss.

"We all do, beautiful." Storm thrust upward inside me again at the same time Hildar thrust his clever fingers, spreading them again as he drizzled more oil over my ass and inside me. I was coated well with the slippery stuff, some of it even dripping down to lubricate Storm's cock as he buried himself inside me over and over again, a slow, sensual seduction.

There was movement behind me as Hildar rose up and positioned himself to mount me. I tensed but Asher petted me with soothing strokes up and down my spine while Hildar caressed my buttocks. His hands were slippery with the oil he'd used on me. As I knew it would, the soothing scents helped me relax to accept what was to come next. It was the one familiar thing amid all these unfamiliar sensations. Though I was enjoying the experience, I welcomed the simple pleasure of my favorite scent. I supposed it helped to ground me, and I was glad of it. I wanted nothing to ruin this experience, especially not my own anxiety.

When I felt the head of Hildar's cock probing my ass, I concentrated on remaining absolutely still, relaxing my muscles so I didn't unintentionally fight him. In a way, I suppose this was the ultimate surrender. Body and mind. And it felt like it was supposed to be happening. If someone had told me after my first meeting with Storm when he was so injured that I'd be in this situation, I'd have called them a godsdamned liar. Not only did I not have any expectation they'd all three take me for a lover, but I never could have guessed I'd surrender myself so completely to *any* man, let alone three. And that I'd not only do it willingly, but eagerly? That I'd make a conscious decision to participate in my own surrender? Yet here I was. And it was perfect.

The head slid past my rim with a smooth motion, my body enveloping Hildar with seeming eagerness. He cried out as I arched into him. All the while, Asher petted me. Storm eased his thrusting to allow Hildar entry but stroked my arms in a steady up-and-down motion.

"Just relax as much as you can, love," Storm encouraged. "You can take him."

"I know," I responded. "I'm good."

I met Storm's grin with a kiss, letting him know I was truly okay. All the while, Hildar worked more of his cock inside me until, finally, I felt his belly against my buttocks. I looked over my shoulder at the beautiful sight of Hildar's sweat-slicked chest and straining muscles. The veins in his neck and arms stood out where he held himself rigid. His head was thrown back in ecstasy, his mouth open as he gave a hoarse shout.

"Fuck! She's so tight!" Hildar's voice was rough, his grip on my hips tightening until I knew I'd wear his fingerprints as bruising on my flesh. The perverse thing? I loved the thought. Grew wet at the thought.

"I know," Storm agreed, beginning to move within me once again.

The two of them soon found their own rhythms. Storm slow and steady while Hildar took a more aggressive position. I was stuffed, but not uncomfortably so. They'd taken great pains to make sure I was prepared for this. I also thought that my own body had been so eager for this that I was more relaxed than I had ever been during sex. Like every conceivable force in the universe conspired to get me in this exact position. To pleasure both myself and my men. Because we were one. We were meant to be together.

Blindly, I reached for Asher, pulling him to me so I could kiss him. He met me with wicked flicks of his tongue, his hands framing my face to slide into my hair. When I finally pushed him away, I reached for his cock, which he willingly gave. Kneeling beside me on his knees, he pulled my hair back to grip it in a ponytail at the back of my head. With his other hand, he gripped the base of his cock and helped me guide it to my mouth.

Again, I had a man groan under my body's ministrations. Again, it was a beautiful sight to behold. There was just something about a man in the throes of passion, out of control and at the mercy of the woman he was with. It was even better when the woman in question was me. Well, when it came to these three men it was.

Before long, all three were taking their pleasure from me. I loved every blistering second! The joy on their faces was worth more to me than I would have been prepared to admit even a week ago. Maybe it was the near-death experience that put things in perspective for me. Maybe it was simply the men. Either way, I wasn't questioning it ever again. If they needed me this way, I would provide. Willingly. Enthusiastically. Because with every second of pleasure I gave them, they gave it back to me three-fold.

Before long, Hildar groaned, "Oh, fuck. *Oh,*

fuck!" His cock swelled inside my ass, making me feel impossibly fuller as he pounded into me. His grip on my cheeks was bruising. He even let go of one side to bring down a hard *smack* across my ass.

The hit startled me, but only stimulated me even more. With a cry, I came, squeezing the two dicks inside me to the point I could feel their heartbeats pulsing. I sucked even harder at Asher's cock, wanting to give him as much pleasure as the other two gave me. He gripped my hair in both hands, tight fists guiding me where he needed me to go. More than once he gagged me, but I didn't care. When he needed to be more aggressive, I simply opened my mouth and let him take what he needed.

"I'm coming!" Hildar bellowed, his cock swelling and swelling until he exploded inside me. Hot seed bathed me inside. I actually felt the heat of it, probably because I was hyper aware of my men now, needing to know every single thing they needed. As Hildar thrust deep, holding me to him to receive every last drop of his cum, I felt Storm swelling, his orgasm not long to follow.

"Uhhh!" Storm grunted. His face, viciously beautiful with blatant masculine lines, was now contorted with that same all-consuming need I felt inside me. The pressure built and built until his muscles seized and he came deep inside my pussy with a groan. Again, I felt the hot spurt of his seed, the same as I had Hildar's. Again, it filled me with satisfaction that I knew I'd only ever feel when meeting the needs of these men.

Did that make me a pet? A creature living only to see to the needs of her master? I honestly didn't know. I honestly didn't care. When Asher tried to pull away from me, his own cock swelling with the need to come, all my attention shifted to him. Did he think to deny me his cum?

"I'm about to explode, beautiful," he bit out. "Let me go."

I gripped his shaft in one fist, looking up at him with what I hoped was a fierce expression. He needed to know that, though I intended to give them everything they needed, I wasn't above taking what I needed as well. Right now, I wanted him to come down my throat more than I wanted to obey him.

"Fine," he bit out. "Take it from me then!"

Pumping my fist and sucking for all I was worth, I did. He came, and I swallowed every scorching drop. His shout was the last of us. Surely the whole keep heard us, but I was exhausted and couldn't be bothered to care.

For long moments, we all lay in a heap. It was Asher who moved to get a rag to clean us with. Hildar rolled off me, pulling me with him as he went. Asher carefully wiped seed from my body before tossing the cloth to Storm and a third to Hildar.

Once cleansed, the three of us lay in the big bed together in silence.

"Tomorrow will be a long day," Storm finally said, breaking the stillness and bringing us back to reality. "You'll be sore after this, beautiful. Do you want to stay here while we do what needs to be done?"

"No," I answered. "I never want you to have to do something like this without me."

"You're truly a wonderful mate," Storm said. I could hear the pride in his voice. "A treasure beyond compare."

"And to think you thought you were to only be a pet." Hildar chuckled, as if the whole notion was the height of absurdity.

Should I tell them of my epiphany during this last round of sex? Maybe. But not now. Right now I just wanted to sleep. I gave Hildar a halfhearted slap. "We'll discuss that tomorrow."

"I thought you said you weren't really angry about that," he insisted.

"Never said I was angry. Worry about that conversation instead of the judgments to come."

They all chuckled.

"My little pet," Storm said, earning his own slap. "Our pet."

After a small silence, Asher said softly, "Our... *love*."

Marteeka Karland

Erotic romance author by night, emergency room tech/clerk by day, Marteeka Karland works really hard to drive everyone in her life completely and totally nuts. She has been creating stories from her warped imagination since she was in the third grade. Her love of writing blossomed throughout her teenage years until it developed into the totally unorthodox and irreverent style her English teachers tried so hard to rid her of.

Marteeka at Changeling changelingpress.com/marteeka-karland-a-39

Changeling Press E-Books

More Sci-Fi, Fantasy, Paranormal, and BDSM adventures available in e-book format for immediate download at ChangelingPress.com -- Werewolves, Vampires, Dragons, Shapeshifters and more -- Erotic Tales from the edge of your imagination.

What are E-Books?

E-books, or electronic books, are books designed to be read in digital format -- on your desktop or laptop computer, notebook, tablet, Smart Phone, or any electronic e-book reader.

Where can I get Changeling Press E-Books?

Changeling Press e-books are available at ChangelingPress.com, Amazon, Apple Books, Barnes & Noble, and Kobo/Walmart.

Changeling Press, LLC

ChangelingPress.com